the Widower

the Widower

EMBRI WILSON

27

First Print Edition: November 2025

ISBN 979-8-9930836-0-5 [Trade Paperback]
ISBN 979-8-9930836-1-2 [eBook]

This is a work of fiction. Names, characters, businesses,
places, events, and incidents are the products of the
author's imagination. Any resemblance to actual persons,
living or dead, or actual events is purely coincidental.
Actions within the story are not intended to reflect
real-life situations or provide suggestions for
real-life behaviors.

No AI was used in the research, conception, creation,
writing, design, or editing of this work.

Cover Image by Marina Vorona [Floral]
Cover Image by Vitalik Radko [Model]
Cover design by E.M. Wilson
Copy Editing by Nicola Hodgson
Proofreading by Jade Hemming

To those who have lost the irreplaceable.
May you find someone who understands.

Author's Note

Dear Reader,

The following story contains explicit language, and on-page depictions of BDSM practices, including but not limited to bondage, breath play, pegging, and CNC. This is a work of fiction meant for entertainment and depicts an individualized sample of what is otherwise a vast and diverse practice and community.

This story also contains mentions of grief, loss, death and disease, and contains topics for which some may have moral or ethical objections. Please know that I approach every part of this book from a sincere and personally painful place.

With love,
Em

One

The pink slip in my hand was the end of my career *and* the start of my new life, but at the time, all I could think was: *Fuck*.

Me, Aubrey Nielson, the girl who left her small town in Maine for New York City, graduated top of her class at both Dartmouth and NYU, the lauded teacher devoted to her students, had been fired two months into the semester by a piece of mail.

When I called to confirm, they told me the district had to downsize due to low enrollment—double-talk for budget cuts—and being the last in, I was the first out. They were kind enough to give me access to my retirement savings, but at thirty-two years old and having only worked in the district for a year, my account totaled a whopping eighteen hundred dollars.

I had spent my morning crying in the apartment I could no longer afford to rent, mourning a life I had built brick by brick, only to have it knocked down to its foundation on a random Tuesday afternoon. I loved my life in New York, loved living in Brooklyn and teaching in Harlem. Weekends in Manhattan felt like stepping into a dream every time I walked along the crowded streets beneath the towering skyscrapers. While rats and traffic and subway dancers might be too much for some, it was all the opposite of the home I had left behind. In New York, I could be who I wanted to be. My past wasn't painted on my forehead, my lifestyle wasn't a source of gossip. I was one of many. A small fish in an ocean of people just as fucked up as I was.

But, like all dreams, it faded away to reality with one hell of a wakeup call.

With no money, no job, and no prospects, I had just two weeks left until I had to move back to Maine and stay with the only family I had left: my best friend Crystal and her two little boys.

As much as I loved her, I wasn't looking forward to running into the rest of our high school class, or having to answer questions like, "Why'd you get fired?" or "Why aren't you married yet?" or "Don't you want a family? Clock's-a-tickin'."

I hadn't given up hope yet. So much could change in two weeks.

So much could change in two *days*.

"It didn't sell?" I asked the dock attendant when he returned.

"Nah, I'm sorry," he said in his weathered voice. "No one's been looking for an old boat like that."

My dad's jon boat was nothing fancy. The utilitarian metal with an engine that would likely run forever, but it was nothing to balk at. I hadn't kept it up the way I should and had barely used it since I moved, but it was one of the last physical pieces of my father I had left.

"I'm still willing to take it off your hands," he added.

"Thanks, I'll think about it. I'm going to take it out for a bit, okay?"

With a nod, he left me to it.

Stepping into my boat felt like stepping into the last moments of my childhood. The little engine was temperamental, but the current of the St. Lawrence was slow enough to let me paddle back to shore if needed. With a practiced smack, it sprang to life, and I steered away from the dock. The chilly spring air carried the citrus scent of the fir trees on the Canadian shore. The smell always brought back bittersweet memories.

My dad started bringing me out here when I was thirteen, a few months after my mom passed away. We lived by the water in Maine, but the river was an escape from the stress of Dad's job commercial fishing in the Atlantic. We would take the little boat as far down the St. Lawrence as the gas would take us, marveling at the yacht houses the size of hotels, and the mansions that looked like castles towering over the old trees; the former homes of railroad barons and hoteliers, still standing and inhabited over one hundred years later.

We would trade stories of what our lives would be like if we were as filthy rich as the people living in those mansions. He'd always tell me that we were the rich ones, because time with each other was far more valuable than money. At the time, I found it absurd that he believed money wouldn't make our lives better. When he passed away three short years later, moments like those became my favorite memories of him. Returning to these islands showed me how truly lucky I had been.

In the middle of my daydream, the engine sputtered to a stop.

Damn it.

I smacked the side of the engine again, but nothing responded. Looking over my shoulder, I saw the current had drifted me toward the rocky coast of one of the largest islands, and uncomfortably close to one of the ancillary structures jutting out into the river. Running aground was the last thing I needed. I pulled out the paddle to steer away just as the engine spurred to life at full throttle.

I fell back into the boat, the paddle flying from my hand. The boat careened toward the structure, and as I screamed, it smashed into the side of it, tossing me into the water.

• • •

I only realized I had been knocked out when I woke up. The rocks of the shoreline scraped my palms, and my clothes were soaked. Lifting my head almost caused me to black out again. The pain was so sharp in my skull, I could think of nothing else for a few moments. I uttered every curse word I knew.

When the pain subsided, I stood up slowly, carefully. My head throbbed, but it was bearable. Looking around, my heart ached more than my head. My boat was out of the water, mangled between the rocks of the shoreline and the weathered wood wall of the damaged structure. I reached into my pocket to call for help, but my phone wasn't there.

My series of curse words expanded into other languages.

There was only one option left. I stared up the hill at the towering stone mansion in the distance, and my stomach turned. If someone lived there, like my dad had said, they would have a phone.

After trudging through a line of trees, my view opened up to a sprawling green lawn dotted with patches of manicured bushes. Eventually, I crossed paths with a group of workers tending to the plants. One spotted me and gaped with a look of horror. What I thought was water trickling down my cheek coated my hand in crimson when I tried to wipe it away. The sight of my blood—and the amount of it—gave me the same reaction as the worker.

A man ran to me and started pulling me with him toward the house. *"There is a doctor inside,"* he said in Spanish, though I would have followed his lead without an explanation.

Once inside, an older woman shuffled toward us. "What's this fuss? What happened?"

When she came into the light, my heart fluttered in my chest. She had the same shape as my mother when she was healthy, wore similar half-rimmed glasses, and had the same gray pixie haircut. Her pale skin, narrow nose, and English accent were nearly to *opposite* of my mother, but the visual reminders were oddly comforting during a day like today.

"I'm so sorry. I was on my boat, and the engine malfunctioned and ran into one of your buildings," I explained.

"Oh, my dear," the woman cooed. "I was asking about your head."

• • •

Inside the castle they called a mansion, a doctor inspected me and concluded I had a mild concussion, but to my luck, the source of my bleeding was due to a very small yet unfortunately placed cut on my scalp. A terrifying problem solved by a single stitch.

The older woman, Mildred, sat with me the whole time, seeming genuinely concerned about my well-being. She kept me calm and talking, asking me about my work, my hometown, and, eventually, my career despair. Without realizing it, I was spilling my life story to her; everything from my parents to my hesitation to move back home to Maine. She made me feel so safe, I forgot to call anyone to come pick me up.

"You are so young. There's no reason for you to fret over

a family just yet." She was either flattering me or she couldn't tell my age.

"Do you have kids?" I asked her.

"None from this body, but I've raised my stepson since he was five." She handed me a cup of tea. "And I've been this family's nanny for years. I see the master's children as my own as well."

"Children live here?"

"Three! One's a teenager, but he'll always be a babe to me. I started with the family when he was two, back in London."

I glanced through the door at the sprawling foyer, watching the people tidying up inside it. Dark mahogany covered the floors and walls, a grand marble staircase led to a mezzanine and rooms above, and a crystal chandelier the size of a boardroom table dangled overhead. It was hard to believe a place like this existed in America, or that this was a family home.

"Who does this place belong to?"

"Mr. Augustine Montgomery."

Augustine Montgomery? How does a name *sound rich?*

"Is he here? I should explain what happened and apologize."

"He's away for work, but he should be back later this weekend," Mildred said in her charming accent. "We can tell him about the damage when he's in a good mood. Shouldn't be a problem."

Something about her phrasing made her words land coldly on my skin.

A sudden flurry outside caught Mildred's attention, then her eyes grew wide. "He's here? He wasn't supposed to be back for another day!" She stood and started gathering the tea set, even snatching my cup from my hand. "Stay here, love," she instructed me in a frantic tone.

She shuffled out of the room and stopped suddenly.

"Mr. Montgomery. We weren't expecting you until tomorrow," she said.

"I was told there'd been an accident." The baritone British accent vibrated in my chest, as well as much lower, piquing my interest.

I leaned through the doorway to see him, and felt lightheaded again—this time, not because of the concussion. It was because the man standing with Mildred was even sexier than his voice.

Mr. Montgomery was tall and well-tailored. A black suit that looked like it cost more than my car flattered his broad shoulders and sat well against his slender waist and hips. His dark hair was cut short on the sides and left long on top, the structured waves lying in an effortless style. His angled jaw was softened by a bit of scruff and a pair of luscious lips that stayed parted as he waited for an answer from Mildred.

When my eyes landed on the silver band on his left-hand ring finger, my excitement waned. *He's off-limits.*

Mr. Montgomery looked like a dream, as if David Beckham and a young Johnny Depp had a child who grew up to take over Wall Street. It was a cruel joke that a man rich enough to own an island would also be sickeningly attractive *and* married. I reminded myself not to forget that last part.

He looked over at me with dark green-hazel eyes, and I felt anything but cold. "And who might you be?" he asked in that alluring voice.

When I remembered how to speak, I held out my hand to him. "I'm Aubrey. Nielson," I said, almost forgetting I had a last name.

"Hello, Ms. Nielson." He gave me a brisk handshake and added, "A pleasure to meet the person who trespassed upon and vandalized my private estate."

Rich *and* a prick? Shocking.

In the minute I had spent with him, I knew him better than I cared to admit. I had been around too many men like him not to recognize the archetype.

"I apologize for my presence and the damage. It was truly an accident," I told him in the demure way I assumed he'd expect. "I'm more than willing to pay for any damages."

"You have twenty thousand dollars tucked away in your pocket?" he asked.

Twenty . . . ? What the— "Twenty thousand dollars? For a shed?" I asked without thinking.

He looked down his nose at me as if I had offended him. "It was a greenhouse constructed in 1904." He narrowed his eyes. "Not a . . . 'shed.'"

"Sir." Mildred popped back in to save me. "I believe there are other ways Ms. Nielson could pay you back." I looked at her with wide eyes, hoping she was not suggesting prostitution. "You've been looking for a tutor for Matthew for months," she explained. I relaxed a bit.

"Yes, Mildred. I am aware." He started to walk away, and Mildred followed him without question. For some reason, I followed as well, stealing a glance at his tight backside as I did. *Damn.* He was a dangerous one.

"Ms. Nielson is a teacher and is currently looking for employment."

We walked into a room with large windows overlooking the gardens. A small lounge area with two antique-looking sofas sat before them. At the back of the room, Mr. Montgomery walked around a desk, the only signifier that this room was an office.

"What makes you believe she is qualified to be Matthew's tutor?" he asked without looking at me.

Mildred nudged me to answer. "Oh. Well, I have a Master of Education from Dartmouth," I said.

He continued thumbing through his mail.

"Most recently, I was a calculus and advanced language instructor at a private school in Manhattan. I speak French, Spanish, and Italian fluently."

He peered at me from the side of his eye, still unamused. "*Pensez-vous que vous maîtrisez français?*" he spoke easily. *You think you've mastered French?* Of course he spoke it too.

"*Assez bien pour corriger votre gammaire,*" I quipped. *Well enough to correct your grammar.* After that, he *almost* looked impressed.

He set the mail down and leaned his hip against the desk, crossing his arms over his chest while he appraised me from head to toe. My body stirred under his scrutinous gaze. I ignored it the best I could as the silence extended to an awkward length.

"Send your CV and contact information to Mildred, and I will consider it."

Consider it? I can't consider whether twenty thousand dollars will magically appear in my bank account. "Great," I said sarcastically.

Mildred took my arm and led me from the room. The smile on her face seemed out of place, given what just transpired. She glanced over her shoulder before saying, "He liked you."

"*Really?*" I asked with genuine surprise. If that was how he treated people he liked, his enemies must already be in their graves.

"I could tell. He's a bit rough around the edges, but he takes care of his staff quite well," she told me. "A position like this is just what you need! It'd at least keep you from moving in with your friend."

For someone I had met an hour ago, she seemed far too happy for me. Knowing nothing came for free, I waited for the catch. "Won't I need to meet with his wife as well?".

Mildred stilled for a moment, then continued. "The children's mother passed away a few years ago," she said with a rueful expression.

A familiar ache spread through my chest; the pain that came every time I remembered my mother and how it felt when I lost her. Knowing three kids were living through that now, somewhere inside these walls . . .

It was then that I knew, money owed or not, I couldn't turn down the job if it was offered.

Two

"He looked like *what*?" Crystal asked me.

My best friend of decades knew everything about me: the good, the bad, and the sordid. Our weekly phone call had come early due to the wealth of information I needed to share. "That's what I'm saying. He was *gorgeous*." Packing my clothes into my suitcase kept me from getting too worked up. My uniform of black, high-waisted pencil skirts to hug my best features, and light-colored blouses to make up for the lack of blessings on my upper half. "Handsome face, perfect hair, amazing ass . . ." I shivered at the memory.

"So, what's the prob—hold on," she said over the sound of her youngest screaming.

As she handled that situation, I leaned in closer to my broken mirror and tucked a short curl behind my ear to finish applying my lip balm. My freckles were still noticeable as my brown skin had yet to warm to its summer shade. In the depths of winter, I was the perfect midpoint between the rich umber features of my mother and my honey-haired, freckled father.

"So, what's the problem?" Crystal finished.

"He still wears his ring."

"Oh, no . . . Oh, god, that's so sad." Growing up with a

widower who never accepted the loss of his wife, I had seen both sides of that struggle—his and my own. "I feel awful for those kids."

"Me too." The painful memory ached in my chest again. "I can't stop imagining three little versions of me sitting in that house, lost and scared."

"You turned out all right, though."

"Because I had you, your parents, and all the therapy money could buy," I reminded her.

Crystal's family was my stability when life was otherwise out of control. They took me in, cared for me, gave me space to feel what I needed while ensuring I was never as alone as it seemed. Every child who lost a parent deserved that same feeling of security while learning to navigate the chaos of grief.

"You really want the job, huh?" Crystal said, pulling me from my thoughts. "You want to help those kids."

There was no use in denying it. "I really do. It's not an ideal position, living with a family I don't know, but a chance to work with kids like me feels like kismet," I said. "But the widower... I don't know if grief is the cause of his temperament or if he's just an asshole. If that's the way he always acts, I'm afraid he'll fuck it up for me."

"Fuck it up, or fuck *you*? We all know you can handle both."

"Stop. Those days are over for me," I said, unsure of how truthful my statement was. "I've learned to get my rocks off in other ways."

"No one kink shames you like you, Aub." Maybe that was true.

My phone buzzed with another call. *Private Number* graced the top of my screen. "Oh shit, I think they're calling me!"

"Already? Oh my god. Answer it!"

"Love you! Bye!" Switching to the new caller, I cleared my throat to sound casual. "Hello?"

"Ms. Nielson?" a charming accent asked.

"Mildred?"

"Yes! Hello, darling. Mr. Montgomery has agreed to have you on!"

Joy spread through me like a sunrise. "Are you serious?"

"Yes! This wonderful news. We'll send a car to pick you up tomorrow morning, have you meet the children and discuss arrangements with Mr. Montgomery. I can't wait!"

Neither could I.

• • •

The next morning, I was vibrating with nerves. A Rolls-Royce came to pick me up—an interesting contrast to the usual Civics and Priuses that lined my block—then, a few hours later, I was on the St. Lawrence headed back to the island.

Mildred was the first to greet me. "Ms. Nielson. Welcome!" She hugged me. The warm gesture didn't feel overly familiar. "Come. He's waiting for you."

My mood dipped when I realized who she meant.

She led me down the hall by the arm to the office. Inside, Mr. Montgomery paced as he spoke on the phone in what sounded like Mandarin, wearing a crisp white shirt tucked into a well-fitting pair of slacks. He wasn't wearing a tie when we met either, but this time, he had his sleeves rolled up to his elbows. His casual look, I presumed. With a raised finger, he gestured for us to wait. It annoyed me, but Mildred complied with a smile.

"*Xièxiè*," he thanked whoever he spoke to and ended the

call. "Ms. Nielson," he greeted me while still peering down at his phone. "A pleasure to see you again."

"Likewise," I lied.

"I'll leave you to it." With a bow of her head, Mildred left the room, leaving me in awkward silence with Mr. Montgomery and the sound of him texting.

"I have reviewed your CV and ran a thorough background check. You can never be too careful when strangers appear in your home uninvited." He never looked up from his phone as he spoke and barely paused from his typing. "All references said you were well-qualified, and I would be stupid not to take you on."

There was a compliment in there somewhere. "I'm happy to hear that."

He finished his text, the swooshing sound signaling its departure. "I'd like to start you on a two-month trial basis. My eldest, Matthew, is the greatest concern at the moment. His marks are dismal, and he is at risk of being held back. If you could aid in raising them before the term's end, we can discuss keeping you on."

"That seems fair."

"As for compensation," he began. "The damage to the greenhouse was less extensive than expected. However, estimates were still upward of nine thousand."

I swallowed loudly. *Fuck.*

"Mildred and some of the other full-time staff live on the premises—an offer I will extend to you as well, if you accept the trial position. Unpaid."

He stared at me while I processed his proposal. *No rent, but also no pay?* A pinging sound called his attention to his phone once more.

"Do you find those terms acceptable, Ms. Nielson?"

"Yes, indentured servitude sounds quite convenient," I said under my breath.

"What was that?"

"Yes," I recovered. "I accept."

"Brilliant," he said flatly. "Are you ready to meet the children?"

My mood lifted. "I am."

He gestured toward the door.

We left the room. Mildred followed us with another staff member, the company easing the nerves that riddled me while in Mr. Montgomery's intimidating presence. Five or so people were buzzing around the foyer, cleaning, rearranging, or carrying something. The smell of wood polish filled the room with a cozy, antique scent. There seemed to be more people in the house for upkeep than people who lived in it.

Mr. Montgomery led us up the grand staircase and down another hall. As we walked, my attention was trained on the massive crystal chandelier hanging above the stairs. My house growing up must have cost less than that thing did.

We entered a large room full of toys. Two small children played on the floor. The girl looked up and broke into a wide grin. "Daddy!" she yelled and ran over to Mr. Montgomery.

He leaned down and picked her up, swinging her into his arms. Then, I watched him do something I hadn't seen him do before: smile.

The little boy ran over and hugged his father's legs. Mr. Montgomery ruffled his hair. "Children," he said, setting his daughter back onto her feet. "This is the new tutor, Ms. Aubrey Nielson." He gestured to me. "Ms. Nielson, this is Tabitha and Sebastien."

Their names sounded European to me, but the girl didn't seem to have an accent. I leaned over to greet them at eye level.

15

"It's so very nice to meet you both," I said with a smile.

Tabitha smiled back, swaying back and forth as the velvet plumes of her princess dress danced around her. Sebastien grinned but remained in a safe position behind his father's leg. They weren't quite the same size, but I knew they had to be twins.

"How old are you two?" I asked.

"Six," Mr. Montgomery answered.

They shared the same heart-shaped faces, blue eyes, tawny brown hair, and a kiss of freckles against their noses and cheeks—features they had not received from their father.

"Where is your brother?" he asked them.

Tabitha shrugged in response.

"We will have to hunt him down, then."

"It's nice to meet you, Ms. Aubrey," Tabitha said. Her little voice melted my heart. The two were so precious and well-mannered; if they curtsied, I wouldn't be surprised.

"I'll see you soon, Tabitha," I said with a wave. "Goodbye, Sebastien." When I waved to him, he turned away with a blush. In different company, I would have squealed over his cuteness.

After tearing myself away from them, we set off down another hall. It took a while for us to reach the next room, and by that point, I felt horribly lost.

"I must warn you, Matthew is more of a handful," Mr. Montgomery said. "He is fifteen and experiencing a bit of teenage angst."

"I remember those years fondly," I joked.

He gave me a sideways glance that made it clear he was not a fan of my sarcasm. Noted.

We walked into a different type of game room. A billiards table stood near the door; further in, a sprawling sectional sofa sat in front of a TV the size of a car. A music video with scantily clad women in inappropriate positions played quietly. A boy sat with expensive headphones, playing a handheld video game.

"Matthew," Mr. Montgomery said to the boy, and was promptly ignored. "*Matthew,*" he repeated louder. He walked over and stripped the boy of his headphones, blaringly loud music spilling out of them.

"What the fuck?!" Matthew yelled in response.

"Mind your language. We have a guest," his father reprimanded him. I would have been six feet under with no teeth had I said anything close to that word in front of my mother, let alone a guest.

The boy turned to look at me. His face was a softer, more youthful version of his father's. They shared the same dark hair and eyes, though he had fairer skin and freckles like his siblings. He, too, had no accent. The family must have moved here before the kids arrived or soon after Matthew was born.

"Who are you?" Matthew asked with petulance.

"This is your new tutor, Ms. Nielson," Mr. Montgomery said. I held my hand out to him, but he didn't take it. He turned around and resumed his game. "Say hello, Matthew."

"No."

Mr. Montgomery looked frustrated. "Last I remember, you had lost privilege of this." He pulled the game from his son's grasp.

Matthew turned and snatched it back. "Well, when no one is here to enforce the rules, I do whatever the hell I want."

Mr. Montgomery's nose scrunched ever so slightly with a sneer. He must have been used to his son's attitude, but he did not appreciate it. "Your lessons begin tomorrow evening."

"Cool," the son said sarcastically, tapping the buttons of his game.

"It would be lovely if you'd greet your new tutor."

"When are you leaving again?" Matthew asked his father.

Mr. Montgomery glared at the back of his son's head, then cracked an insincere smile. "Tomorrow."

"Good." He put his headphones back on.

Mr. Montgomery closed his eyes with a sigh, then turned back to me. "I take it you'll have no issue working with this kind of behavior?"

I knew he meant the behavior of his son, but it seemed *his* behavior was just as in need of correcting as anyone else's. "Fucked up" only began to explain this family's dynamic. It made me more excited to delve in.

"No issues at all."

• • •

Later that evening, Mildred showed me to my room. It was quaint by castle standards; just large enough for a queen-sized bed, wardrobe, and a window that overlooked the water. While the room was bare, the old-world aesthetic was opulent compared to my studio apartment.

"We'll send for the rest of your things in the morning," Mildred said.

"I don't have anything else." I gestured to the three suitcases. "Just this."

"Well, that works out nicely. My room's just up the hall. Don't be afraid to come find me if you feel uneasy. Old houses can be a bit intimidating at first."

"Thank you, Mildred."

She smiled and took her leave.

I turned back to the plain room, wondering what I could do to make it feel more like home. My sheets would help.

Maybe a few scented candles to cover the smell of dust and wood polish? Maybe a heater to cut down on the draft?

I set out to unpack and get settled in. Hanging my clothes was an easy enough task. I lifted a stack of dresses and, beneath them, found my chest of secrets. My stomach fluttered at the thought of what lay inside. Not something I should have around the kids, but not something I could give up either.

My private life was always well separated from my professional life, but this place was my home *and* my place of employment. This room was the only privacy I would have.

I ran my hand over the intricate lid and scolded myself for not being able to part with its contents.

"Everything to your liking?"

I flinched when I realized who was standing in my doorway, turning to hide the chest behind me. "Yes."

He studied me for a moment, an unreadable expression on his face. I stared back, feeling naked beneath his gaze.

"Well, then," he finally muttered. "Goodnight."

"Goodnight."

He closed the door as he left. With shame, I tucked the chest away at the bottom of the wardrobe and lined my shoes in front of it. Out of sight, out of mind, I hoped.

Too bad the same wouldn't work with Mr. Montgomery.

Three

Almost a month passed, and I had settled in nicely. Whatever hesitations I had over the living arrangements were unfounded. Being in the same house with the kids made for a comfortable routine, even though my responsibilities kept expanding past what was typically expected of a tutor. Mildred and I woke up with the kids and got them off to school with everything they needed. When the twins returned in the early afternoons, I took turns with Mildred helping them with their basics—math, reading, and Spanish—then switched my focus to Matthew when he got home in the evenings. My days were long but rewarding, with plenty of time for naps and afternoon tea with Mildred.

The kids made it worthwhile. Tabitha was an astute student in all subjects, at the perfect age when little girls honed their thirst for learning. Sebastien was the opposite, mainly due to his attention span, but he showed an impressive aptitude for music. Mildred taught him piano for over two hours every evening. I enjoyed the sound of music coming down the halls during my time with Matthew.

The angsty teen got home around five, and I usually spent

the next two hours coercing him into finishing his homework. He was a challenge, but one I knew exactly how to handle.

The work came naturally, and my bond with the kids developed quickly. The only part of the job I disliked was that Mr. Montgomery had been gone all but four days since I started. Apparently, that was the norm. So many of Matthew's behavioral issues could improve if he had a father who was home more than a handful of days per month.

In hour two of my time with Matthew, he had finally resigned to etching lines on his math homework. We sat at the table, and I watched him pretend to struggle through the problems. He was intelligent and a quick learner, but he tried to hide it. I had a theory as to why.

Raindrops tapped against the window in time with the beginning bars of Debussy's *Clair de Lune* from Sebastien's practice up the hall. I got lost in the dream-like combination for a moment, then glanced over to find Matthew staring down my shirt.

"Stop it," I snapped at him.

He gave me a sheepish grin. "You're hot. I can't help it."

I cringed and fastened the next highest button. "I'm old enough to be your parent." A young parent, sure, but plenty of my classmates had babies in high school.

"My dad hired you because I needed a tutor, not a stepmother," he teased me further. "Just because my mom's dead doesn't mean you can take her place."

"Why would you say something like that?"

"I know you have a crush on my dad."

I barked out a laugh. "I certainly do not have a crush on him."

"Whatever you want to call it. You'd hop on his dick in a minute if you had the chance."

21

"I would not."

He snorted. "Yeah, okay."

Don't give in to the anger, Aubrey. When I was a teenager, I said every awful thing I could think of just to see how far I could push the boundaries. Matthew had lost a parent too, and the other was gone so often it was as if he wasn't alive either. What he needed more than anything was someone who cared enough to push back.

"Why do you do so poorly in school?" I asked him.

He looked up at me and gave me the same condescending eyebrow quirk as his father.

"I know you're doing it on purpose."

He laughed me off, but I saw straight through it.

"You're a smart kid and have so much available to you—if you would just *try*."

"I'm a rich kid with a dead mom. The only way I could be more of a cliché is if I started wearing glasses and fighting crime at night."

I leaned a cheek on my balled fist. "But being the rebellious 'bad boy' in class isn't a stereotype?"

He gave me a sideways glance but said nothing.

"Failing in school isn't a way to punish your dad. It only punishes you."

"Whatever," he grumbled and continued doodling on the margins of his homework.

"Look. There are two ways this can go," I said. "Option one: you do poorly in school, don't graduate, and all your friends think you're cool. Then, three years later, you can't find a good job without a diploma, and you're short on rent. So, the little misunderstood bad boy comes crawling back home to Daddy to ask for money."

Matthew's side-eye turned into a glare.

"Or, option two: you stop pretending like you don't give a shit, because you do. You study, get good grades, and have the pick of any college in the world. You leave home, Daddy might pay your tuition, but you are as far away from him as possible, with the freedom to do whatever you want with your life."

He stared me down, but I knew nothing spurs a kid into action like telling them they'll be stuck in the same hell of their teen years if they don't do something to get themselves out.

"The choice is up to you. Let me know when you've figured it out." I stood up and started to leave, knowing he would stop me.

Before I could reach the door, he piped up. "Wait."

• • •

After dinner, I sat in the comfortable confines of my room. My mail had finally started being forwarded to the mansion— something I hoped I wouldn't have to redo in a month. The pile of letters and bills sat in a heap at the end of my bed; the newest, a box from a distant cousin in Maine, wrapped tightly in layers of tape, likely some family heirloom to chastise me for "giving up on my hometown" and all the bullshit that comes with that school of thought.

There are two types of people in the world: those who leave their hometown and those who don't. Everyone who left and ended up moving back acted as if I was insulting them when I made the choice to stay away. But that was for reasons other than career growth. In fact, it was almost always to avoid judgment for the private parts of my life.

After changing into my sleepwear, the curiosity got to me. *What is in that fucking box?*

I took the package and meandered down the dark hallway

to locate something sharp enough to cut the tape. Mildred and I spent all our time with the kids, keeping us separate from the other staff and areas of the house in which they worked. I had frequented three types of dining rooms and four types of lounges, but had yet to find the kitchen. In a house designed for a different time, it had two spaces that rarely overlapped: those of the owners and those of the servants. One hundred years ago, people like me would never have had the chance to experience life on this side. I hadn't had the time or courage to cross the boundary for a glimpse into the abject past, choosing to put my energy into the kids and learning from Mildred.

The next best option for a knife was the letter opener in Mr. Montgomery's office. Had he been home, I would be hesitant to enter it, but the room sat dark, door open, same as it always was when he was gone.

I went inside and scanned the desk for scissors, but found none. Setting the box beside me, I leaned over the top of the desk to peek into the cup tucked beside the computer's monitor, finding the top drawer sitting halfway open. An intricate gold frame sat atop some papers. Inside it was a picture of a much younger Augustine standing with a woman near the Arc de Triomphe, wearing laughing smiles as if they were having the time of their lives. A message was scribbled across it.

To my Gus,
Forever my favorite day.
Love you always.
Paris, 2011

My eyes fixated on the image and the thousand words it shared. *Gus? Paris, the year Matthew was born?* I was looking at Mrs. Montgomery.

I had always imagined what his wife looked like; the type of woman who could enamor an austere man like Mr.

Montgomery and make such beautiful children. The picture in my mind had been a modelesque, gaunt beauty with a face as intimidating as her memory; the archetype so often seen with a wealthy man. But the woman in this photo looked much different. She looked approachable, kind. Surprisingly *normal*. She wasn't gaunt, but rather an average size 12 or 14. Her blonde hair was in a bun atop her head, her crooked smile warm and friendly, freckles on full display without a lick of makeup on. I stared in surprise.

"Looking for something?" Mr. Montgomery's voice rumbled in the quiet room.

I jumped with fear and quickly closed the drawer. "S-sorry, I was looking for scissors," I stammered as I turned to face him.

Reaching down, I found my shorts had ridden up much higher than I thought. *Shit.* My heart raced with the embarrassment of knowing my employer had just walked in to find me ass up and snooping through his desk.

He stalked over slowly, never prying his eyes from me. Without looking, he dragged a pair of scissors from his penholder and held them out to me on the tip of his finger.

Somehow, I found his gesture flirtatious. As he was tall and devilishly handsome, most of his actions seemed sexy to me.

"Thank you," I said, then began to cut the packaging tape from the box's joints. When I glanced up between cuts, I found him still peering at me, expressionless. "I'm sorry for coming in here. I can never seem to find the right room for small things like this."

He said nothing in response. I didn't know whether to run out or make small talk, so I defaulted to the latter.

"When did you get back?"

"A few minutes ago." He stepped forward and took the

scissors from my hand. The small brush of his fingertips against my palm made my skin prickle. As he placed the scissors back into the holder, my eyes drifted over his crisp, white shirt while my mind imagined the body hidden beneath.

"Was there something else you needed?" he asked in his posh accent. "Or are you simply entertaining your habit of stumbling into places you shouldn't?"

There was no appropriate reason to still be standing half-dressed in his office in the middle of the night. My cheeks warmed with embarrassment. *What he must think of me.*

"No, sorry, just the scissors." I gathered up my box to leave. "Thank you again."

"Goodnight, Ms. Nielson," he said as he ushered me through the door.

With a smile, I said, "You can call me Aubrey, Mr. Montgomery."

He peered down his nose at me with a look of annoyance. "Goodnight, Ms. Nielson," he repeated. With that, he shut the door in my face.

Regretting everything that just happened, I fled down the hall and back up the stairs to my room.

Once inside, I closed the door and leaned against it to catch my breath. Something about him got under my skin. It always did.

He was rude, cold, and domineering. He reminded me of the men with whom I used to spend my time. He reminded me of *how* I used to spend my time with them. Still breathless, the memories sent a chill over my skin and a warmth between my thighs.

You don't need that anymore, I reminded myself. Once I pushed the lewd thoughts from my mind, I locked my door and walked over to set the box on my bed.

Inside it was nothing but a college hoodie.

Really? I made a fool of myself over a piece of clothing.

I threw the box onto the floor and still couldn't shake my nerves—the humiliation tempting me toward old predilections. The pull in my core grew as the desire nagged in my mind. Even my clothes sliding against my skin with every breath felt like a tease. When I could stand it no longer, I walked past the box and went to my dresser.

Inside the chest, I found the silken rope and the wand, and my excitement bloomed from an ember to a flame. I stared for a moment, trying to remind myself they weren't needed, only wanted. But what is the point of denying ourselves what we want?

I grabbed both and returned to the bed. After plugging in the wand, I looped the satin around my neck. Holding the ribbon's tail in my hand, I pulled harder until the tie added more pressure against my throat. My excitement burned into arousal. Placing the wand between my legs, I gasped.

The perfect vibrations hummed on my clit, giving me just what I wanted. The smooth yet unforgiving material around my neck made my breath shallower. As the pleasure built inside me, I choked out a quiet moan, sacrificing critical air in the process.

I panted and turned the intensity up a level. Trying to catch my breath, the vibrations teased me further, the grip around my neck tightening the more I strained with pleasure.

When my breathing was nothing but tiny gasps, the fear sent a rush of adrenaline into my veins, heightening my senses, blinding me to everything but the hot pressure building in my core. My legs shook when I moaned again, and with my last bit of air gone, I turned up the intensity of the vibrations once more.

The feeling was too much, my body shivering in time with the vibrations pressed against me. I let it drown me, holding my breath, focusing on my climax and my inability to call out in ecstasy. When my vision began to narrow, I let go of the bind. A rush of air entered my lungs, along with a burst of sensation between my legs.

I grabbed a pillow and smothered my moans while the orgasm tore through me, my body shaking, shuddering. Wave after wave of deep pleasure washed over me each time my sex clenched and released around nothing.

We all have secrets, I suppose.

Four

Breakfast the next morning was more awkward than usual. Regardless of last night's events, the mood always felt tempered when Mr. Montgomery was present. Even the kids seemed different when their father was around. Mildred and I enjoyed breakfast and dinner with the kids every day when they weren't running off in different directions, but with Mr. Montgomery at the table, the energy was off-kilter.

Two more of the staff came in and set down the plates of our selected breakfast foods. I had yet to get used to eating eggs and toast at a table with silver candle holders, crystal glassware, and fine china place settings. Excluding the presence of Matthew's hoodie and cell phone, their lives looked like an episode of *Downton Abbey*. The kids never seemed fazed by the opulence that surrounded them, but this was their normal. The only thing out of place was me.

Matthew texted his friends while eating, and Tabitha giggled as she made a smile out of an orange slice at Sebastien, making him laugh until their father sent a glance their way. They quieted and returned to eating.

Mr. Montgomery lounged in his chair at the end of the table, shifting his attention between an international paper and his phone each time it pinged, subsequently ignoring his family. He was gone most of the time, and now that he was here, he still paid them no mind. Mildred seemed unbothered by it, but I couldn't understand how a family could share a meal together and not say a word.

"Tabby, did you show your father what you learned in dance class this week?" I asked.

She shook her head with an excited smile, then got up from her chair to run to his side. He peered down at her as she raised her arms and spun into a wobbling pirouette.

He set his phone down to give her a light round of applause, but picked it back up right after. Tabitha went back to her seat, her smile beaming. The twins loved any attention he gave them. Why wouldn't they?

"Bastien, you should perform your new song after breakfast," I said. He brightened over my suggestion.

"I'm afraid that will have to wait until tomorrow," Mr. Montgomery said from behind his paper. "Daddy has a conference call with Beijing." *And* Daddy *needs to reassess his priorities.*

I watched Matthew sneer with similar thoughts.

"Tomorrow, then," I told Sebastien.

The silence that stretched after was uncomfortable. I sipped on my orange juice as I tried to formulate small talk that wouldn't piss him off.

"Where did you just return from, Mr. Montgomery?"

He glanced at his expensive-looking watch, then went back to his paper. "*Roma,*" he said in an Italian accent.

"Is that Rome, Daddy?" Tabitha asked with a giggle.

"Yes, my love."

It was usually so easy for me to read people—the subtle

nuances of body language and behaviors—but there was something about him I couldn't figure out. It fascinated me.

I watched as he picked up his piece of toast, balancing the triangle between his attractive fingers. He set it onto his tongue before sinking his teeth slowly through the corner. Augustine was a man who could make a flinch look like flamenco. As he chewed, his hazel eyes suddenly looked into mine.

"*L'italia è un paese meraviglioso, no?*" I remarked to cover my staring. *Italy is a marvelous country, isn't it?* That, at least, got him to stop looking at me long enough to roll his eyes.

Glancing over, I found Matthew making an obscene gesture suggesting I wanted to perform oral on his father. I glared at him until he stopped.

• • •

Later that afternoon, Mildred sat with me in the downstairs tea room. She had gotten into the habit of showing me around and telling me things about the house in our downtime, which led us to have tea in a new location each time.

There were almost one hundred rooms in the mansion, she told me once. I knew the main rooms well enough, but the secret connections and the old-worldly nomenclature fascinated me. Parlors, a cloakroom, the drawing room. Hidden pathways and stairs, places for servants to move through the house without being seen by the family or guests. Rooms opened onto other rooms in ways that didn't always make sense in modern usage; bedrooms opening off lounges, spaces with interior stairs to bathrooms on the floor above. It was a world I would never truly understand, nor did I want to.

Mildred and I were treated as extensions of the family, separating us physically *and* socially from the rest of the staff.

In the solitude caused by such passé formalities, I understood Mildred's excitement to have me join the staff and finally give her a companion.

"Across there's the ballroom. Behind it's another catering kitchen that connects to the main kitchen on the ground floor," she explained. "Behind that is the Master's Chambers."

As proper as the term was, my ancestors would never allow me to refer to anyone as "master," regardless of the context. Calling him by his name was the most anyone should expect from me.

"That's Mr. Montgomery's bedroom?"

"It was. He hasn't slept there since . . ." She didn't need to finish her sentence. "He stays in the former guest quarters behind his office."

"And where is the best place to find scissors?"

She laughed, the cheery sound echoing in the room. "You're better off buying your own. Never look for something small in this house."

I smiled in response. "Good to know that now. I had an awkward run-in with Mr. Montgomery in his office while looking for some last night. I didn't realize I was snooping around outside of his bedroom, too."

She placed her hand on my arm. The intensity behind her eyes confused me. "Mr. Montgomery's a very private man. Always has been," she told me. "He has little tolerance for people poking into his business. Give him half a reason and you'll be out on your arse before you can count to three."

"Haven't you been with him for more than a decade?"

She nodded. "I know Mr. Montgomery better than most," she told me, "which is why you'd be good to trust my advice." Her smile lessened the harshness of her words. She took her hand from me.

Last night's mistake gave me plenty of reasons to avoid him, but no one who knew me well would classify me as well-behaved. "Well, it's easy to stay out of his way, considering how often he's gone. Where does he go anyway?"

"He does multi-national business consulting. Don't ask me what that means exactly, but he's always flying between Europe, Asia, and the States. Beijing, Paris, LA, London, Rome, Seoul . . ."

"No wonder he's never home."

"Yes. His schedule's been so busy, he purchased a loft in SoHo to keep close to the airport."

"He has a place in Manhattan, too?"

"Yes, of course," she said as if it were common knowledge. "He didn't always travel quite this much. His time away has increased significantly since Mrs. Montgomery passed. Many things haven't been the same since she left us. God rest her soul."

With as much as Mildred talked about my parents and what took them from me, it felt odd that she was so tight-lipped about Mrs. Montgomery.

"How did she pass?" I asked.

Instantly, Mildred's brow creased. She shook her head to signal she couldn't talk about it.

"I'm sorry, I didn't mean to pry, I just—"

"I know, dear. You've felt loss the rest of us could never understand." She looked at me with a teary smile, then patted my cheek lightly. "Mrs. Montgomery was a kind woman, loved by everyone, but no one loved 'er more than Mr. Montgomery. That's all you need to know."

I had no doubt about that. Dealing with her loss was likely the source of most of the family's pain *and* their bad habits. Having been there myself, I wanted to help them in whatever capacity I could. They clearly needed it, but whether they realized that or not was a different matter altogether.

"More tea?" Mildred changed the subject.

I smiled as she poured it. Then, suddenly, she stopped.

"Ms. Nielson." The deep voice behind me grabbed my attention.

I turned around to find him standing behind us, wondering how long he had been there. "Hello, Mr. Montgomery."

"Come to my office, please. I'd like a word."

He left the doorway without awaiting my response. My heart dropped. *He heard it all.*

I looked at Mildred with a frightened gape. She had a very similar expression. She closed her mouth and patted my arm. "I'm sure you'll be fine," she said. That only made it worse.

I stood and raced after him as fast as my heels would take me, catching up with him at the door of his office.

He pulled out a chair in front of his desk and circled it to sit in his own. "Please, have a seat."

I did as I was told while my heart pounded nervously, convinced he was going to fire me. He picked up a small stack of papers and said, "Matthew is doing very well in school."

That was not what I expected. "He is?"

"Yes. I received his report card today."

Augustine slid the small paper toward me. A list of Matthew's classes, followed by one A, three Bs, and two Cs. Even I was impressed. "This is the last one he received prior to your arrival." He aligned another paper with the first, this one containing a smattering of Cs, Ds, and an F. Pride swelled in my chest.

"I . . . I'm in shock," I said. "I can't believe this."

"After a mere month, neither can I." Mr. Montgomery had a rare grin on his face. "You are doing a wonderful job with all the children, especially Matthew. I think he respects you, and he does not seem to provoke you the way he does me."

"It's normal for teenagers to push boundaries," I assured him. "He just needed a little encouragement to push in a more productive direction."

Augustine laced his fingers together on the desk as if ready to do business. "I would like to offer you a salary to keep you on."

My heart leaped in my chest. "Really?"

"I appreciate the effort and attention you have put into my children's individual needs, and I believe it is only fair I match what you would receive at a comparable establishment," he said. "Does one hundred and twenty-five thousand seem fair?"

I nearly choked. *Does he mean dollars?* My last job paid me fifty, and that was a private school where families paid more tuition per semester than I did for my undergraduate degree. The pay he proposed, without any of it going toward rent, would allow me to put more into my savings than I had my whole career.

"I think that's more than generous," I said, but hoped he'd disagree.

"*Too* generous?" he asked sardonically. "Would you prefer to continue working without pay instead?"

He was challenging me. I wondered if he thought that amount per year was laughable, if it was only a starting number, and his way of testing my confidence. Was I bold enough to say I was worth more than the watch on his wrist?

"Forgive me for my lack of business acumen," I said, "but does this conversation typically invite negotiation?"

He smirked. "It does."

"So, I should. Negotiate."

His smirk widened into a grin as he leaned back in his chair. "You should."

Had I known him any better, I would have thought he enjoyed watching my timidness while stepping into his area of expertise, but unfortunately, I couldn't read him past that. What was an appropriate rebuttal to an already outrageous offer?

A wild number flew into my head and out of my mouth. "Two hundred."

"One fifty," he came back. His grin remained. I hadn't offended him *or* embarrassed myself.

"One seventy-five."

"*One fifty*," he said again, more sternly this time. Negotiation over.

"I accept."

"Good. I'll have the contract sent to you this evening. I look forward to having you on for the foreseeable future."

I brushed my hair out of my face as I nodded, the smile pulling at my cheeks. "I look forward to that too."

• • •

"One hundred and fifty thousand dollars?!" Crystal shouted through the phone. "That's what lawyers make, not a damn teacher!"

"I know."

"Jesus Christ, that's a lot of money."

"I *know*." I sat on my bed with my knees curled up, still coming down from the day's event.

"Damn rich people, just throwing out money like it's— wait . . ." She paused for a moment. "Do you think he's paying you more so you don't complain when he makes a pass at you?"

I laughed at her joke until I realized she hadn't told one. "Of course not. He barely says two words to me. He'd never make a pass."

"When was the last time you got laid?"

Of course you'd turn this on me with a question like that. "I don't know."

"You don't know because it's been so long you can't remember, woman! Maybe I shouldn't be worried about *him* making a pass," she said. "You better find some dick before Mr. Mont-Money offers his up and you can't say no."

I laughed. "Fuck you, Crystal."

"Fuck someone, Aub." We hung up.

Crystal knew me better than anyone, but she didn't know *everything*. I had chosen to leave my old life behind, and I was not going to change my mind over a man who was now paying me an obscene amount to live in the house he occasionally visited.

If anyone was safe from my bed, it was Augustine.

Five

With all the stress that came from dealing with a moody teen full-time, two first-graders were a welcome change of pace. Tabitha and Sebastien tumbled around on their oversized plushies as they laughed. The sound of their small giggles brought an uncontrollable smile to my lips.

Though I hadn't left the house in over a week, and hadn't left Alexandria since I arrived, it felt less confining each day that passed. I had time to talk to Crystal more often than I did with a traditional school schedule, and Mildred was always around to keep me company. Imagine getting cabin fever while living in a one-hundred-room castle.

My phone buzzed against the cushion of the window seat. I picked it up and looked at the screen. *Rianne*. Usually, I would ignore her like all the other times, but I was in a good mood this morning.

"Hey, Kitty," I answered.

"Bunny! How are you? How's Maine treating you?"

"I'm not in Maine," I told her, though I should have known better. "I landed a teaching job in upstate."

"That's amazing! I'm happy you didn't have to move back with all those prudes."

Out of all the reasons I had given for not wanting to move home, she was most concerned with the lack of sex. With Crystal having the same worries, it made me question how I came off to my friends.

"Well, if you're still in New York, you know you can come by the club and pull a shift whenever you want. We miss our Bunny," she purred.

The memories of that place always made me smile. It wasn't necessarily my clients or the staff, but how natural the job felt; how good it made *me* feel.

Working for Rianne had been a great way to bring in some extra income, especially during the summers when school was out. But now, I didn't need extra money, and I didn't need to be pulled back into a scene I was trying to leave behind. My gaze returned to Tabitha and Sebastien as they squealed with joy. Helping *them* was all the gratification I needed right now.

Emotionally speaking, at least.

"I wish I could, but it's a long drive from Alexandria."

"Oh, you're in *upstate*," she said. "I'll give you a weekend shift if you'll come visit." The coveted weekend shift. A possible month's rent after tips.

"I can't right now. Maybe some other time?"

"Whenever you're ready, Bunny. You just let me know."

"I will."

"Kisses."

When I ended the call, I saw the time and went to gather the twins. "It's time to get ready for bed, little ones." They frowned but made no sounds of protest. "You can't be sad on a Thursday night. Tomorrow's the second-best day of the week, remember?"

Their smiles returned. Tabitha came up and hugged my legs before running out of the room. To my surprise, shy Sebastien did the same. I stroked my hand over his hair, partially to return his hug, and partially to thank him. When he ran out, I felt a sense of pride.

The more I bonded with the kids, the more I started to chip away at the family's walls. Mildred had years on me, but I was making noticeable progress. One hundred and fifty thousand dollars per year progress, some might say.

Mildred had yet to show up this evening. Being late was very unlike her. Rather than leaving the playroom a mess, I started cleaning it on my own. I picked up the toys and noticed a run in my stockings. Tossing the toys into the trunk, I bent down to take a closer look at the tear.

A little snag at the inside of my ankle. Most likely my heel caught it. *There goes another pair.*

I took a moment to stretch my hamstrings, judging how stiff I had become with months away from my yoga routine. *No need to keep up my flexibility if no one is going to take advantage of it*, I chastised myself. Sliding my hands up the back of my legs as I stood, I ran them over my backside to check the placement of my skirt. I glanced over my shoulder and gasped when I found a figure standing in the doorway. "Mr. Montgomery."

"Ms. Nielson."

I dropped my hands and felt my cheeks warm. *Why does he always manage to walk in on me with my ass in the air?* "Good evening."

"Evening." He walked closer, his hands in his pockets, while he stared down at my feet. The smell of his delicious cologne wafted into my nostrils and lulled my senses. When his eyes bounced up to mine, I felt warmer and colder at the same time.

I cleared my throat and attempted to find the words to

apologize and make my exit at the same time. "Was there something you needed?"

"I need you," he answered.

My eyes widened with surprise.

"Will you be joining us for breakfast tomorrow?"

"Yes, of course."

"Good." He shifted his weight closer to me and crossed his arms. He looked down at me with an expression I couldn't read. "I'll be needing additional support now that I've let Mildred go."

I flinched with surprise. "*What*? You let her go? Why?"

He looked out of the window as if watching her leave. His expression was neutral as he explained, "It was her time. With the success you've had with Matthew, you will assume her responsibilities with ease, I'm sure."

Heartbroken and in shock, I couldn't understand his thought process. How could he be so callous? "Is she already gone, or can I say goodbye?"

"She left this afternoon," he answered. "I will give the news to the children at breakfast tomorrow. It would be helpful if you'd assist with any emotional outbursts they may have." *Emotional outbursts? That's what he wants to avoid?*

I stared at him in disbelief, the news still gripping my throat. He wanted me to help him tell his kids that yet another person in their life was gone and never coming back. How could I do that with a straight face? I couldn't. I wouldn't.

"I'm sorry, but I think it's best you break the news on your own."

As I walked away, he caught me by the arm, his grip loose yet firm, as if keeping someone from leaving without permission was second nature to him.

"I wasn't asking," he said. His dark eyes stared into mine. "I will see you tomorrow morning."

No question, no room for negotiation. This time, it was his way or nothing at all. With that, he let me go. I left the room while blinking back tears.

Mildred was my only friend in this place. Now, I truly felt alone.

• • •

It took me until late that night to calm down. Emotionally speaking.

Mr. Montgomery got under my skin like few people ever had. My attraction to dominant men had always been my downfall, even when I knew their need for control usually came from deep-seated feelings of inadequacy—one that manifested as a desire to feel needed and in control. But something about him felt different. He was so mercurial, it was as if he had two sides to his personality. The provider-protector and the avoidant-absentee. Maybe he was struggling to find a balance between the loss of his wife and the needs of three children. Maybe he was used to having control so often, he was afraid to lose it. Maybe he was just a Gemini. All I knew was that every time he challenged me, every time he embarrassed me, it got me *very* worked up.

I swirled my hips against the vibrator I had wedged between my pillows, teasing my clit and grazing my entrance, unable to push it inside, only to torture myself. On my phone screen, the "real" couple fucked hard and fast while wrapped in their poorly affixed bondage paraphernalia. The woman's expression was twisted between pain and pleasure, her partner's hips slapping loudly against her as he nailed her to the mattress. *God, I miss that.*

I tugged my nipple between my fingertips, twisting it until I gasped with pain. The man pinned the woman's legs to the side and pulled out to start thrusting deep.

As I moved faster against the toy, an exhilarating heat built inside me. *Maybe I'll be able to do it this time. Maybe I won't need to—*

My thoughts were interrupted by a small rap on my door. I froze and waited to see if I had imagined the sound. When it happened again, I knew someone was knocking.

"*Shit, shit, shit,*" I whispered as I hid my silicone friend beneath my sheets. I pulled my panties up, my shirt down, and threw on a robe.

When I opened the door, I was surprised at what I found. "Tabby? What's wrong, sweetheart?"

She looked up at me with tears in her eyes. "I had"—she hiccupped—"a bad dream."

"Oh, honey . . ." I lowered myself to my knees and hugged her against me. "You're okay now. Dreams aren't real. They can't hurt us if we don't let them."

"Mildred wasn't in her room. Will you come sleep with me?"

Damn it. I couldn't tell her why Mildred hadn't answered, and that filled me with an awful sense of guilt. In my silence, Tabitha cried more, and my heart splintered in my chest.

"Let's get you tucked back in."

I walked with her down the long hall and around the corner, the only light coming from the moonlight sparkling off the hallway's sconces. This house would give me nightmares, too, if I thought too much about it.

I followed her into her room where Sebastien was fast asleep. After I helped her back into bed and tucked the sheets around her like my mother used to do for me, she reached for my hand.

"Please don't leave me," she begged through her tears. Her little hand gripped mine so tightly, I knew I couldn't go.

"I won't." I lay on top of her duvet and pulled the throw blanket over my legs and waist. "You know what my dad used to say about nightmares?"

"What?"

"That they don't come true if you tell someone about them. Do you want to tell me what happened?"

Her wet lashes batted a few times before she nodded. "I had a dream that I fell into the water outside."

"The river?"

"Yes," she answered in a whisper. "We were walking in the garden—Bastien, Matthew, Daddy, and I—and it started raining very hard. I slipped and fell down the hill and into the water."

"That's scary."

"Matthew and Bastien tried to help me, but they were too small to reach me. But then Daddy—" She stopped short.

"But then what, sweetheart?"

She looked at me with welling tears. "Daddy walked away. And I started to drown."

My heart sank to the floor. Even in her dreams, he was abandoning her.

"Well," I said, stroking my hand over her hair to comfort her. "That's how you know it was just a dream. Your father would never let you get hurt. He'd catch you before you ever got close to the water."

Her eyes cast down, her nod much weaker than before. "But, if he didn't . . . you would save me, right?"

I stared at her and hid my emotions the best I could.

"Of course I would, Tabby," I told her. "I'd jump into that water in a heartbeat."

She snuggled up next to me. "Thank you, Aubrey."

Soon after that, she fell asleep, but I couldn't sleep at all. I was at my limit, and all of it was about to boil over right onto the widower.

Six

The next morning, I stood outside the parlor while Augustine gave his kids the news, fully expecting the worst. Leaned back against the wall by the doorway, I couldn't hear him as he spoke, but when Matthew yelled, "Why?" I knew it had happened.

"Matthew, calm down."

"You always do this! You never care about what we want, you always do what you want to do!"

"Well, when you can support the entire staff on *your* income, you can have a say."

The flustered grumbling that followed told me the conversation was over. I tried to scurry away, but Matthew stormed from the other entrance and nearly bumped into me. His face was reddened with anger, but underneath his scowl, I saw his sadness.

"Matthew," I sighed, gripping his arms to keep him with me.

"Did you have something to do with this?"

"No," I assured him. I placed both of my hands on his cheeks and looked into his eyes. "Mildred was my friend. I wanted this to happen as little as you did."

"Yeah, sure." He pulled my hands from him and pushed past me, shoulder checking me as he did.

My rage simmered deep within. I wasn't mad at Matthew; I was mad at the person who had hurt him in the first place.

Augustine walked out with a look of annoyance. If he had a heart, it was too calloused to feel anymore. Or at least that's what he'd have people believe. Losing his wife was no reason to harm the people who had lost their mother.

The twins sat at the table, Tabitha comforting Sebastien as he cried. I rushed over.

"Are you two okay?" I asked them.

They both hugged me, crying onto each of my shoulders. Seeing the way they mourned Mildred brought tears to my eyes. It reminded me of the pain I felt after losing my mother. But I was thirteen then. Knowing it must be that much harder to understand as a six-year-old, I hugged them tighter to me and comforted them the only way I knew how.

"I'm still here. I'm not leaving."

• • •

When I had the twins settled in their room again, I went looking for their father. I found him in his office, shoving things into his designer travel bag.

"Are you leaving again?" I asked gruffly. This time, *he* was the one who looked surprised by my presence.

"Yes," he answered. "To London."

"So soon? You just got back."

He didn't respond, and that enraged me further. I was angry at him for leaving me as the sole caretaker of his family and even angrier that he didn't realize that's what he was doing.

"You work so much your children hardly get to see you.

Did you not plan to spend some time with them after sending their caretaker away?"

"They'll be fine. They have you, do they not?"

His simple, hollow threat showed his cards. It was proof he wouldn't fire me. Who else would be here to raise his children for him?

"I'm a teacher, not a nanny."

He tossed me a condescending glance. "You are whatever I pay you to be."

Taken aback, I felt my coy façade slipping. Once again, he got under my skin and would soon find the part of me I buried inside.

I stormed around his desk and snatched the bag from his grasp. "You are fucking up your kids. You know that, right?"

He stood up straighter and looked me up and down as if searching for where my audacity came from. He placed his hands on his hips, daring me to continue.

"Your kids need regularity and structure. They need consistency. If they keep having people come in and out of their lives, they'll never be able to trust that someone will stay."

His scowl deepened. "You don't know what you're talking about."

"I know more than you think." What happened to my parents was only half of what made me qualified to iron out this fucked-up family dynamic. "I had to sleep next to Tabitha last night because she had a nightmare you let her drown. Your six-year-old is having dreams that you don't care about her."

"It was a dream. Don't be childish."

"Don't be childish? She *is* a child," I seethed. "They lost their mother, and their father is too busy working to acknowledge their presence. They need a real parent in their lives. Not a placeholder their father pays."

He looked at me for a moment, then started to laugh. "You have quite the pair of bollocks on you, don't you?"

"I don't need balls to know when you're being a prick."

His smile faded. He held out a hand, asking for his bag, but I didn't give it to him.

"Stay until tomorrow. You owe them that much."

"I cannot change my plans each time my children cry."

"Then maybe you should stop being the reason they're crying at all."

The last semblance of amusement drained from his face, leaving a deathly glare in its place. When he reached for his bag, I pulled it away from him again. Then, he snapped.

With a hand on my chest, he shoved me against the wall— the surprising force made my heart race with fear. His hand slid up my throat to the base of my jaw as he leaned in closer to threaten me.

"I am not someone to be fucked with, Ms. Nielson," he growled a mere inch from my face.

Blinded by rage, I grabbed his belt, pulling his hips forward to meet the swift upward kick of my knee between his legs.

With a gasp, his strength left him, but I kept him standing with a grip on his belt and the collar of his shirt. "Neither am I, Mr. Montgomery."

He braced himself against the wall, his expression strained under the pain I inflicted. I stared into his eyes, daring him, loving the groan of pain and pleasure he let out.

"I'm not fucking with you when I say your children need you. Stop worrying about work and start worrying about being a better father," I fumed, letting out all the anger I had been suppressing over the past few days.

I let him go, and he fell back to rest against his desk, his hand falling to his manhood to soothe it. He glared at me from beneath his brows but failed to hide the smile curving his lips.

"Enjoy your trip, Mr. Montgomery," I said.

With that, I strutted out, aware he watched me the whole time.

Once in the hall, I stopped suddenly when I saw Matthew. He stared at me for a moment, brows furrowed with indiscernible emotion. Then, without saying a word, he hugged me.

I stood in shock for a second, hugging him back when I understood what was happening. He pulled away and ran up the stairs, but not before I caught a glimpse of his tearful smile.

As fucked up as this family was, that day taught me two important things: They needed my help, and they knew it.

Seven

"I did something bad," I told Crystal.

"Did you fuck him?" she asked, sounding far too excited.

Over a week had passed since *the incident.* Augustine had returned from his business abroad yesterday, and the elephant in the room grew larger each hour that passed. I needed Crystal's advice, which meant I had to fess up.

"No. I sort of . . . kneed him in the balls and told him he was being a shitty father."

She stared at me for so long, I would have thought our connection had frozen if her hair wasn't blowing in the breeze. "You did *what?*"

"I know." I pressed my palm to my forehead in shame. "I wasn't thinking."

"Babe! You know what happens when you try to dominate a dom."

"Yeah, I know." A sadistic standoff wasn't something I needed to have with my employer.

She let out a breath through pursed, smiling lips. "You want it to happen, don't you? You're gonna keep pissing him off, hoping he'll blow up and give you exactly what you want. You kinky bitch."

"No!" *I mean, maybe I've thought about it a little.* "It wasn't like that. He pushed me, and I snapped." Replaying it in my mind made it no better. "I expected him to fire me on the spot, but it was almost the opposite. Challenging him is the only time I get him to emote like a human."

"He's probably been taught to repress his emotions like every other man. Anger may be the only way he knows how to communicate his feelings. Besides, what's the worst that could happen? We all know the way to a man's heart is through his penis and you've almost forgotten what one looks like, so . . ." She giggled.

"Seriously, Crystal . . ." I trailed off when a staff member walked onto the veranda where I was sitting. "Let me call you back."

"Ms. Nielson, there's a call from Matthew's school." He handed me the phone.

I took it from him and mouthed *Thank you.* "Hello?"

"Hello. With whom am I speaking?"

"This is Aubrey Nielson. I'm Matthew's, uh, guardian." I hated saying "nanny."

"Is something wrong?"

"Matthew has gotten himself into some trouble and needs to be picked up immediately."

Shit. "Okay. Someone will be there shortly." I closed my eyes and took a breath. *I have to talk to his father.*

Spewing every curse word in my vocabulary, I went inside and down the grand staircase toward the office.

My heart pounded nervously as I approached. Returning to the scene of the crime was less than desirable, but either I told him now or risked hearing it from someone who wouldn't seek to protect Matthew from the blowback.

I tapped on the door, but it didn't catch his attention.

When he started rattling off Italian, my hesitation faded to annoyance. He was working, as always, too concerned to notice anything else happening around him.

Augustine glanced at me approaching, and his speech stumbled to a stop. He looked away from me and got back on track. I stood in front of his desk and waited for him to stop lecturing the person on the phone about "selling in a bear market." When he reached a pause in his conversation, he looked at me expectantly.

I took that as my cue to speak. "There's an issue at Matthew's school. I can handle it if you'd like."

He started to answer, but looked away and started yelling into the phone once more. With a frustrated huff, he covered the speaker and looked at me once more. "Please."

His aggressive conversation resumed, and that was the end of it. I escaped unscathed.

• • •

It was an odd experience taking a boat to Matthew's school. The dock along the edge of the campus suggested it was a common way to commute. The affluence of the student body must have been staggering.

Matthew's school was as otherworldly as the mansion. The gothic archways of the main hall looked like something you'd see in the great halls of Yale or Columbia. Someone walked out of the office's door and held it open for me. Matthew sat inside the office, slouched in the chair with his arms crossed, donning the same look of indignation his father often had.

"Matthew," I called to him. When he faced me, I gasped. His left cheek was purple, his eye swollen. "What happened?"

"Nothing," he said like a typical teenager. I shot him a *don't mess with me* look, and he rephrased himself. "I got in a fight, but it wasn't a big deal."

"It *was* a big deal," the administrator said. "Which is why he's suspended for three days."

"Suspended?" His father was going to kill him. Or me. Whichever was easiest. "Is there something else we can do instead? He can't miss that much school this late in the semester."

"He said he would rather take the suspension than stay late the next two weeks for after-school detention."

Kids, I swear. "No, let's go ahead and sign him up for that detention."

"Aubrey, no!"

I shot him another look, and he sat back in his chair, silent.

• • •

I took Matthew to a café farther up the river by the twins' school to give us an opportunity to talk. The waiter was kind enough to bring a bag of ice with our coffee and pastries.

I stared at Matthew over my latte as he leaned against the bag in his hand. He avoided my gaze, but behind his guilty face hid a thinly veiled layer of pride. As much as he denied it, I knew he craved his father's attention. The problem would come when Augustine ultimately denied him of it once more.

After a moment, Matthew's eyes flickered up to mine. I waited, sipping my coffee, letting him fill the space with whatever he wanted to say.

"Why are you being nice to me?" he asked.

My brow furrowed. "Why wouldn't I be nice to you?"

"I don't know. Because I'm a fuck-up? Because I don't listen? Because Dad just fired Mildred and now I'm ruining things for you too?" Even if those were legitimate reasons, it still wouldn't be enough to make me chastise him. "Please, please don't tell my dad."

I set my cup down with a sigh. "If you didn't want to get into trouble, then why were you fighting, Matthew?"

His eyes dropped from mine with guilt. "There's a guy in my class who likes to talk shit and I was tired of it."

"What kind of shit does he talk?"

Matthew's brow furrowed, but I watched him force it downward into a scowl. "He likes to call me 'orphan.'"

My heart fell into pieces in my chest. Kids never seemed to understand how they perpetuate their own pain by directing it at others. Only someone with an underdeveloped pre-frontal cortex would think to joke about the death of his mother and—what I now saw was common knowledge—the absence of his father. Fighting only worsened problems, but sometimes, people deserved to be punched.

"Did you make him bleed?" I asked.

Matthew hesitated. "Yeah, a little."

I looked him in the eyes and said, "Good." A smile returned to his face.

I pushed my coffee aside. "Come here." I took Matthew by the chin and pulled his face closer to me. While inspecting his eye, I tried not to laugh at the breathless look of yearning on his face.

"I'm not going to kiss you, dork, I'm going to hide that bruise."

His eyes fluttered away. "Oh."

Digging into my bag, I found my concealer at the bottom—the lightest shade I used was still a bit too dark for him, but it was better than purple. As I unscrewed the cap, he leaned away in protest. "Do you want to wear makeup, or do you want your father to see your black eye?"

"If he even sees me today."

That may have been true, but I wasn't about to agree with him.

I ran the stick beneath his bruise, making him flinch when I hit a sore spot. I evened it out with my finger and gently pressed on a layer of powder to set it. Though the swelling was still noticeable, it was much less so than before.

"There." I held up the compact mirror to show him.

"Wow! You can't even see it!" he said. "Wait . . . Does that mean you're hiding something too?"

I laughed for reasons he didn't understand. "Let's pick up the twins and go home."

•••

At dinnertime, I sat alone with the kids the way I'd usually do when Augustine was away. He was often late to dinner—if he even showed at all. Tabitha sat next to Matthew rather than beside her twin. I watched in amusement as she and Sebastien spoke in their silent twin language. Matthew finished his plate and grinned, knowing he was going to get away with it. He'd feel different when detention started.

We were nearly done eating when Augustine made his appearance. He was glued to his phone as he sat at the end of the table beside me. Only when he lifted the cloche from his plate did he look away, but his gaze returned to it right after. His avoidant silence made me want to knee him all over again.

He grabbed his glass of red wine while his thumb flew over the keys with that annoying sound. I returned my attention to my own glass. Grinning like a mouse that got the cheese, Matthew's shoulders shook with silent laughter.

"May I be excused?" he asked. "I have homework to finish."

Augustine finally looked up. Confusion creased his brow when he saw his son. "Yes, of course."

"Thanks." Matthew stood up and left the room before his father could say anything else. Augustine's puzzled leer followed him all the way out. *He knows.*

"We're all done, too," Tabitha said for both twins. "Can we go play?"

Augustine's phone screen lit up, drawing his attention again. "Thirty minutes, then it's off to bed."

"Okay, Daddy."

Tabitha held her hand out for Sebastien, and he took it. She closed the door behind them, the way I taught her to do with their playroom, not the cage in which I was trapped with her father. I wanted to leave, but my conscience whispered for me to stay. The silence stretched too long, the elephant trumpeting loudly in the corner of my imagination.

"Mr. Montgomery," I said, my voice tighter than intended. "I've been meaning to apologize to you."

He smirked. "For what?" he asked disingenuously. "Sending my balls to my stomach?"

The way he pronounced "balls" was both comical and mortifying. The embarrassing memory made my cheeks warm. "Well . . . yes."

"You meant well. Besides, I'm quite fond of women who can put me in my place." He stared at me while taking a slow drink of wine.

"Oh?"

His phone buzzed against the table, and he picked it up.

When he started typing, I moved to leave, but he stopped me by asking, "Was that makeup on my son's face?"

My mood dropped again. I turned back to him in my chair. "I think you know the answer to that."

A deep laugh rumbled in his chest. "And was that makeup covering a shiner?"

"I think you know the answer to that as well."

"This was the 'issue' you remedied?"

"It was."

He took another sip of his wine and set it down to grab his silverware. I watched him prepare a bite, behaving as if he had no interest in learning more.

"Do you care to know why your son got in a fight?"

He hummed an indifferent response. "Boys will be boys, as they say."

"They will if men continue to expect nothing more from them," I quipped.

Augustine's eyebrows rose.

"If you think he did this simply because he is male, you are tragically overlooking the real issue here."

"And what might that be?"

"That he was fighting because of *you*."

He shot me a look of annoyance. "Brilliant. Tell me how I'm ruining my child this time?"

"A kid at school was calling him an orphan—making fun of him for the fact that *both* his parents are gone."

Augustine stared ahead, pulling the contents off his fork with his teeth.

"He hurt someone else because *you* are hurting *him*."

He gave me a look that could kill. "Do not chastise me for situations you know nothing about."

"I can't know what you refuse to tell me. All I know is how Matthew feels and how little you seem to care."

He set his fork down with a bit too much force. I had angered the beast, just like I wanted.

"Even when you're here, you aren't *really* here. You're on your phone, hopping between meetings, making plans to leave again. It isn't fair to him. It isn't fair to any of them."

"I am trying, Aubrey."

"Then try harder."

I pushed away from the table to leave, but he caught me by the wrist. When I tried to yank it away, he stood and pulled me closer. "What makes you think you can speak to me this way? Do you want me to fire you?"

"And what would you do without me?" I threatened him. "Take time away from work to raise your own kids? How horrible."

The second the words left my mouth, I knew what would happen.

Augustine shoved my back against the wall, stood between my legs, then pinned my wrists against the wall beside my head. The X position he had me in made my thoughts stutter, the sudden arousal leaving my mind in a haze. Overtaken and stimulated, that deplorable part of my brain was in heaven. This was Augustine in his most dominant form. Against all rational thought, I wanted him to do more.

He leaned in closer, his snarled lips a mere breath from mine. My eyes bounced between his lips and his intent gaze.

"There are things about me that you do not understand," he said. "I have every intention of doing what is best for my children, but I am not as in control as I seem."

The irony made me laugh. "That's bullshit and you know it."

My attempt to pull my wrists from his grasp only caused him to tighten his grip. My breath shallowed, and the heat between my thighs became harder to ignore. This was my favorite game: the infliction of pain with the hidden promise of pleasure.

He must have seen it on my face. His scowl faded with recognition as he looked down his nose at me.

"Are you *trying* to anger me?" His question was an accusation. My teeth in my lip failed to pin my smile. He stepped closer and pressed his body against mine. "Do you find some sort of enjoyment in it?"

I pushed my hips forward, feeling his erection throb against me. I looked him in the eye, finding in him a mirror of myself. "Don't you?"

A quiet growl rumbled in his chest.

In one swift move, he pulled me from the wall, bent me over, and slammed my chest down onto the table. The force knocked over my glass of wine, dribbling the last sip against the wood a few inches from my face.

I stared in shock. My heart raced when my mind registered his hands still wrapped around my wrist and flat against my back, pinning me down.

"*This* is what you want?" he asked. His aggression scared me, but more unfortunately, it turned me on.

He stepped closer and pressed himself against me. I wriggled my backside against him, feeling his hard cock at my seam. His hand traced slowly down my spine, then left to grip my hip and stop my movements. I whimpered to suppress a moan.

Drunk on ecstasy, the lack of personal gratification caught up to me. My resolve languished in my helpless position. I had been longing for a man to take me, roughly and mercilessly, and here Augustine was, the embodiment of all my darkest desires, bending me over a fucking table.

Our heavy breaths filled the otherwise silent room. I looked back at him and saw my thoughts reflected in his expression, full of shame and lust. We stared as if waiting for the other to stop it, for one of us to make sense of the situation and behave justly.

But neither of us did.

He cursed under his breath. His hand left my wrist and went to his fly. As he unfastened it, I reached down and began to pull up my skirt.

"Daddy? Aubrey?" Tabitha called from outside the door.

Augustine let go of me, and we quickly moved away from each other. He resituated his pants while I did the same to my skirt. "In here, my love," he called to her, sitting down in his seat again. He shot me a look before she skipped into the room.

"Aubrey!" She beamed when she saw me. "Will you read us *Le Petit Prince?*"

Still flustered, I crouched down to her level and took the book from her hand. "Yes, of course I will."

She took my hand and led me out of the room with her. Augustine looked at me from the corner of his eye as we left.

I walked with Tabitha, thankful she had pulled me from a mistake I was more than willing to make. Fuck my stupid brain for being attracted to men I knew would do nothing but hurt me.

• • •

After reading to the twins for over an hour, they finally drifted off to sleep. I turned off the lights, leaving the door cracked when I left.

As I meandered down the hallway, my body still buzzed with desire. I couldn't wait to lock myself away and ease the noxious ache with the company of my chest of secrets. My body stirred, my mind flooded with erotic scenes I knew were too reckless to reprise. Tearing myself from my thoughts, I rounded the corner. Then I saw him.

Augustine stood at the top of the grand staircase. Though I meant to sneak away, my heels clicked loudly against the wood floor. He looked over his shoulder and caught sight of me.

He turned to face me and leaned against the banister, his delicious body twisting in a way that made my mouth go dry. I watched his eyes scan me from head to toe, his tongue wetting his lips as he did.

We stared for a moment, neither of us moving, neither of us capable of walking away from the opportunity standing right in front of us. Finally, he made his move, stalking over with the slow, deliberate pace of a dom who knew he was in control.

I swallowed the lump in my throat. "Mr. Montgomery."

"Ms. Nielson." He walked closer to me, but he didn't touch. As I stood breathless, he peered down at me with a dark gaze.

He brushed my hair from my face, the backs of his fingers tracing down my cheek. Firmly, he gripped my chin and scrubbed his thumb over my lips. When he slipped it into my mouth, I sucked it, watching a wicked smile curve his lips. I knew exactly what he wanted, and what role he wanted me to play to get what *I* wanted too.

No matter how much I tried, I couldn't fight the temptation of a man like Augustine. I was a moth ready to set myself aflame just to feel that sadistic heat again.

Augustine's thumb slipped from my lips, his hand leaving my face. "Come on then," he said in a growly whisper. With a turn, he began his descent down the stairs, never looking back to see if I'd follow.

And he didn't need to.

Eight

I'd like to say this was part of my plan—that giving into my attraction to Augustine was a crucial piece of my plot to get through to him—but that wasn't the truth. I was lonely, horny, and Augustine was . . . Augustine.

Following him was an out-of-body experience. As if floating through a dream, my body behaved on its own, my brain numb. I was in his office before I could feel my feet on the floor.

He stood at the open double doors near his desk, unfastening the buttons on his wrists. A wordless invitation. The confidence he had taunted me as much as it tempted.

Inside, the room was eerily plain. Only a grand, four-post bed centered on the back wall with side tables, an armoire, and two antique chairs positioned in front of a tall arched window that matched the ones in his office. No rug, no curtains, no paintings on the walls or decorations on the tabletops. It was a larger version of my room that looked even less lived in. Temporary lodgings.

The doors closed behind me and a lock clicked. I looked over my shoulder at Augustine as he stalked closer. In the darkness, a sane woman would fear a man with his temperament, but it only made me want him more.

Augustine weaved his fingers into the hair on the back of my head and tugged it gently, making me look up at him.

"This is what you want?" he asked. "To be fucked by someone you know will hurt you?"

He made it impossible to nod, so I said, "Yes."

My heart pounded in my chest as he placed his hand gently on my throat. "I thought you were smarter than that." Then, he kissed me.

His lips felt like pure bliss and tasted more decadent than expensive wine. With a trace of his thumb against my chin, he parted my lips and slid in his tongue. I had to fight myself to keep from moaning.

He kissed like a Frenchman. Passionate, sultry, with plenty of tongue. It was the kind of kissing that reminded me of sex—the heated teasing that created a desperate ache between my thighs. Every time I thought I should stop, he placed a more delectable kiss on my lips.

The hand on my throat traced down the center of my chest, a finger teasing between my breasts. He plucked at my buttons, one by one, the material sliding from my shoulders as he did. I returned the favor with quivering hands, feeling lucky that a few buttons were already undone. He pulled his shirt off and I moved to undo his belt. Our kisses deepened, our breaths becoming heavier as his fingers made quick work of my bra and my skirt's zipper. His hands ran over my ass before sliding his fingers beneath the side of my panties and ripping them down to my thighs.

When our lips parted, he stared down at me as his hand slid between my legs. A quiet hum rumbled in his chest.

His finger slipped inside, touching me where no one had in months. "Already wet for me?"

"Are you not already hard for *me?*" I reached forward to finish unfastening his pants, but he grabbed my hands and pulled them from him. I looked up at him in surprise, then gasped when he picked me up by my thighs, carrying me to the bed and dropping me onto the edge of the mattress.

The muscles of his strong arms and chest flexed as he unfastened and removed his pants. As he leaned up, my eyes traced down his toned core to a delicious V that pointed to what I wanted most. A thick erection strained against his thigh beneath the thin shield of his underwear. He gave it a squeeze as if to tease me.

That was about the time it stopped being about getting through to him. I didn't care who he was or what we were to each other. I just wanted to fuck.

He moved closer. I closed my eyes in expectation of a kiss, but his only touch was a hand against my chest, pushing me down onto the bed.

My teeth sank into my lip, while I watched him peel my stocking down my leg and, in a painfully slow motion, wrap it around his hand and pull it from my foot. He did the same with the other, then lifted my ankles and dragged my panties up and off my legs. A gentle push against my feet told me to drop them to the sides. I did so, exposing my most intimate area to him, feeling like a virgin under his scrutinous gaze. The way he licked his lips while staring down at my sex made it hard to breathe.

He leaned onto his hands to hover above me. His mouth found my neck, then trailed down my chest, then my stomach, then lower, lips tickling over my thigh as he tracked slow kisses down toward my aching center. When he made it to the apex of my thigh, I hissed when he dug his teeth into my sensitive flesh.

I tensed with the delectable pain, but when his teeth left me, he lowered his mouth to my sex. When I closed my eyes, my senses heightened to the feeling of his tongue sliding through my folds, his lips nipping and sucking as he teased up toward my clit. Once there, he sucked it over and over, teasing it with the tip of his tongue. I moaned and gripped my breasts, tugging my nipples between my fingers. Though I almost never came from oral sex alone, the pleasure was so deep I felt I could come apart right then and there.

My hips trembled when the pleasure rushed through me. When I looked down in astonishment, his dark eyes found mine. He stared at me while his tongue slid up into view, the muscle in his shoulder flittering as he stroked himself. I let my head fall back onto the bed and moaned.

With an arm around my waist, he moved me up higher on the bed. Sitting back on his heels, he positioned himself between my legs and hiked my knees up and apart. I remembered I should ask him to use a condom after he was already pushing himself inside me.

"Ah!" I arched back when he slid in deeper. I was wet, more than ready, but he was big—*much* bigger than expected— his girth stretching me to my limit. The tinge of pain made me whimper. It had been months since I'd been penetrated. It was a self-obedience practice I had adopted to make vanilla interactions like these more enjoyable, and holy hell did it pay off.

With nothing between us, I felt every inch of him as he pushed deeper. His head fell back with a quiet *Fuck*, displaying his similar sentiments.

"You take me so well," he said, easing his cock slowly in

and out. His fingers dragged up my hip and thigh, spreading me wider for him, then they found my throat. "Does it hurt?"

"Yes," I whimpered.

He breathed out something between a sigh and a laugh. "And do you like that?"

Fucking hell. I nodded. "Yes."

He leaned forward onto his hands. I lifted myself onto an elbow and pulled his face to mine. He allowed me a single kiss before he pushed me down by the chest again.

"I am going to fuck you. *Hard*," he said as a warning, though it felt like he was fulfilling a request. With no add-ons, no *real* pain, he could rip me apart, and I would still want more. "Stop me if I get too rough."

Proof he knew nothing about me. I relaxed back, submitting, letting him take me in any way he wanted. "You won't."

With a hard thrust, his hips crashed against mine, sending a shock of pleasure through my core. I mewled. His pace quickened, his cock stroking deep with every quick pump of his hips. The flood of pleasure made my eyes roll back, stealing my breath while I drowned in the blissful sensation.

"Oh my god," I whimpered. "Oh my fucking god." I couldn't remember having vanilla sex that felt this good.

I reached down to touch myself, circling my fingertips against my clit, my sex gripping him as I moaned. His fingers dug into my ass as he pulled my hips up in time with his downward thrusts, stroking in all the right places. I pressed my feet against the mattress and lifted my hips from the bed, swirling them as he retreated, and pushing down as his hips crashed against me.

The bed shook, the headboard tapping against the wall

with every thrust. I fisted the sheets, my moans verging on screams. The heat of my pleasure built hot and fast inside me.

My legs began to tense, and I knew I was right there. As he used my body for his own desire, I watched him, finding his eyes squeezed tight, his beautiful lips agape as he panted, his brow twisted in a look of torment. It was as if fucking me to pieces brought him pain as well.

And with that, I lost it.

I arched back, crying out as the orgasm ripped through me. I came hard—so much harder than I expected. Each wave of pleasure pulsed through my body in time with the clenching of my sex around him. My body shuddered and shook in a blissfully erotic dance.

Augustine groaned every time his cock stroked inside me. I kept rubbing myself, enjoying every second of my climax as it wrecked me. He grew larger inside me, fucked me harder, then finally, he pulled out of me with a moan.

Warm sprays of semen fell onto my chest and stomach over and over as he came. His warmth trickled off the side of my hip while he stroked himself dry. A bead of sweat trailed down the center of his heaving chest as he sat back on his heels.

He looked down at me with disdain as he panted. The look of a dom disappointed in himself for letting me make him come so hard.

Feeling thoroughly fucked, I was at a loss for words. I stared down in adoration at the carnality. It felt so wrong. So dirty. So . . . *hot.*

Augustine rolled to his back beside me, then reached for the tissues on his side table. He wiped his mess from my stomach and then tossed them into the trash. As his breathing slowed, he looked at me as if expecting me to say something.

I was out of breath and out of brain cells—language escaping me completely.

He turned off the light without a word. I drifted off to sleep before I knew I was doing so.

• • •

An unfamiliar alarm jolted me awake. When I opened my eyes to a room that wasn't mine, it all came flooding back to me.

In the bed next to me, Augustine sat up and turned off the alarm with a sigh. He peered down at me, his face devilishly handsome but void of emotion. I hid my body beneath the sheets and stared back at him, not knowing what to say.

He appraised me neutrally. "It's best we forget this happened, don't you think?"

His words crushed my spirit, but I agreed with a nod. He left the shield of covers and walked naked into his bathroom, shutting the door behind him. My fantasy was over, and the reality was harsh. He left me shamed and embarrassed, as per usual.

I left the bed, put on my clothes, and fled back to my room.

That morning, I showered longer than usual, trying to scrub away the part of me that enjoyed being used by my employer last night. It was one thing to have rough sex with a stranger, but I had sex with *my boss*—and unprotected sex at that.

With that thought, I scrubbed myself again.

• • •

My skin ached with anxiety when I took the twins to the dining room for breakfast. Tabitha held my hand even after we sat, and the shame I felt made my stomach turn. I calmed myself with a sip of juice.

Matthew walked in looking tired. I glanced at him, my surprise staving off some of my guilt.

"Your eye," I said. "Did you not want me to cover it up again?"

"It doesn't matter," he said. I gave him a curious look until the servers came in and set down four plates.

My mood dropped. "Your father isn't joining us?" I asked, already knowing the answer.

Matthew shrugged and started shoveling food into his mouth.

"Where is Mr. Montgomery?" I asked a staff member.

"I believe he left earlier this morning, ma'am."

"Oh."

I couldn't decide if it was better or worse that he was gone, but I knew if he wanted to do worse than use me and toss me aside, he would. Nothing was sacred to him. Everything was replaceable; everyone had a price. He wouldn't fire me until Matthew finished his semester, at least.

"When is Daddy coming back?" Tabitha asked me.

"I'm not sure, sweetheart."

"Then can we play outside today?" she asked with a smile. Sebastien turned to look at me with the same expression.

"Of course we can," I told them, making them cheer. "Finish your breakfast first."

They did as they were told, inhaling their food so we could leave as soon as possible.

Seeing how something so simple brought them joy caused my guilt to return. I cared for them as much, if not more, than they seemed to care for me. If Augustine let me go, they'd lose yet another form of stability in their lives.

I couldn't put them through that pain again. I had to give him a reason to let me stay.

Nine

More than a week passed, and Augustine hadn't returned.

When I asked the butler, Warren, he told me something about springtime being a busy season for corporations. Hirings, firings, acquisitions, taxes? Maybe finalizing contracts before spending summers on their yachts? I wasn't sure what exactly Augustine did for work, but it gave him plenty of excuses to stay away. I loathed his inconsistency and, most days, him.

Every part of our night together was a mistake. Though I had full faith in my IUD, I feared waking up with an itch. I didn't know his status or his preferences. I didn't know much about him at all, and yet . . .

His allure was too strong—a brand of man I had fallen for before, and one that only got worse for me as time went on. There was a chance Augustine was pulling another typical dom move by ignoring me until I crawled back to him, but I didn't want to play that game again.

I wanted an equal. A toxic, inexperienced dom was beneath me. Figuratively speaking.

It had been nearly two weeks of me living in the shadow of my mistake, and I still hadn't built up the courage to tell Crystal what happened. Sick with guilt, I decided it was time.

When I grabbed my phone to call her, I found something surprising on my screen.

Crystal: I gave your number to someone.

I video-called her immediately, glaring at my screen until her conniving smile appeared. "You did *what*?" I hissed.

"Okay, but before you get mad, he has a full head of hair and a good job."

My anger fizzled. "What kind of 'good job'?"

"He's a *doctor*," she said with added emphasis. "He's cute, and even if it doesn't work out, he's a guaranteed lay. He's a regular at Cuff." A well-known New York City fetish club.

"But is he a top or a bottom?"

"I'll let you have fun figuring that out."

I sneered. Blind dates were awkward enough without an undefined power exchange. But I was horny and my ego was damaged—not a good combination to have when Augustine finally decided to come home. I'd need to find some way to resolve it. If not this, then something else.

"If this goes badly, I'm blaming you," I told her.

She snickered. "Mm-hmm. Love you too."

When I hung up, I felt worse. I still hadn't told her what happened with Augustine. The longer I went, the more she'd think I was trying to hide it from her. *Was* I trying to hide it from her?

After my moment of contemplation, I unlocked my phone again, the screen remaining on the list of my recent calls. Beneath my thumb, Rianne's name stared at me enticingly.

She offered. I could just accept.

I hovered over her number for what seemed like minutes as I debated with myself. Though her offer for a weekend shift came with many, many cons, shaking off the dust and regaining some confidence felt like a much-needed pro.

Finally, I called her. She picked up immediately.

"There's my best friend!"

We were great coworkers, but I wouldn't call us friends. I laughed. "You only call me that when you need a favor."

"Well . . . I do."

"What do you need?"

"A dominatrix. I'm short one tonight."

"*Tonight?*"

She hummed a yes. I'd have to leave in the next couple of hours if I wanted to make it there in time.

"Why did you call me, Bunny? Was it because you missed me?" she purred. I could hear her pout. "Or because you wanted that shift I offered you?"

I *was* calling her in the hopes she'd give me the shift, but now that she had, I was hesitating. "I don't know . . . I've been trying to get away from all that."

"For what? So you can settle down with some vanilla bitch and have kids?" She cackled. "Please. I know you better than that."

She didn't need to drag me that hard, but I understood her game. "You really need someone tonight?"

"Not just someone. I need the best." She really knew how to flatter. And manipulate. "So, can I count on you tonight?"

I let out a slow breath. "Yeah."

• • •

With or without a scheduled date, I had planned to take a weekend to return to the city for a little Me Time. After arranging for a babysitter for the twins, I started to regret my decision to leave for the weekend. The thought of being away from the kids made me want to change my mind and stay, but

I knew taking care of myself would make me more capable of caring for them.

Two nights away would give me time to get over the mistake I had made with Augustine—a chance to wipe it from my memory and stop replaying it every time I laid down at night. *It was a one-night stand*, I told myself. *They're always messy.* Having another would prove that.

I packed an overnight bag with the essentials: a change of clothes, lingerie, a pair of flats for when my stilettos proved too much to handle on the Manhattan sidewalks, condoms, and toiletries. When I was packed up and ready, I zipped it up tight and went to check on the littles.

Tabitha sat in a chair while Sebastien practiced piano with his instructor. I interrupted him. "I'm heading out," I told them as I kneeled to their level. "May I have a hug before I go?"

They ran over and squeezed me tighter than expected. My chest ached.

"When are you coming back?" Sebastien asked.

"Sunday."

His brow furrowed, and his chin quivered. The sight gripped my heart and didn't let go.

"Please don't be sad, sweetheart. You're going to have so much fun this weekend, and you'll barely notice I'm gone because I'll be back so fast."

He hugged me again, and I let him hold on as long as he wanted. Tabitha held my hand until he stopped, then took his place, her head resting on my shoulder for a long moment. They made it nearly impossible to say goodbye. More reason to ensure I'd only be saying *See you later.*

Fighting back tears, I waved goodbye to them and went to the lounge to check on Matthew, finding him sitting on the couch playing video games.

"Where are you going?" he asked when he saw me. "Do you have a date or something?"

"Yes, 'something.'" I pressed a kiss to the top of his head. "Be good."

"*You* be good," he teased.

It's a little late for that, kid.

• • •

Leaving the island felt like time travel. A short boat ride and a six-hour drive brought me back to my past. A life I thought I had left forever.

The Manhattan fetish club, Risqué, hadn't changed one bit since my last shift over a year ago. The club was invite-only, focused on satisfying a VIP clientele with a diverse range of S&M and bondage kinks. Even after forty years in business, it had unparalleled notoriety in the scene, always keeping it in competition with the newer establishments that cropped up each year. I remember feeling like a celebrity when I became part of the staff.

Although sex and fluid exchange were prohibited in the club, the job gave me the satisfaction I couldn't get from many of my past relationships. When my real world was full of men who wanted submissive women—ironic how often life comes full circle—I came here to enjoy life as a domme. My love of both roles, when balanced, validated my switch identity.

Teachers often had second jobs to supplement our shitty pay. Once I got the job at the private school, I decided it was time to go "legit." Working at a school full of wealthy families meant there was a good chance one of the dads was my client. One report that I was a sex worker, and my job was gone, as if the same parents weren't making siblings for their kids while they were in the next room. Had I known my job would be gone soon anyway, I would have made the same choice, though maybe not as abruptly.

In the changing room, I fastened the multitude of buckles on my thigh-high boots while watching Rianne slide her lubricated body into a latex catsuit, inch by tedious inch, making me thankful for the freedom of my high-cut bodysuit. A leather mask with molded bunny ears added a bit of whimsy to my intimidating look, playing on the nickname given to me for my preference to "hop" between roles. I always felt most like myself in fetish wear—the same preference that made it impossible to rid my personal closet of stilettoes and thigh-high stockings.

"Please tell me you're getting your back blown out in upstate," Rianne said suddenly. I appreciated her bluntness, even when it was cutting. In character and behind our masks, it was easy to confuse us. The only difference was her 4a texture and mastery of flexi rods that made me want to hide my curls in a bun.

I started in with my bobby pins and gave a vague answer. "Kind of."

"Details."

"I had a one-night ordeal with a dom. It was good for what it was, but it's never happening again."

"Says everyone before it happens again."

I shot her a look through my mask.

"A dom, huh? What's wrong with him? Is he poor? Bad job?" she asked.

"Nope. C-level and filthy rich."

"Is he a dog?"

"No," I answered with a rueful sigh. "He's offensively attractive."

"But he's got a tiny dick."

"Also no. Not *at all.*" My sex ached at the mere thought.

Rianne's face was twisted with confusion until something clicked. "Oh, so he's married."

Her words panged in my chest. "Yeah." In his mind, which was all that mattered.

"Okay, phew. You really had me thinking you found a unicorn or something," she mused. "Well, congratulations, homewrecker. Was the sex satisfying at least?"

She was only teasing, but I hadn't been able to relieve the shame of that night. I deflected her question by saying what I knew to be true. "I'm rarely satisfied by a dom."

"But you're still dedicated to your lack of dedication?" she asked, alluding to the fact that she didn't consider being a switch a true preference.

"I am."

She put on her matching mask. "Well, I'm glad you haven't given up on this side of yourself, at least."

Yeah, I thought. *I've just given up on all of me.*

• • •

Dealing with new clients was a skill not everyone possessed. Reading subtle cues, getting someone to push past their shyness or society-induced shame to communicate their desires properly. Like teaching, it was less about the result and more about understanding motivation. People rarely let the full truth speak first.

This client knew he wanted someone to watch him, embarrass him, and punish him, but he didn't realize what he really wanted was to be *seen* while doing what others had always told him was wrong. Nothing within the rules was "wrong" in this place. No judgment, only communication and understanding. I would never shame one of my clients, yet there I was, shaming myself.

My pet was calm, balls drained, a smile glued to his face. A sign I had given him everything he needed. After releasing him from his shackles, he asked, "Can I see you again, Mistress?"

I ran a finger beneath his jawline. "Only if you're good." A little slap punctuated my sentence and widened his smile. I exited the room, jealous of his satisfaction.

Laughter drifted up the hall from the dressing room, but I wasn't in a social mood after my conversation with Rianne. I walked into the smaller changing area and stripped off my borrowed gloves to check them back in. After a thorough wash and dry of my hands and arms, I checked my lipstick in the mirror, getting distracted by my eyes instead.

Even behind my mask, I looked tired. Not by exhaustion or fatigue. I was tired of the bullshit.

Leaving this scene had been my goal, yet I always ended up back in it in one way or another. I couldn't let this part of me go. Maybe it was time to admit that I didn't *want* to.

Laughter boomed from down the corridor, as if the other girls had heard my thoughts. My mood dipped even lower. A drink sounded better than gossip, so I settled for a quick public appearance.

In the greeting room, I strutted to the bar, enjoying the lingering stares I got while doing so, and leaned my elbows onto the counter.

"Can I get a glass of wine?"

"Is red okay?" the bartender asked.

"I'll always accept a red."

Missing my joke, she went to fetch it for me. Sitting on a nearby stool, a masked man sipped what looked like scotch, making me wish they'd allow me to drink something harder before my shift ended. The bartender put down my glass, and I lingered over my first, disappointing sip.

"Is my British bitch ready?" I heard Diana ask.

The man beside me turned and answered, "More than ready."

His familiar baritone reverberated through me, sending a fearful chill up my spine. I turned to look at the man as he walked past me. Beneath his mask was a set of sculpted lips, and on his elegant hand, a platinum wedding band. My breath left me in a rush.

Augustine.

My heart raced for minutes on end. A single glass of wine was nowhere near sufficient to calm my nerves. I knew it was him, knew what he was paying to have done to him, but I had to see it for myself.

I snuck through the back room and into the corridor meant for security and training. Through the two-way mirror on the wall, I stared at the man cuffed, collared, and strapped down against the cushion, Diana whipping his reddened ass with the flogger, his erection bobbing with every lash. His face turned in my direction as he groaned, and my jaw dropped.

Augustine wasn't a dom after all.

Ten

Augustine, for lack of a better term, had me fucked up.

He didn't know me, didn't have any idea what I was capable of, yet he had me twisted up and believing his lies like an amateur. Shocked was too light a term for what I was feeling. Lost between anger and thrill, I was disappointed in myself for not being able to figure it out sooner. I stared at myself in the mirror for an hour when I woke up, trying to figure out if I had seen him or if I had projected my contempt for him onto a stranger.

A dominant-masochist wasn't the most uncommon occurrence, but it was rare to see a true dominant pay to be topped so aggressively. Sexual preferences can be fluid, and people can spend money on experiences they don't enjoy, but I knew Augustine better than that.

He wasn't dabbling in the gray area between. He liked both. If he truly preferred to sadistically top and masochistically bottom the way I did . . . I was in for some real trouble.

In my stupor, it took me so long to get ready I was almost late to my date. Stockings weren't the best look with the jersey dress I had packed, but I didn't have the energy to care. It was a miracle I was still holding my sanity together after Augustine tipped my grasp of reality on its side.

Colin drove me again in the Rolls. After seeing the looks from patrons, I realized I should have had him park up the street and let me walk to the restaurant on my own. What I must have looked like stepping out of a house-priced car wearing a fifty-dollar dress.

A man approached me. "Are you Aubrey?"

"Yes. Hi," I greeted my date.

He gave me a coy smile that screamed *submissive*. Not what I hoped for, but I could make it work. "Want to go inside?"

You? "Absolutely."

• • •

Dinner started off nicely enough. The wine was delicious, though it could have come from a prison toilet and I'd still drink it all the same. As I sipped as slowly as I was able, he held the conversation well, asking me the usual questions about my interests, my educational background, and my job. He was handsome, either biracial or light-skinned like me, but with tight curls and dark brown eyes. Unfortunately, that was where his attractive qualities ended.

As time passed, more about him started to bother me. Squirrely was the best way to describe him. His eyes darted around when he spoke, he chewed with his mouth open, didn't match his wine with his food, and didn't pause his sentence when the waiter came over to check on us. Pettier still, his laugh—a high-pitched, feminine-sounding giggle that was unexpected from someone with a voice as deep as his—made me cringe.

When my patience began to run thin, I stared at him, waiting for his eyes to stop bouncing around the room as he told another pointless story of how he had become the uninteresting person he was today. I could get off on forcing him to stare at me while I smacked the squirreliness out of him.

During another one of his unending sentences, I stroked a finger over the back of his hand, trying to call his attention. When his story failed to wrap up, I grabbed his hand in mine. Finally, he stopped talking.

"Tell me how long you've been into . . . what we're into," I said.

His cheeks gained a tint of rosiness. "Two years now. My last girlfriend introduced me," he said. "Once I tried it, I couldn't go back."

"Same," I agreed in sentiment. I was far from new to this game.

"You're a . . ." He leaned in to whisper. "You're a domme, right?"

"I can be if that's what you'd like."

His brows furrowed in confusion. "What does that mean?"

"I'm a switch, technically. I assume both roles well and enjoy them equally."

The pause that followed lasted far too long. "Oh." I knew exactly what that meant.

Doms were usually the worst about it, laughing off my insistence, acting as if wanting both was a habit I needed to be trained to give up. I enjoyed letting them try, but it was never going to work.

"So, you . . . you like to top sometimes but not always?"

"It depends on the dynamic with my partner. I prefer a balance of both, but that won't affect what we do tonight."

His eyes widened. "Tonight?"

"Yes. That's what this date is for, right?" I scanned his

bewildered look with confusion, trying to figure out what I had done. "Did I say something wrong?"

He let out another annoying giggle. "No, of course not." He checked his watch. "Damn it, I just remembered I have early rounds tomorrow morning. I should really get going."

"Right now?"

"Yes. Sorry." He called for the check, then set a few bills onto it, avoiding more conversation while waiting for the waiter to return. "I'll call you?"

An early appointment. The top excuse in the first date playlist. "Sure," I agreed with his lie.

He pressed a kiss to my cheek—my *cheek*—and left. I watched him walk away, then downed the rest of my glass of wine.

Why did this keep happening? At what point did I become the one who got kicked out of bed or left alone in a restaurant?

The waiter came by to collect the check and I stopped her. "May I have another glass?"

"Of course."

"You know what? Make that a bottle."

"The date didn't go well? His loss," she said with a wink. "I'll have the bottle over soon."

The date was the least of my problems after a week like mine. At least I'd have alcohol to keep me company.

• • •

Sitting in the corner of the patio alone, I drowned my sorrows while I waited for Colin to pick me up. With no need to drive and most of the next day to sleep off a hangover, I was in no rush.

I watched couples at a nearby table cast glances of pity

my way. At another, two college-aged boys had been watching to see when I'd be drunk enough to approach. Little did they know, I was already two drinks past that point. I clinked my nails rhythmically against my glass while they smiled, but never approached.

Why aren't they coming over? Is it because I'm so fine it's intimidating? Or, do I look like I show up on a first date saying I'm lonely and horny but want a wedding and a baby—in that order—within the next eighteen months? I pondered that for too long. *Nah, I'm hot as fuck.*

At the end of the bottle, a text from Colin buzzed on my phone to tell me he was outside. Perfect timing. Any longer and I'd get sloppy. I stood and quickly found I was more intoxicated than expected, making my five-inch heels quite the challenge. Carefully, I staggered out of the restaurant, finding Colin waiting at the curb. He helped me to the car and opened the door for me.

Only when I plopped down into the seat did I realize I wasn't alone.

Augustine sat next to me, tapping away on his phone. The harsh light pierced the darkness of the car, illuminating his handsome face marred by that vacant expression—the same face he had when he kicked me out of his bed. Immediately, my mind went back to last night, watching all my questions get answered by the whip marks on his ass.

I hadn't planned on seeing him so soon after my discovery. A shame he caught me when I was too intoxicated to hold my tongue.

"Hi, Augie," I slurred, calling him by Crystal's nickname. At least I had the wherewithal not to call him Mont-Money.

Augustine glanced at me from the corner of his eye. "Ms. Nielson. Get a bit pissed tonight, did we?"

Drunk me couldn't translate between British pissed and

American pissed. "My date was a waste of time. Of course I'm mad."

"Were you this drunk on your date?"

"Don't blame this on me when dude was a whole-ass rodent." My quip garnered a hint of a smirk from Augustine. "He 'remembered' he had an 'early appointment' and left," I said, air quotes and all. "I drank after to numb the ache of my poor, empty vagina."

Not a chuckle, but a full laugh escaped him. He was most likely laughing at my expense, but I was too far gone to notice.

"Even if I had been drunk, I'm still hot. Admit it." I leaned closer to him. "I mean, you fucked me. I can't be *that* ugly."

"Jesus Christ." He pressed the button to roll up the partition between us and Colin, then glared at me.

"Oh, sorry. I forgot we were supposed to forget it happened."

Without a response, he looked back at his phone and started typing again.

This man didn't know how much his indifference made me want to choke him. More than that, he didn't know how much we'd *both* enjoy that scenario. The thought made Drunk Me *very* horny.

I scooted closer to him and leaned against the back of the seat near his shoulder. The hem of my dress rode up enough to show the top of my stocking, but he didn't take notice.

"Does it count as remembering if I tell you I want to do it again?"

He sighed but never stopped typing on his phone. "Yes."

I hummed my discontent. "I don't like you, Augustine. But I do like your penis, and I *really* want it inside me tonight." I stroked my finger in little circles on his chest. "I'll let you choose where."

His expression never changed. "You're drunk."

"And you have a dirty little secret."

"Oh, do I?"

"Mm-hmm."

The blue strobe of the streetlights through the window washed over him, his lips casting a curved shadow against the scruff on his chin, his sharp nose perfect in profile, the light reflecting off the few gray strands in his otherwise dark hair. His visage mesmerized me.

He continued to ignore me, the way he always did, the way that drove me crazy. Now, I knew it was all part of his game. It was laughable he thought I didn't know how to play it better.

My fingers unfastened the next button of his shirt, opening it to the middle of his pecs. He didn't flinch a bit, nor did he look my way.

"Why do you hate me, Augie?" I asked.

"I don't hate you, Ms. Nielson."

"Then why didn't you like fucking me?"

"It's not that I didn't enjoy sleeping with you," he answered. "It's that I don't feel the need to sleep with you again."

His words were a knife to my ego. *Who the fuck does he think he's talking to?* I slurred even in my mind.

"Fuck you," I spat. "I let you fuck me raw, risked my health for *vanilla* sex. If you think I'm not worth fucking again, you're a fucking idiot."

My overuse of "fuck" made him chuckle, but I was out of vocabulary *and* patience.

I climbed up in the seat and swung my leg over his lap to straddle him, interrupting his text message. He started to scold me, until he looked down, his words evaporating as he watched me lower my hips onto his lap.

"You think you don't want to fuck me again because I'm

just another submissive woman. But you've got me all wrong," I said. When he glared, I ran my fingers into his hair and yanked his head back. His eyes widened as he looked up at me. "You act like a big, mean dom, but I know what you really are."

"And what's that?" he challenged.

I placed my other hand at his throat and tightened my grip on his hair. He stared me down while my lips hovered a breath away from his. "You're a switch," I whispered with a smile. "Just like me."

He held my gaze, his expression unchanged, but his silence gave me all the answers I needed.

I released my hold on him, then dragged my nails down his chest. Closing the small space between us, I kissed him.

His hands gripped my hips as I moved against his lap, and he subtly flexed his hips toward me. While he continued to hide his desire for me, barely returning my impassioned gestures, he never pushed me away either.

"You're drunk, Ms. Nielson," he said against my lips.

"And you're—" The car lurched, and a wave of nausea hit me like a punch in the stomach. "Oh, god."

I reached for the window control and Augustine pressed it down for me. I slid from his lap and retched through the window onto the street below.

Sexy, Aubrey.

Lucky for me, I didn't remember the rest of the night.

Eleven

The following morning was as clean as it was a mess.

I woke up in an unfamiliar bed, surrounded by fresh white linens and fluffy pillows. Through the window, I recognized the signature streets of SoHo. *Who put me up in a fancy hotel?*

My memory flooded back, accompanied by a wine headache. I remembered exactly who had put me up. This wasn't a hotel, but rather the SoHo loft Mildred told me about months before. Augustine had taken me home with him.

I found myself in my dress and stockings from last night. My panties were on and uncomfortably dry. It was foolish to think Augustine would take advantage of me in my inebriated state, considering he would barely take advantage of me when I *begged* him. Cringing over both memories, I stripped myself of the wretched nylons and went to the bathroom to wash off last night's makeup—and shame.

Hair up, face washed, and teeth brushed, I was in the best shape I could be with only the toiletries in my purse. A fluffy robe gave me enough bravery to step outside the room. When I stumbled into a hallway, I stopped in surprise. To my right, the long hall extended past two doors in line with mine, leading to a third at the very end. To my left, bright light poured from an open living space. As I walked toward it, my eyes took in every inch of the room.

Tall windows with gridded mullions and arched tops set in an exposed brick wall. The window's black frames matched the black metal handrails of a floating staircase. Rustic hardwood floors added warmth to the otherwise ultra-modern aesthetic. Past the blockage of the stairs, the living space expanded two-fold, fully open to a kitchen and dining space. At the end of a long table sat Augustine.

I had imagined the SoHo loft as a small bachelor pad he slept in between flights instead of a second home large enough to house the whole family. Wishful thinking, perhaps.

Augustine lifted his gaze from his phone and spotted me. "Good morning, Ms. Nielson," he greeted me.

Unable to escape, I padded over to the table. "Good morning, Mr. Montgomery."

He appraised me as I approached, a hint of a smirk tilting his lips. "Care for some coffee?" He gestured to the chair beside him.

"Sure." I pulled the chair over and sat, hoping to maintain as much distance from him as possible.

He poured the coffee from the French press into my cup. "Cream?" he asked. "Or, do you prefer your coffee like your recollection of last night? Black."

I rolled my eyes. "My memory is just fine, thank you. I believe it's *you* who wants clarification."

He set his phone to the side and peered at me—the kind of attention I rarely received from him while clothed. "You made quite the claim last night."

I blew the steam from my mug to hide my smile. "It wasn't a claim," I corrected him, "British bitch."

The silence that followed brought me such joy. With the

smirk drained from his face, he leaned his elbows onto the table, and in a warning tone, said, "Care to say that again?"

"You heard me." I took a welcome sip of my coffee, letting him stew. He did just that, sneering all the while. "This is your loft, right?"

He maintained a scowl. "Yes."

"Mildred told me you had this place. I expected it to only be big enough for you."

"The children all have rooms. As will you. If you manage to maintain your employment," he threatened.

"I always hated this neighborhood. It felt pretentious— like the people who moved here were trying to prove they had money and taste, though they were really only convincing themselves of the latter," I explained just to annoy him. "My apartment was in Brooklyn, because teaching didn't pay enough to live near my school in Manhattan, so I got a second job working at a club called Risqué. I'm still close with the staff, so I fill in on occasion. Which is why I was there Friday night."

"Friday?" he asked in an anxious tone.

"Yes. You know, the night you had Ms. D tie you down and whip you until you came."

His practiced stone façade faltered for just a second. "You saw . . . ?"

"Everything?" I finished for him. "Sure did."

As he continued to leer, I stared him down, letting him know it was me who had the upper hand. He leaned back in his chair, looking away with a chuckle and a shake of his head. His thumb rubbed circles against his forefinger—the only visual cue of his nervousness. He both loved and hated when I outwitted him. How had I not figured him out sooner?

"You called me a switch," he said.

"I did."

"How do you know I'm not simply a masochist?" he asked.

It was the way he pinned me down on that table, the look on his face when he realized he could be rough with me and I'd pull my skirt up and ask for more. The enjoyment he got from knowing it hurt when he fucked me.

"Because a masochist doesn't fuck like you do," I said with confidence. His smirk confirmed my claim. "I'll admit you're a hard read. But apparently, so am I."

"Apparently so," he agreed, his eyes fixed on me as if I were the only thing in the room. I had his full focus, and, quite possibly, his admiration.

"I blame myself," I told him. "We had sex before we had time to communicate what we wanted. We were both holding back, which is most likely why you—as you so kindly put it—didn't feel the need to do it again."

With a chuckle, he agreed. "I suppose."

He looked away with a smile, and the sun shining behind him made his eyes look green rather than the true dark hazel they were. The smile curving his lips made me lick my own, but my curiosity still tugged at my mind.

"How long have you been in the scene?" I asked him.

"Two years. A bit less, perhaps," he answered. "I'm not as experienced as you, I'm sure, but I have been well trained and know exactly what I like."

I put my coffee down. "And what would that be?"

He leaned his elbow onto the table, subconsciously getting as close to me as possible. "I believe you have me pegged, Ms. Nielson," he admitted. My mind went to a different place than he intended. "Impact play, sensation play, orgasm control, bondage . . . I like rough sex and I like it to be cruel," he explained. "Being dominant is in my nature. Bending people to my will is a pleasure for me in both business and the bedroom, but . . . I enjoy when a woman can do the same to me."

"You enjoy forced submission," I said, not asked.

"Very much so," he agreed. "Even from the bottom, I have a habit of attempting to top—but only because I like to protest. Often. And, more so, to be punished for that protest."

"You're a brat?" I asked with a chuckle. "I would expect more class from a man like you."

"We all have our vices, Ms. Nielson," he said with a playful grin. "And you?"

Where do I even start? And how much am I willing to tell?

"I started the way most do, with an older partner who was already in the scene," I said. "I'm a natural nurturer, but to me, that means being a disciplinarian when needed. Giving someone exactly what they need, watching them come harder than they ever had in their life because I could read their body like a book . . . that got me off. But then I made the mistake of letting a dom beat me into submission. I didn't realize how much I enjoyed being bound, choked, beaten, and humiliated . . . I didn't realize how much I wanted someone to hurt me," I admitted with unabashed truth.

The mere thought sparked warmth between my thighs.

Augustine shifted in his chair with a similar reaction.

"After a few years doing it for fun, I linked up with someone at the club, and eventually, a spot opened up. Switching between being a domme one day and being someone's submissive the next was the most sexually fulfilled I had ever felt."

The smile on Augustine's lips showed me he felt the same. "What an interesting situation we find ourselves in."

"Interesting indeed."

His eyes drifted over me as if he were seeing me for the

first time. "I'd love to show you something. If that's all right," he said.

I knew what he was going to show me. What I didn't know was whether I'd be able to walk away after I saw it. "Go ahead."

He led me across the room, past the bedroom I woke up in, and down the hall to the door at the end. He pulled a key from the pocket of his trousers and unlocked it. Inside was a lounge space that opened into a bedroom.

The billowy, white bedding looked stark against a black slatted headboard and matched the panels hung along the walls. Sound dampening. A more aesthetic version of what we used in the private rooms of the club. Augustine was about to get me into some serious trouble.

A door in the corner was propped open to an aesthetically consistent white bathroom. Light gleamed off the marble tiles and glass shower enclosure, but what gained my attention was the door on the other wall.

A large, walk-in closet with a central dresser sat nearly empty except for the meticulous line of suits and shoes. When he unlocked one of the drawers and pulled it out, my mood lifted once more. Inside, leather bondage sets were laid out perfectly as if they were designer silk ties. In drawer after drawer was more leather, ropes, clasps, and fasteners of various uses, followed by toys as diverse as their leather counterparts.

As I appraised his collection, he opened another door at the end of the room. It swung open to reveal a lounge. Black, velvety, tufted fabric covered the walls, a table, and a couch. Metal bars crossed along the top of the room like an elaborate sculpture. Multiple surfaces for fucking, playing, and punishing, all draped in warm, dim lighting.

I salivated.

"Like what you see?" he asked in a growly voice.

The grin tugged on my cheeks. "Did Samira design this for you?" I called Manhattan's leading sex room interior architect by her first name. Nearly everyone in the city went to her, and I had sent at least four of my clients her way. She owed me a coffee.

Augustine let out an amused huff. He was the visitor stepping into *my* world.

"I can't say I'm shocked," I said, "but I am amused."

He watched me eye the contents of his drawers. "You don't prefer leather, I assume?" he asked.

"For punishment, yes. There's nothing wrong with the classics. But from a bondage standpoint, I find it lazy," I replied.

He cocked an eyebrow. "Lazy?"

"Pedestrian."

Though he tried, he couldn't hide the erection straining against the thigh of his trousers.

"Did you show me this as intimidation?" I asked. "Or was it an invitation?"

He stepped closer. "I'd rather enjoy a redo. A chance to show you the real me." He took my face in his hands, turning my head to look at him instead of the lesser temptations next to us, then let his hands trail down to linger on my neck. His fingertips left a trail of embers in their wake. "If you're interested."

It was harder to breathe when I looked at him. "I could be persuaded."

Twelve

Augustine had me shower before our scene, giving me free range in his spa of a bathroom. As my mind ran wild with the seductive possibilities, hot water ran over every place I wanted to feel him. There were always nerves when it came to a new partner, but Augustine wasn't all that new. He could get me off on his own. This time, it was all about what *I* wanted.

When the ache in my sex became too needy to ignore, I turned off the water and left the steam of the glass enclosure. My clothes were missing from their previous location on the vanity. Predictable. Taking my cue, I dried off, wrapped myself in the towel, and gave my hair an unhelpful fluff in the mirror.

Sliding the bathroom door open felt like I was the main attraction walking onto the stage, but when I found Augustine sitting in a chair, staring at his phone rather than at me, I got the sense of who was running the show. I pulled the towel from me slowly, letting it drop to the floor. Finally, he looked at me. An evil smirk twisted his lips.

"Turn around," he said with a swirl of his finger.

I did so, giving him a view of the part of me he seemed to appreciate most.

"Come here," he said. When I took a step toward him,

he stopped me with a hand. "No, no. I want you to crawl."
My eyes narrowed into a glare. With a hand massaging the gift
between his legs, he lounged back in his chair and wet his lips.
"Hands and knees, Ms. Nielson."

Maintaining my look of contempt, I lowered myself to my
knees and then my palms.

Augustine watched with careful eyes and slowly unfastened
his belt. "Hate me all you want," he said. "It will only make
it better."

With every demeaning step I took toward him, the sight
of him in his sexiest form sent a chill over my skin and heat
between my thighs. *Fuck, I want this. I want him.*

When I was at his feet, I ran my hands over his thighs while
he unzipped his fly. He reached behind my neck and pulled me
closer, while his other hand pulled out his cock and rubbed it
against my lips.

"Impress me," he said.

Like a good pet, I took him into my mouth, keeping my
hands on his legs. I slid him deep to wrap my lips around the
base, then sucked as I made my way back up to the tip. Fresh
and clean like the scent of his cologne, the tip salty with his
excitement for the pleasure I would give him, he tasted better
than I had imagined.

As I continued, he watched me intently, hazel eyes heavy
with lust. The audible sigh I gained from him made me suck
even harder. His hips flexed toward me, and his cock strained.

"Just like that." A simple sentence I had heard one million
times before somehow sounded like poetry when leaving
Augustine's lips.

Hungrily, I fisted the cinched material at his hips, devouring
him until my jaw ached. When I went down again, he held

me there and shoved himself against the back of my throat. I looked up at him with a pitiful expression.

His girth restricted my air just the way I liked. His grip tightened in my hair and on the nape of my neck as he moved. Quick and rough, he thrusted deep, keeping me from breathing. Then finally, he pulled himself from me, a trail of spittle still connecting us.

My breath returned in a gasp. He leaned forward and pulled me into a luscious kiss. While his tongue teased mine, I couldn't fight the grin that pulled at my cheeks. We were off to a good start.

With a deep hum, his lips left mine. He tucked himself back into his pants and stood up, pulling me with him. He took me by the hand and led me into the closet.

Inside, with the door closed, Augustine turned his attention to the drawers, opening one after the other, his eyes dancing over each item as if they were passages in a book he was referencing. Standing naked in a room full of clothes, my body ached to be touched.

By the time he closed the last drawer, an array of leather sat atop the dresser. Before I could take it in, he pulled me against him, gripping my chin and tilting it up. He looked down at me, appraising my face with his dark eyes.

"I want you bound and pinned while I spank you. *Hard.*" His fingertips tickled as they slid over my jaw. "Is that all right with you?"

I swallowed and said, "Yes."

"Good." He lifted a harness and wrapped it around me. The suede inside of the leather caressed my lower back while he fastened the first buckle around my waist. "Choose." He nudged his head toward the dresser.

A line of paddles and floggers sat lying in wait. All of

them were too gentle for what I needed. His belt still hung unfasted around his waist. I took either end of it in my hands. The smooth, beveled shape of the expensive leather was sure to hurt.

"I want this," I said, giving his belt a tug.

His eyes lifted to mine, his tongue wetting his lips to hide his smile. "Interesting choice."

Therapists have had a field day unpacking how my lack of corporal punishment growing up led me to seek it out as an adult to help me disassociate from the childhood I lost too soon, but here, none of that needed to be explained. In this world, all that mattered was pleasure.

"With your permission, I won't respond to 'no' or 'stop,'" he explained. He pulled the strap tight against my thigh. "Rather, I'll rely on your safe word."

"That's fine with me."

"What is it?"

"The usual: Red. Yours?"

"The same. And when gagged?" he asked.

I lifted my hand in a peace sign—a noticeable plea for mercy I rarely needed.

"Understood."

He turned me around, placing my wrists into the cuffs at my lower back. The pressure on my belly, thighs, and arms made the ache inside me gnaw and burn. The neediest parts of me were left exposed, untouched. After finishing with my restraints, he slid his hands down to cup my ass, gripping it tight, fingertips digging in, but not enough to hurt.

"Ready?"

He didn't wait for me to answer before pushing me into the next room. I looked back at him over my shoulder. "Don't be gentle with me," I told him. "I mean it. Nothing like last time."

"Last time was gentle to you?"

"Very."

His smile spread before his hand slapped against my ass. "Then be a good girl and bend over."

I leaned over the padded table, falling the last few inches without the balance of my arms. My breasts pressed into the soft velvet, my hands gripped into fists behind me, ready for what came next.

The sudden snap of a belt made me flinch. He noticed. "Tell me your limit," he said. "And don't be bold."

"I want it as hard as you can give me," I answered. "Just don't break the skin."

A chuckle rumbled in his chest.

I stood in silent anticipation for a moment before feeling the bite of the first lash. It stung against my cheeks and made my heart pound. When the belt hit me again, my legs quivered with the pleasure that shot through me.

"Too much?" he asked.

"No," I moaned. "Not enough."

"Good."

He hit me harder, making my hips clash against the table, and the pressure on my thighs and bladder stroked at the heat deep inside me. I tried to reach forward and brace myself for balance, but my wrists simply tugged at the harness. Bound and helplessly pinned by gravity. The combination teased me in a way that made the muscles in my core clench exquisitely.

Again and again, the belt smacked against my ass, and the more tender it got, the more the pleasurable pressure built inside me. The next spank made me cry out in pain.

He paused, and his hand smoothing over my sensitive

cheek made me twitch with surprise. He pressed his erection against me as he checked in. "Is there something you need to tell me?"

I was hot, wet, drunk on the pleasure so few people were ever willing to give me. "More," I begged him. "I'll come if you don't stop."

He growled as he moved away. "My pleasure."

Augustine gave me just what I wanted. Lash after lash in just the right spot. My ass went numb except for the dull sting every time the belt made contact, a harder, yet teasingly empty version of being fucked roughly from behind. Better yet, my pleasure seemed to bring him his own.

His moans mimicked mine after a hard spank, and a curse left him sighing deeply. The desperation in his voice increased when I felt a string of my wetness land against my inner thigh.

The pleasure peaked with the next hit, a loud moan escaping me, my legs tense and shaking as I teetered on the edge. I looked back at him, begging him to give me what I wanted. He did.

The belt hit against my sex once, surging pleasure through me, twice, building it stronger, and the third time, exploding.

The orgasm flooded through me in a rush. He moved to stand behind me, and as I tried and failed to catch my breath, I heard his breath just as labored, accompanied by the sound of his fly unzipping. "I'm not done with you yet."

He pushed himself into me in one hard thrust. My legs curled up, and my sex squeezed around him in response.

Wasting no time, he pumped his hips against me, his cock stroking hard against my sensitive walls, never letting me come down before pushing me close to the edge once again. His hand wrapped around my hair and yanked back. My posture strained until I could barely breathe. His hand gripped my sore ass, then smacked hard against one cheek and then the other. He groaned as his relentless pace never slowed, never broke. I pushed my hips back to increase the intensity.

"Oh, my fucking god," I cried when I felt him grow harder inside me. The head of his cock rubbed hard and perfect against a needy spot deep inside. "Ah! Fuck, you feel so good."

"Then come for me, again," he breathed. "Right now."

I did as he asked, letting the second orgasm tear me apart. My whole body shook, and my feet lifted off the ground as I squeezed tight around him over and over in violent, pleasurable waves. He continued to fuck me hard, his hips clashing against my ass until he could take it no longer. Abruptly, he pushed deep with a moan and began coming inside me.

The sound of him finding his own pleasure was a song I instantly knew would become my favorite. As I listened, the rest of my strength left me. My legs gave out beneath me, and I tumbled to my knees, his warmth trailing slowly down my thigh.

I sat on my heels and panted, the headiness of my orgasm still clouding my mind and vision. He kneeled beside me and placed soft kisses against my neck. His hand slid between my legs. The slow stroke of his fingers pleased me and calmed me at the same time. I dropped my head back onto his shoulder and reveled in the feeling.

His warm lips nipped my ear. "Was that better?"

All I could do was laugh. "Much better."

• • •

I always wanted softness after rough sessions. Blankets, robes, kisses. Augustine was happy to provide them all. I curled up next to him on the sofa, propping up my knees to sit on my hip, not my sore, freshly moisturized backside.

He pulled my leg forward to drape it over his lap, making my robe fall away. He ran the backs of his fingers over my newly exposed skin, grinning. "You'll be bruised tomorrow," he said.

"Good."

He pinned his smile with his teeth so as not to seem too pleased. "I can't wait to see you on the other side."

In our comfortable yet intimate quiet, I took a moment to appreciate how lucky a predicament I had fallen into. Not only because the impossibly handsome man before me was willing to let me whip him to orgasm, but also the balance it gave us. What was missing from our professional relationship was communication. Trust. And both were the foundation of everything we just did. Everything he wanted to do again.

"If we decide to do this . . . we leave it in the bedroom," I said. "I don't do TPE. Who I am in here has nothing to do with who I am out there." I pointed to the door.

"I couldn't agree more."

"That being said . . ." I trod carefully. "This only works when we communicate. We both got exactly what we wanted because we said what we meant. This could get complicated quickly if we don't talk."

He smirked, but I hadn't told a joke. I climbed over to him, flinging the edge of my robe to the side as I straddled his lap.

"I mean it, Augustine." I brushed my hands over his hair, hoping the soothing gesture would take the sting out of my words. "You are a very private person—which I will continue to respect—but you have to respect my boundaries as well. Talk to me. Trust me. Let me do what you hired me to do, *and* do this, without threatening my employment status every five minutes."

His smirk remained as he gave my sore ass a squeeze. "I'm sure you'll find a way to persuade me if I resist."

"I will."

Thirteen

My weekend in Manhattan had been everything. Secrets revealed, desires explored. It reminded me how magical Manhattan truly was.

Augustine and I had traveled back to the mansion late that night, but had gone in separately to avoid questions. For the next few days, everything was as normal as it had always been. Almost *too* normal.

Augustine hadn't changed one bit. He was always on his phone, late to meals, disappearing only to be found later in his office on yet another call. I didn't need to talk to him to know what he was doing. Avoiding social interactions, hyper-focusing on distractions, especially those that came with a hefty dose of serotonin . . . Preoccupation was his shield against grief, and, inadvertently, against his children as well.

As easy as it would be for me to tell Augustine all about himself, he needed to come to the realization on his own. All I could do was encourage him to get there and give him some positive affirmation when he tried. Or, painful affirmation, if he preferred.

He didn't make it to dinner that night, but I expected no

less. Earlier in the day, I had received an email from him with a contract attached.

The terms were typical of what I had seen with my other formalized kink relationships; copies of our list of interests, experience, and limits, details about his vasectomy and distaste for additional forms of protection, followed by five pages of enough legal jargon to make my head spin. I read it page for page, every sentence pissing me off more than the last. The problem wasn't *in* the contract; it was the contract itself.

He didn't want me to sue him. Understandable. But a signed contract agreeing to a schedule and expectations felt like he was hiring me again.

My job as a domme was sex work, but I never *had* sex at work. When my time was paid for, I was not a human: I was an object, an experience, a fantasy. Power was never truly balanced when one participant was hired. But if I refused to sign, would the deal be off the table completely?

"Have you seen Daddy today?" Tabitha asked as I tucked Sebastien into bed.

"No, sweetheart," I told her. My nerves were on edge. Not seeing Augustine all day stole my chance to read his mood. "Your daddy must be busy tonight."

Sebastien smiled at me. I pressed a kiss to his forehead and turned to do the same to Tabitha.

"If you see Daddy, will you tell him goodnight?" she asked me.

I took a deep breath to maintain my composure. "Yes, I will," I told her with a grin. "Goodnight, little ones."

I left the room and closed the door behind me.

With the kids in bed, my nerves returned. Feeling this way was not in my nature, but I couldn't remember the last time I wanted something so badly. The checklists we exchanged were nearly identical for desires, and though he lacked experience, he was open to everything I wanted to do to him. It was as if Augustine had put all my favorite foods in front of me, letting me pick whichever plate would satisfy me most that night, and all I had to do was sign away my sense of taste.

I went downstairs to the parlor for a glass of wine, intending to go back to my room to prepare my argument right after, but when I made it to the bottom of the staircase, my gaze fixed on the office door at the end of the hall.

The mere thought of touching him again brought a warm ache between my thighs.

"Looking for something?" I nearly jumped out of my skin when his voice rumbled behind me. I turned to find him standing with a pompous smirk on his face. "Or, were you looking for some*one*?"

My eyes drank him in. The scruff on his chin and cheeks was longer than usual, his white shirt a bit wrinkled at the seams. It must have been a long day, but he wore it well.

"I was on my way to bed," I said.

He crossed his arms and took a step closer. I refused to shy away. "Whose bed, Ms. Nielson?"

My warmth turned to throbbing. "Mine. But I'm glad I ran into you."

"Is that so?"

"Yes. I wanted to talk about your contract," I told him.

A devilish smile stretched his lips. "Of course. Join me in my office?"

He led the way up the hall, and the stirring inside me grew more intense with every step I took. Once inside, he locked the door behind us and gestured me toward his desk. Rather than sitting in a chair, I turned and sat on the edge of the desk instead. His gait slowed as he read my intention, his eyes moving over my body while mine did the same to his.

He stopped a few inches from me. "I assume this is about the terms. Did you review them as I requested?"

"I did."

"And what did you decide?"

I breathed in courage and said, "I reject them all."

His confidence fractured with surprise. "What?"

"I work for you during the day, Mr. Montgomery. I don't work for you at night."

The desire to touch him was too great. I reached for him, letting my fingers trace down the buttons of his shirt, lower and lower, until my fingers looped around his belt. He stepped forward to stand between my legs, placing his hands on my hips.

"I'll sign your *Covenant Not to Sue*, but everything else between us will be off the books." As I started unfastening his belt, he failed to hide the heavy rise and fall of his chest. "I told you I need your trust. That doesn't come because you said so on a piece of paper. Give me the range to read *you*, not your legalese, and I will make sure you *thoroughly* enjoy yourself, wherever, however, and as often as you'd like."

He moistened his lips while he watched me unfasten his fly. "Your offer sounds intriguing," he said.

I gripped the front of his shirt and pulled him closer, then slid my other hand down the front of his pants. He placed his palms onto the desk beside me and leaned in for a kiss. I let his lips brush against mine for a split second before I turned my head. He growled and grazed my neck with his teeth. His mouth against my skin sparked fire in my core.

"Should I show you just how *intriguing* it can be?" I massaged him, feeling him throb against my palm.

His lips left my neck with a quiet moan. "I'd like that."

When his hand gripped my breast, I grabbed him by the chin and pulled his face to look at me. "Then I'll see you in three hours."

His heavy eyes blinked with confusion. "Three?"

"Your daughter has a habit of waking up at midnight." I pushed him away and stood. "I'll be back to let you finish when I'm finished working." I patted my hand against his package then listened to his growling chuckle while I walked away.

"Looking forward to it," he said as I left the room.

Fourteen

When the time came, I waited an extra half hour just to annoy him. I wanted him riled up for what I had planned.

Having reviewed his checklist numerous times, I had his limits and desires memorized. Reading between the lines showed me what he would enjoy once introduced properly.

Teaching. My forte.

I got dressed and grabbed the night's paraphernalia from the chest in my closet. Back downstairs, the office light was on, door propped open. I made my way inside, locking the door behind me, and strode confidently into the bedroom.

Augustine stood in a robe, hair damp from a shower. "I was worried you wouldn't come."

Without a word, I stepped past him and set my bag on the nightstand. I stripped off my dress, leaving only the heels and mesh bodysuit. I felt sexy even without the breathless stare he sent my way. On the bed, his selection of playthings for the night caught my attention. A leather paddle, cuffs, and collar. Typical bitch.

"Why are these out?" I asked.

"In case you'd like to use them on me."

God, I love a masochist. "Cute, but I'm not open to suggestions."

I untied the belt of his robe and pushed the material from his shoulders. It fell into a heap on the floor, leaving his masculine frame open for the taking. He didn't move to cover himself, didn't even flinch. He was anything but shy, and I was anything but surprised.

I pushed him back and he fell onto the bed. I crawled over him and coaxed him further up.

Once in position, I reached into my bag and pulled out the three long ribbons. I dragged them over his chest to tease him.

"Satin?" he asked.

"Yes."

"I was hoping for something . . . harsher."

"You'll find there are many ways I can turn your pleasure into pain." I leaned down to place a sultry kiss against his lips. When I sat back up, I smacked a hand against his cheek. "Arms above your head."

He smiled before doing as he was told, reaching above his head and wrapping his hands around the wooden posts of the headboard. A simple tug of his hips made him widen his legs and stretch his arms out straight. He could listen when he wanted. Securing the tie around his ankle and the post was quick work for me. A practiced method to get him in the position I wanted: a helpless one. He could try to flex his hips, try to top me from the bottom, but it wouldn't work.

I moved back up his body and sat on his lap, feeling his cock throbbing beneath me. "Hands." He let go of the headboard and held them out for me. I wrapped the tie around his wrist. While I focused on my knots, he reached down, his hand stroking against my hip and waist as I secured the next tie. "Did I tell you to touch me?" I asked.

"No," he answered. *He really is a brat.*

Once the last tie was fixed to his other wrist, I leaned forward to loop the ribbons around the headboard's posts. I felt his warm tongue circle my nipple through the thin mesh before his lips closed around it and sucked.

The tease warmed in my core and made me long to feel him inside me, but I knew it would be worth the wait, especially when he was almost begging for the forced submission he claimed to enjoy. I'd have him begging verbally soon enough.

I pressed down against his throat, pulling him away from my breast. "Did I tell you to do that either?"

He licked his lips again as he smirked. "No." His hands slipped from my waist to cup my breasts, his thumb continuing the tease in lieu of his lips.

With a roll of my eyes, I swirled the ends of the ribbons around my hands and yanked. His arms flew above his head under the ribbon's guidance. He looked pleasantly surprised, his erection straining against my sex.

I tied the ribbons together and glared down at him. "You need to learn."

"Learn what?" he asked. Cheeky bastard.

"That you should listen to me."

I took the blindfold and slipped it over his head. His lips parted with anticipation. The sight brought a smile to my lips. He was so beautiful this way, bound and blissfully unaware of what I was about to do to him.

I pet his hair. "I'm going to hurt you," I said in a gentle tone. "I'm going to make you want to tell me to stop, all while making you wish I never would." His chest heaved with a labored breath. "Tell me your safe word again."

"Red."

I trailed my fingers down the center of his defined chest. "Use it if you need to."

He smiled. "I won't."

Seeing the aggravating, arrogant Augustine bound and blind between my thighs gave me such a high. My senses sharpened. His scent, every flinch of his muscles, the sound of every breath he took, captured my attention. Tonight, I was the hunter, and he was my prey. I couldn't wait to devour him.

I climbed off him to stand next to the bed, dragging my fingers down his thigh as I did. Then, I waited.

I didn't move—not even a shift of weight—simply watching. He tugged at his restraints, testing them while his anticipation grew and faded in the minute that passed. His brow creased.

"Aubrey?" he called out finally.

"Yes, Augustine?"

His head twitched in my direction. "I thought you had left." I didn't respond.

Padding over to the nightstand, I smiled as his head stayed tilted in the direction I used to be. The lighter clicked, drawing his attention. I lit the wick and watched the wax warm, glistening as it became liquid inside the bowl-shaped divot.

Augustine pulled at his restraints again. When his arms could do nothing but flex, he growled with frustration. I would have thought he wasn't enjoying himself if his cock wasn't rock hard against his stomach.

"Will you say something?" he asked.

My answer came in the form of a drop of wax.

He hissed and bucked when it landed against his chest. "Fuck!"

I climbed back onto the bed and straddled him. Then I lingered, letting him lie anxiously, watching his breath shallow

114

with anticipation. Once his breathing calmed, I tilted the candle again.

"Agh!" After breathing away the pain, he relaxed back onto the mattress. A smirk twitched at the corner of his mouth.

I swirled the candle to verify enough of a pool had accumulated, then let drop after drop fall in quick succession from his nipple down the groove between his pecs.

His muscles flexed and reddened as he expected more. When nothing came, he took a breath. "Sh-shit, that hurts."

"Do you think you deserve anything less?" I asked him. I let another drop fall against his stomach, making him hiss again.

"No. Fuck. I don't." He panted, waiting for the next drop. I obliged.

My tongue traced over my lips while I trailed the drops lower and lower. His fearful groans turned guttural and reverberated in my core.

When I reached the base of his abs, I let the wax pool yet again. The anticipation was palpable in his panting and the glorious sight of his cock swelling and straining with need. I could let the wax fall there, really hurt him, or I could do something better.

I moved the material between my legs to the side and took him in my hand. Slowly, I lowered myself onto him, only a couple of delicious inches.

His breath came in quickly; his mouth parted in a silent groan. Blindfolded, he couldn't see how good he felt, how much it drove me crazy to tease him this way.

When I paused, his legs strained against the satin in a failed attempt to thrust. "No, love. Don't stop."

"Why? Do you want to be inside me?"

"Yes."

"Do you deserve that?"

That pretentious smirk appeared on his lips again. I dripped the wax onto his nipple and across his chest to the other. He gasped when each drop hit, but moaned when the pain faded.

"Do you deserve to be inside me?" I asked him again.

He swallowed between heavy breaths. "No."

"That's right."

I sank onto him, pushing him deep. My head fell back when I lifted myself again, and the feeling of his head sliding against my aching walls made me feel drunk with ecstasy. I swallowed my moan when I rose and let him slip from me.

"No, no, no, please, Aubrey, please," he begged to my sheer delight. "Don't tease me. Fuck me."

An evil smile curled my lips. "I don't think I can trust you to listen to me."

"You can."

"Hmm . . . I don't know."

"Fuck me and I'll do anything you want."

I loved the way his desperation caused frivolous things to come out of his mouth. *Oh, the possibilities.* "Anything?"

"Yes."

"What I want—" I took him in my hand and stroked him slowly. His head fell to the side with a sigh. "—is for you not to come."

"What?"

"Not until I say you can."

He nodded enthusiastically. "I won't."

I lifted him to my entrance and lowered myself onto him again. I couldn't suppress the moan that escaped me, but neither could he. When I finally started to move, the pleasure was too much to stifle. I whimpered when his cock stroked against that sensitive spot deep inside.

As I rode him, I dropped drip after drip of wax onto his torso. His hisses and groans of pain melted to moans. He began to breathe harder, his skin reddening, the veins protruding from his arms. He was close.

It took all my control to rise and let him slip from me again. I slid my fingers inside me to ease the ache. "See? I can't trust you."

"You can, you can," he assured me. "Please, Aubrey."

Watching him beg was officially my favorite form of entertainment.

Setting the candle aside, I slipped him back inside me, raising and lowering myself at first to drive him crazy, finding it did the same to me as well. I leaned back, balancing with a hand on his thigh and rubbing my fingers against my swollen clit. When I rubbed his head against my G-spot, I nearly fell backward with the blinding rush of pleasure.

The heat burned hot and heavy inside me, putting me right on the edge. I moved my hips faster as the pressure built and my pleasure began to drown me.

Stroking him against every aching, desperate spot, both of us moaning in time, I felt him harden and gasped. When I lifted myself off him, he growled in frustration.

"Not yet!" I snapped.

He panted, his brows furrowing with pain above the blindfold. "Please," he said just above a whisper. "Please let me come."

As I rubbed my clit, staying on the edge, my sex quivered and my muscles tensed. I had him exactly where I wanted. Seeing him submit this way made me so hot. I pushed him back inside me and released the restraints on his arms. His hands flew to my hips, feeling me move as I fucked him the way I wanted.

I rode him hard and fast, pushing us both to the edge quickly. His fingers dug into my skin, and the cooled wax on his torso cracked under the pressure of my palms. He moaned in time with me.

"Ready to come, baby?" I asked. When he arched back with a groan, I felt him harden right where I needed him, and with that, I lost it. "*Fuck* . . . Now!"

My head fell back as we exploded at the same time.

My hips shuddered in his grasp as the orgasm tore through me. I drowned in the pleasure, the feel of another flood of his warmth inside me, amplifying it. Rush after rush, I reveled in the all-consuming sensation—and the *power*.

When I started to come down, I circled my hips again, stroking him inside me to come down from my orgasm and coax out the last of his. It leaked from me and spilled onto him. A messy yet rewarding ending.

I removed his blindfold. "See?" I teased him. "Good things happen when you do what I say."

He chuckled but failed to disagree.

• • •

Aftercare almost always verged on intimacy, but with Augustine, nothing was usual. He was strangely quiet. As if meditating, he would lie there, breathing deeply, cooling from his post-coital glow back into that neutral, stony façade. A warm sunset before a winter's night.

With the wax cleaned off his chest, he sighed with content and sat up. The drawer of his nightstand slid open, and his phone magically appeared in his hand once again. I sighed in defeat. "Do you want me to go now?"

"No," he said. "I'd prefer you to sleep here, if you don't mind it."

"I don't. Anything you need."

We had slept together the first night, too. He didn't want to talk, but also didn't want me to leave. A psychologist could have a field day with that.

"I'll be up early to catch my flight. I'll wake in enough time to return you to your room unseen." His last sentence wasn't my concern.

"You're leaving again?"

"That is what I do best, is it not?" he mocked me.

"You're awfully brazen for someone who was begging not ten minutes ago."

He gave me a sideways glance, the smirk twitching on his lips.

I lounged back against the pillows and began making myself comfortable. "When will you be back?"

"Soon."

"That isn't an answer." When he elaborated no further, I added, "Remember that communication requirement I mentioned? Would it hurt to share your schedule with me?"

His gaze lifted from his phone with a look of annoyance, then returned. "My schedule—if it were your business to see—changes daily. Having access to it would affect nothing."

I grunted my discontent.

There was the sound of a sent message before he set his phone face down on the nightstand. He settled against his pillows, running a hand over the exposed skin of his chest and stomach, then down to adjust himself beneath the sheet. I ignored the distraction and refocused on my point.

"You may have forgotten that I'm new to this whole

'nanny' thing. I'm learning on the fly, applying my experience as a teacher, making observations and adjustments as I go."

He assessed me for a moment, reading my intent. "And you have a suggestion for me?"

"More of a question."

His eyebrows lifted in expectation.

"Do you need to work as much as you do? If you scale back a little, you could spend more time at home. The twins are so young. You—"

"I invited you into my bed to fuck me, not lecture me," he cut me off. "I do not recall asking for input outside of your expertise, so I would very much appreciate it if we left it at that."

As short as his temper was, it didn't intimidate me. "Well, my *expertise* tells me your kids would love to have you with them more often."

He stared into space with a smile that didn't reach his eyes. "That's what they think," he said and turned off the light.

Fifteen

A few days later, I sat in the downstairs parlor, having tea alone while watching people dust and polish the grand entryway. I felt a world away from them, missing the company I once had this time of day, the last adult conversation I had replaying in my mind.

Augustine's words had bothered me since the moment they left his lips. *That's what they think.*

Did I have it backward? Rather than prioritizing work and letting it pull him away, was he purposefully distancing himself from them for some other reason?

When my mother passed, my father put all his energy into me, placing his needs aside to make sure mine were met. There were times I had wished for space, for time away from him. It took years of therapy for me to forgive myself for those feelings. I was a kid with no idea I would lose him—no idea the world could be so cruel as to put me through that pain twice.

There was no scenario in my mind where Augustine's presence would affect his kids negatively. Those who did real harm to their children either did it intentionally or were unaware of the damage they caused. Choosing to be away meant he was doing neither.

Grief looked different on everyone, but his was a color I hadn't seen before.

There was no use speculating. Half of what I surmised about that man turned out to be incorrect. My time was better spent focusing on that which was in my control.

After finishing my tea, I left the room and nearly ran into two of the housekeepers, women around my age whom I didn't know and probably never would.

"Sorry," I said. They both stepped backward, apologizing while they removed themselves from my path as if I were royalty. They looped arms as they walked away. Seeing that made me long for Mildred's company all over again.

Suddenly, Matthew burst through the front doors, tearing me from my thoughts and my loneliness. He spotted me and ran over.

My heart swelled over the look of joy on his face.

"I'm done!" he said with glee.

Such a sweet summer child. "You're done with finals, but there's still another two weeks of school."

He sneered. "Do I really have to go to that? They won't be teaching anything new."

"But you still have assignments and papers to turn in."

"That's what email is for," he groaned.

"You're going to class, Matthew."

With a dramatic sigh, he gave in. "You're such a buzzkill. I'm going to play video games."

I laughed and followed him toward the lounge. "You can play for an hour, then you have to start on your paper."

"*Fine.*"

My phone chimed with Crystal's video call attempt. I stared at the screen for a moment, then rejected it, texting her instead.

Me: Sorry! I'm with Matthew right now.

Yes, I was near him, but it was only a matter of time before she figured out I was avoiding her.

My phone pinged.

Crystal: Why are you avoiding me?

Ten seconds was a matter of time.

It was time to call her. "I'll meet you in there, okay?" I told Matthew. "I need to call my friend."

"You have friends?" he quipped. My little Augustine.

Much like I did with his father, I didn't dignify him with a response. Instead, I left him for the other end of the hall and stepped out onto the balcony. The sun was glaring, the air hotter than expected. I tucked myself under the awning and called Crystal.

"Hey, I'm sorry," I said when her face appeared.

"You're sorry? I haven't talked to you in, like, two weeks. Are you okay?"

"Yes, I'm fine. I'm sorry because . . ." I looked around me and back through the windows. With no one around, I still whispered, "I had sex with Augustine."

Her jaw dropped. "Oh my god, *you did?*"

"Yeah. A few times now."

"A few—*a few times?*" she stammered with astonishment. "How long has this been going on?"

I hung my head in shame. "About a month."

She closed her eyes and took a deep breath. "A *month?*" she repeated slowly in that punishing, parental way. "Girl, if you do not give me the details, I'm going to drive down there and murder you."

I rubbed a hand over my brow, not sure where to start. "Well . . . he's not a dom."

"He's not?"

"No. He's a switch."

"Fuck my ass. Are you serious?"

"Yep."

"You're not fucking with me, right? This is real life—it's really happening? Augie and Aubrey are having kinky, switch-y sex?"

"It's really happening," I assured her. I was counting down the seconds until it happened again. "He let me top him last time he was here, and it was good. *Very* good. We balance well."

"Oh my god, yes!"

"Don't get too excited. We balance in bed, but not so much when we're not in it."

"Why's that?"

"Him being the person who signs my paychecks makes things a bit complicated," I said. "He sees both sides of me, yet I only see one side of him. I can't figure out why he thinks providing for his kids and being there for them is the same thing." I shook my head with annoyance, still trying to understand his last words. "It's like he thinks he's saving them from him. As if being around them too much would harm them more than being gone."

Her brow furrowed with confusion. "What's that about? The wife?"

"I think so. He never talks about her, but he still wears his ring . . . Something happened, and months later, I still have no idea what that 'something' is," I admit. "His kids are magical, and I want to see them thrive. All the twins want is to be with him. Matthew is being very pubescent, but I know he wants his father around too, whether he sees that or not."

"We knew Mont-Money was paying you to stand in for him. Can't you tell him that's not how it works?"

The day I got that man to listen to me when I wasn't naked would be one of the greatest achievements of my life.

"He's letting me get a little closer, but I don't know if he trusts me enough to open up and tell me why he doesn't want to be around them."

"Yet," she added.

"Yet." My mouth twisted. Vulnerability was hard for some people, especially people with a lot of pain tucked away inside them. I would know that better than anyone. But as long as I was caring for his kids, I wouldn't give up trying to get him to be more present with them.

"You're a badass, Aub. He's a puzzle, but you can figure him out. I know you can."

As much as I wanted to believe her, it didn't feel that way, but it was either I be the voice of reason in his ear, or let him continue being his stubborn, detached self until he ultimately found an excuse to tear me from the kids, and ruin his last chance of having a relationship with them.

"I should get back. Matthew has a paper to write, which means I have to stare at him until he does it," I explained.

Crystal giggled. "Go do what you do best. And call me more often, please."

"I will, I promise. Love you."

"Love you too."

We ended the call, and I took a moment to collect myself. A tinge of guilt ached in my chest when thinking about Augustine. I worried I might have encouraged his bad habits; that sleeping with him gave him another way to ignore his issues, rather than address them. But wasn't I doing the same?

When I made it to the lounge, I plopped myself onto the couch next to Matthew. He looked at me expectantly. "Keep playing," I told him. I pulled his head closer to me and pressed a kiss to his temple. He smiled and went back to shooting zombies.

I would always encourage him to hold onto any innocence he had left. The lord knew I had thrown mine in the fire long ago.

"I did it, I did it!" Sebastien ran into the room yelling. So out of character for a child as shy as him.

"You did what?" I yelled back with excitement.

He held a piece of paper out to me. "I get to play at Carnie the Hall!"

I giggled at his mispronunciation. When I took the official paper from his grasp, I read it and was overcome with pride. "You get to play at Carnegie Hall!"

He jumped up and down, a huge smile on his face. "Will you come watch me?" he asked.

"Of course I will! I wouldn't miss it for the world."

"Will Daddy come too?"

The hesitation I felt before answering was telling. "Of course he will, sweetheart."

He reached up and hugged his little arms around my neck. I'd be damned if I turned out to be a liar.

• • •

Later that day, I called the infamous absentee father and was surprised when he picked up. "Montgomery."

"It's Aubrey," *you twat.* "Sebastien has been invited to play in the Children's Musical Showcase at Carnegie Hall," I said proudly.

"Just a moment." There were muffled voices and laughing. "Sorry. When?" His tone was lackluster, yet it still showed interest. I accepted the small victory.

"Next Saturday. I was hoping you'd be home by then."

"I was set to be in London."

"Then can you please try to rearrange your schedule? He's excited and wants you there more than anything."

The pause extended too long. "Yes, I will see what I can do."

"This is important, Augustine. It's a huge honor and a once-in-a-lifetime kind of memory. Do not make him remember you not being there."

"I said I'll see what I can do," he hissed and then ended the call.

We'd both see.

Sixteen

It was an hour before Sebastien's performance, and Augustine still had not made it to the loft. He had changed his flight, that much I knew, but whether he had made that flight or not, there was no way to know.

"Where could he be?" I asked Colin, our transportation for the night. "Did he plan to meet us there?"

"I don't believe so," he said.

I sighed. "How much longer can we wait before we're late?"

"About fifteen minutes, ma'am."

"He's not coming." Matthew strolled in, looking dapper in his tuxedo. His hair was gelled and styled like his father's. He even had the signature Montgomery look of annoyance on his face.

It bothered me how alike they were, yet they couldn't get along to save themselves. I walked over to straighten his bow tie, lifting his chin when his gaze fell to my chest. "He will be there. Have a little faith."

Matthew gave me an incredulous look.

• • •

I spent the rest of our time taking pictures of the kids together and solos of Sebastien in his tiny tuxedo. All three looked immaculate, and Sebastien was beaming. If not for anyone else, I would frame the pictures for myself.

When it was time, Colin dropped us at the performers' entrance, and we made our way backstage. Once we reached the check-in, Sebastien pulled me to a stop, squeezing my hand with both of his.

His eyes were wide with fear. I kneeled to his level.

"Are you nervous?" I asked.

He nodded, his brow furrowing.

"It's good to be nervous sometimes. It's how we know we're doing something that matters."

"It is?"

"Yes." I ran my fingers over the front of his hair to make sure it stayed in place. "I was nervous the first time I met you. Because you matter to me." His mouth turned up into a smile. "I cannot wait to see you on that stage. You are going to do great."

"But what if I mess up?"

"Mistakes are okay. They are a part of life—an *important* part. But no matter what happens out there, I will still be so, so proud of you."

"You will?"

"Of course I will. Always remember that." I kissed his cheek. "Break a leg," I whispered to him.

He grinned, his fear gone, then went backstage with the attendant. I watched him disappear down the hallway, taking a piece of my heart with him.

"Are you Sebastien's mother?" a woman asked me.

I turned to her, my smile pulled down by the gravity of her question. "Oh, no. I'm his nanny."

"Oh, my apologies," she said. "I just wanted to let you know how lovely he has been in class. He is surprisingly humble for someone with such talent."

"That's wonderful to hear. Thank you."

"Please give my regards to his father. He raised a star student."

I smiled politely as she walked away, then, under my breath, muttered, "He didn't raise shit." I turned to find Matthew smirking at me. "Don't tell your father about any of this."

He laughed. "I won't."

• • •

We were ushered to our seats on the balcony, and I was let down again when we found it empty. I sat and waited. And waited.

When the show began, the first young artist played Bach's *Suite No. 1 Prelude* almost flawlessly. A string quartet by a group of students all near the age of ten followed. Performance after performance, I had to remind myself that these were children—young children at that.

After another few performances had passed, I glanced down at the program. There were only three more acts before Sebastien's, and still no Augustine. I pulled out my phone and sent him a message.

Me: Where are you???

I hoped my additional punctuation added emphasis.

As time passed, I glanced back down at my phone every two minutes to no avail. The lights came up, and Sebastien walked out. Matthew cheered, and Sebastien waved in his direction before he took a seat. The piano dwarfed him.

He stared at the keys. I held my breath in anticipation.

As he began to play the memorable, slow lilt of his well-practiced Chopin's *Nocturne Op. 9 No. 2*, a figure sat beside me. I turned to find Augustine.

"You made it," I whispered to him. He nodded and looked down, watching his son intently. I did the same.

Sebastien's fingers danced skillfully across the keys, his hands lifting above them after a series of notes. A little man rather than a child. The familiar ache washed over me. Remembering that someone was absent and unable to see this moment, whether it was projection or not, made my chest hurt. I hoped he didn't feel it too.

The song's robust—and *difficult*—portion heightened my emotions. I felt a tear roll down my cheek, but couldn't blink, afraid to miss even a second of this moment. He was playing so well.

Sebastien finished his song and the crowd erupted with applause. I stood and clapped too eagerly, but could not contain myself. Luckily, others joined me, and more did the same on the level below. A standing ovation. I was bursting with pride.

I dabbed my eye with the side of my finger to not ruin my mascara and caught Augustine's gaze.

His expression was unreadable as he assessed me. He looked away soon after.

• • •

Sebastien was on cloud nine the rest of the evening. He had a perfect performance under his belt and a belly full of pizza. What more could a six-year-old ask for? The closer we got to the loft, the more the kids gave in to fatigue. Even Matthew yawned every few minutes until we arrived back right after eleven.

Matthew locked himself away to do whatever a fifteen-year-old does before bed. I tucked the little ones in and waited enough time to ensure they were fully asleep. Once satisfied, I left.

Treading lightly down the hall, I found Augustine's door cracked open, as if he were inviting me inside. I accepted, closing the door behind me and locking it.

Past the lounge, he stood near the bed. "Ms. Nielson," he greeted me from behind his phone. "Come to show me how pleased my presence has made you?"

I tutted. "You want me to commend you for being late? We were lucky you showed up at all."

He tossed an annoyed glance in my direction. "We're onto this again?"

"Yes, this. Always this."

"Nothing I do for my family will ever be satisfactory, in your opinion."

"Maybe. But showing up on your own volition would be a good start."

He put down his phone to glare at me. "I was there."

"The best you could have done was to be there on time."

"I was there!" he roared.

Crossing my arms, I stared him down, waiting for him to regret his tone. His anger simmered before me.

"You were late." I walked toward him and pushed him back to sit on the bed.

I straddled his lap and lowered myself onto it slowly. He slid a hand up my thigh. I picked it up and flung it away from me.

Untying his bow tie, I mused, "You think I'm going to let you fuck me tonight?" I chuckled.

He flexed his hips beneath me. "I do."

"If I give you kudos for tardiness, what will make you want to be better?" I pulled the tie apart and dropped it to the floor beside me. Starting with his top button, I fingered the small medallions before slipping them through their sheaths. "You're lucky you wear a tux so well. Otherwise, I'd have two reasons to make you my bitch tonight."

He throbbed beneath the tight fabric of his pants. It was clear who would be topping whom tonight.

I stood and left him for the door. "Go wash yourself. *Everywhere.* I want you clean and naked by the time I get back," I commanded. "And wipe that fucking smirk off your face. You are not being rewarded tonight."

The smile slinked across my cheeks when I closed the door behind me.

• • •

I took my time preparing what I needed for the night, leaving the best part in a bag on top of the dresser in the closet. I walked out in time to catch him coming out of the bathroom. A towel hung in his hand, covering nothing but my favorite part of him.

I walked over and pulled the towel from his grasp, laying it on the bed. He looked me in the eyes, watching my gaze drop to the gift moving rhythmically between his thighs.

"On your knees," I said. He tilted his head with a smirk, challenging me. "I won't ask again."

He maintained his haughty expression but slowly lowered himself to the floor. There were few things in this world hotter than bringing a powerful man to his knees.

"Hands," I said. He lifted his wrists to me, and I placed

them in the cuffs. Once the buckles were fastened, I let them go to fasten the matching collar around his neck.

I unzipped my dress and pulled the thin straps from my shoulders, letting it fall from me like water into a puddle around my heels. He licked his lips, his eyes affixed to the apex of my thighs.

Stepping closer, I caught him by the hair when he tried to lean in for a lick. "You think you deserve to taste this?"

"Yes."

I crouched down with my knees spread wide and lifted his chin so he'd look me in the eye. "And what makes you think that?"

That pretentious smirk returned. "Because I pay you one hundred and fifty thousand per year."

I dropped my hand from his chin and slapped him hard on the cheek. A low growl in his chest showed his upset *and* his enjoyment.

Taking him by the jaw, I made him look at me again. "Do you think this is a fucking joke? That I won't whip you to tears and leave you unsatisfied?"

"Not at all."

"Then apologize."

He smiled just to irritate me. "For what exactly?"

I stood and yanked him up by the collar. He stumbled to his feet. I pushed him onto the bed, pressing him down by the throat, then looped his leash around my wrist and pulled it tight.

"Challenge me again and it won't end well for you." I leaned down to threaten him. "I own you tonight. I deserve your utmost respect and obedience. When I tell you to do something, you do it without question. Do you understand?"

The smirk remained on his lips. "Yes, mistress."

"Good. Now bark like the dog you are," I commanded.

He chuckled as if I had told a joke.

I pulled the leash until it choked him and dug my fingers into his cheeks to force him to look into my eyes. His expression grew serious when I leaned my knee onto his chest to add more persuasion. "I said bark, bitch."

His face reddened and his scowl deepened while he debated whether debasing himself was worth the pleasure he knew I would give him.

He glared for a moment, playing our ironic game of cat and mouse. Then quietly, disdainfully, he gave in. ". . . Woof."

I laughed at his misfortune. Nothing breaks a brat like a little humiliation.

I climbed off him, snarling with distaste for his actions. He avoided looking at me. I was only getting started.

"Lie on your stomach," I said.

He did as he was told.

"Not there, on the towel."

"Why on the—?"

"What did I say about questioning me?"

He swallowed his rebuttal and followed my instructions, inching over on his elbows and knees. With his ego defeated by his desire for me, I had him right where I wanted him.

I secured his cuffs to the bed, then looked over my handiwork. His arms flexed as he tested his bonds, his hair uncharacteristically disheveled. He was powerless. And he loved it.

"Now stay," I teased my pet.

In the closet, I pulled the real star of the show from my bag. I tightened the leather bands against my thighs and hips, checking to make sure it was secure. We were both going to have fun tonight, I was sure of that.

When I walked back out, he took one look at me and pulled against his restraints in fear. "What the bloody hell is that?"

"Your new best friend," I answered, stroking the narrow phallus of my strap-on.

Seventeen

Men were often basic creatures. Simple, easy to read, easy to please. But not Augustine. Topping the ever-loving *fuck* out of him was my reward for dealing with mediocrity for so long.

I climbed onto the bed and kicked his knee up with mine, teasing him by laying the toy against the seam of his ass.

"I didn't agree to this," he said like a true brat.

"When do you ever agree with me?" I teased him. I feared I enjoyed the forced submission he requested just as much as him. "You want this, you just don't want to admit it. Now, shut up or I'll gag you."

He stewed quietly in his restlessness.

I poured the oil—silicone-based, as we would not ruin his ass *or* my prized toys tonight—into my hand and warmed it between my palms. I rubbed it over his back until his skin glistened under the dim lighting. Moving lower, I slid a hand down to his backside and gripped it. His flinch pleased me. My pet was nervous.

He looked back again, eyeing the strap. "It's too big, love. I don't—" I silenced him with a hard slap on the ass, leaving my hand stinging.

"Are you telling me to stop?"

He didn't respond.

"Then Daddy just wants to be gagged, I see. So be it."

I took the leash and pulled it up between his teeth. He growled, making me smile. I wanted to fuck his ass as hard as I could manage, but that would be selfish.

With more of the oil on my hands, I massaged his shoulders and leaned forward to whisper into his ear, "Signal if you want me to stop, but I hope you don't. If you trust me, I promise you," I moaned quietly while switching to his other ear, "I will make you come harder than you've ever imagined possible."

Augustine looked at me with his dark eyes, a growl rumbling quietly in his chest. Then, a nod.

I ran my hand between his cheeks, watching him twitch. I stroked my hand back and forth until he relaxed, then slid in a finger. He gasped reflexively, but my hand was more than enough lubricated to avoid any uncomfortable friction. His muscles clenched around my finger as I slid it deeper, but when I found the magic spot, he relaxed with a sigh.

"That's right," I encouraged him. "Feels good, doesn't it?"

He dropped his head onto the mattress as I massaged my fingertip against his prostate. His sighs turned to heavy breathing, his heavy breathing to a single, reticent moan.

I removed my finger slowly, stroking the toy with my other hand to cover it in the lubricant. Placing my ankles on his thighs and squaring my hips with his, the devilish smile pulled on my cheeks. Fuck, I missed doing this. And with him, it was sure to be even better than before. With the help of my hips and a hand, I pushed the toy inside him.

He tried to fight me at every inch, but what fun would he have if he didn't? I watched his hands as they stayed balled into fists. There was no signal because he didn't want me to stop.

"Relax, Daddy," I teased him while I spread his cheeks wider. "Let it happen."

His fists stayed gripped, but his breathing slowed. His muscles relaxed under my hand and the toy slipped in further.

I dribbled more of the lubricant, giving it another coat as I eased it in and out, circling my hips in an even tempo. His grip tightened against the sheets, his face reddened, teeth bared against the gag, but he never gave the signal to slow down. He stared back at me, glaring, holding onto his ego until he could fight it no longer.

He gave in. He gave himself to me.

The pleasure of his submission made a moan slip between my lips, then one escaped his as well. I reached beneath him and stroked his cock for a moment, pulling it off to the side beneath his hip to watch my progress. Moan after moan growled past the gag. I grew wet, the toy sliding in a circle against my clit as I continued pumping my hips. When his moans grew louder, I could barely hold on.

Digging my fingers into his hair, I pulled his head back. I pumped my hips faster, stroking the toy in just the right place, fucking him just the way I wanted.

When his body suddenly bucked, I looked down to see his pleasure shoot from him. He moaned loudly beneath me.

Letting go of his hair, I ran my fingertips down the muscles of his back, drunk on power and ecstasy. I removed the leash from his mouth, pulled the toy from him slowly, then climbed off and turned him to lie on his back. He lifted a leg to place his foot on the bed and his arms behind his head, smiling while he tried to catch his breath. He wouldn't have a chance to do that.

I dribbled more lubricant onto the toy and pushed in again. His eyes went wide.

"More? I can't," he pleaded breathlessly.

"You can and you will." I pushed the toy deeper.

"*Fuck*," he sighed and laid back onto the bed, giving in to my control once again.

Seeing the collar around his neck, the leash lying between his pecs and along his abs, while I rolled my body between his thighs as he fully submitted to me, was rewarding beyond measure.

Stroking him with one hand, massaging him with the other, the combination made him harden and his balls stay tight. His chest heaved for air while I pushed my hips harder, just where he needed it. His face screwed with ecstasy, and I knew he was there.

With a pained moan, he came again, spilling himself onto my hand. I stroked the head of his cock hard and fast, ruining his orgasm in the best way.

He moaned loud and deep from his chest, dancing under my relentless grip. His hips bucked from the bed, his stomach quivering as he fought between his pleasure and pain, moaning over and over until his head fell back and the last of his orgasm flowed from him.

I slowed my strokes, easing him from the torment I just put him through. His eyes found mine.

"Does Daddy want to thank me now?"

His lips tilted into a smirk. "Thank you, mistress," he growled in his sexy accent.

I released the straps from my legs, then crawled up to straddle his face. "Thank me better."

He wasted no time putting his mouth on me, pulling my hips down to get a deeper taste. With a gasp, I dug my fingers into his hair and gripped it, enjoying every thankful lap of his tongue until I came apart.

• • •

Augustine hadn't let me leave his arms since we finished. His hand gripped my ass while he kissed me slow and deep. I tasted myself against his tongue from the last half hour he spent with his head between my thighs.

Each kiss was slower than the last, his body growing heavier on top of mine. He was behaving the way *I* did after a scene, wanting a soft make-out session before sleeping like a rock. I felt like the one being rewarded beneath a two-hundred-pound weighted blanket.

I broke the kiss. "You need to shower before we go to sleep."

He grumbled but listened, placing one more lingering kiss on my lips before leaving the bed.

After pushing him as far as I had, I wasn't sure how he would react afterward. The last thing I wanted was for him to *drop*—to mentally or emotionally crash from the high of our scene—so I gave him space while staying close, watching him carefully without hovering.

While he rinsed off in the shower, I cleaned the toy in the sink. He was quiet, but the heavy look in his eyes as he peered at me through the glass showed me he was still mine. At least for a few more moments. My focus returned to the toy.

The water stopped. The shuffle of a towel in my peripheral gained my attention, but I still didn't look his way. After a moment, his hands appeared on either side of me against the counter, followed by his body pressing against my back.

"How are you feeling?" I asked him.

"Spent." His lips nipped my ear. "Ms. D has nothing on you."

I smiled to myself. "I know."

He trailed his thankful nipping down my neck. Men were always more pliant after sex, but Augustine was putty in my hands. If only I could get him to be this way more often. *If only.*

"I meant to ask you . . . Does the family stay here during the summer?"

He hummed his "no" against my skin.

"Would it be possible to do so?"

His eyes bounced up to find mine in the mirror. "Why?" His fingers looped through the thin strap of my dress and pulled it down to allow his lips to tickle against my shoulder.

"I've been thinking," I started. His smile spurred me on. "If we could catch you between flights, we'd be able to do this more often. And . . . maybe the kids could see more of you, too." I held my breath.

"You think I can't tell what you're up to? Fuck me, then ask for favors?" His chuckle grumbled with his kiss on the nape of my neck. "You sound like Lar—"

He stopped short, his body going as still as stone.

I watched him in the mirror, his gaze never lifting as he stepped back. "Excuse me," he said and left the room.

The look on his face sent ice through my veins. I knew the start of a drop when I saw one. I finished rinsing the soap from the toy and dried my hands on the towel.

When I walked out, the bedroom was empty, the door hanging open. I tiptoed down the hall past the kids' rooms and into the living space. It, too, sat empty. *Where the hell did he go?* I wanted to call out to him, but I couldn't wake the kids.

The sound of a door closing came from upstairs. I took the stairs for the first time, stumbling into an office space with a desk and two chairs. At the back of the space was the door in question.

It opened onto a rooftop deck, and there he was. Augustine stood against a railing, the material of his robe ruffling in the wind.

"There you are," I said as I approached. He glanced at me over his shoulder, a cigarette hanging between his fingers. I leaned against the railing beside him. "You smoke?"

"Not often. But many afflictions from my youth seem to have reappeared as of late," he mused. He placed it between his lips and lit it, then set the lighter aside.

After an inhale, he offered it to me, but I refused with a shake of my head. He took a long drag as he stared at the city glimmering before us. His gaze, while cold, was subtly morose. It didn't take a genius to figure out why.

It wasn't my place to ask, so I stayed silent, letting him say as much or as little as he wanted.

"Lara is—*was* . . . my wife," he corrected himself with a disappointed close of his eyes. "I assume you've put that together."

"I have," I said as gently as I could manage.

His hand quivered as he lifted the cancer stick back to his lips. I stood in silence, afraid any word from my mouth would shatter him.

He took another drag, licking his lips before he exhaled, the smoke disappearing quickly in the wind. "Thank you for tonight," he said, "but I'd like to be alone now. If that's all right."

"Of course, but . . . I need to make sure you're okay before I leave you." I placed my hand on his arm. He pulled it from me inconspicuously to flick the ash from his cigarette.

"I'm fine." His eyes never moved from the view.

"Fine" and "okay" were not the same, but I knew I had already pushed him too far. "I'll trust you, then. If you need me, you know where I'll be."

"Goodnight, Ms. Nielson."

We were back to formalities.

"Goodnight, Mr. Montgomery."

He didn't look at me when I walked away. As I left him behind, I worried I had let him slip from my grasp completely.

Eighteen

"Your father is going to kill me."

I stood in the foyer with the twins and a guilty-looking Colin. The little ball of brown fluff wriggled in Sebastien's arms. He looked up at me with pleading eyes. "Can we keep him?"

I leaned down and stared at the puppy, considering all the ways in which this would end badly.

Augustine had left the loft early in the morning to resume the business we pulled him from with Sebastien's performance, and hadn't been back since. Back in this dark expanse of empty rooms, my guilt festered. I had let him drop. And worse, I had let him leave directly after. My first words to him would not be *Surprise, you have a dog now.*

"Does it not have a collar?" I asked Colin. He shrugged.

"What is this?" Warren came up behind me. I waited for Colin to answer, but he didn't.

"There are no animals allowed in this home!"

"Mr. Montgomery doesn't allow pets?" I asked him.

"No, ma'am. No pollen or dander permitted in the mansion."

I looked back to Sebastien. The puppy whimpered to be set down. "Let me see him."

The tiny poodle mix was kind of cute. The curls over his body and most of his face made up for his inability to be still. Under the fluff, a small medallion hung off the collar.

"He has a tag, little ones," I said. "That means he already has a family."

"We can't keep him?" Tabitha asked.

"Someone else is probably looking for him, worried sick." I tucked him into the crook of my arm, and finally, he settled down. His tiny pink tongue danced while he panted. "We should help him get back home, shouldn't we?"

"*Yeah,*" they both agreed, the word drawn out with their disappointment.

"It was very kind of you to make sure he was safe. Now, go upstairs and play. We'll get him home to his family, okay?" They knew better than to protest. Instead, they left with exaggerated pouts on their faces.

"Really? You let them bring a dog inside the home?" the butler snipped at Colin. "What if Mr. Montgomery were here?"

"I'm sorry. The kids had him when I picked them up. I didn't know what to do!"

"The word 'no' slipped your mind?"

"I thought that was Mrs. Montgomery's rule."

Both Warren and I flinched at her mention. Not since this week had I heard her name spoken so casually and so often. My brow stitched with conflicting emotions.

"The rules are the rules," Warren said through his teeth. "It isn't your place to decide which ones are worth obeying."

"Enough. I'll handle it," I jumped in. The two men looked at me as if I had just shown up. This was the most I had talked to either of them, and I was breaking up their fight. "I'll call

146

whoever is on the tag and see if I can locate the owners." Colin's face melted with gratitude.

"All right," the butler agreed. "The transportation of this mutt is coming out of *your* pay," he pointed at Colin, then walked away.

"Thank you," Colin said to me. "And I'm sorry."

"Don't worry about it."

"I'm not good with kids. They had it with them already, and I didn't know what to do," he rambled. Kids are easy. It's the adults who are hard to deal with. "I knew Mr. Montgomery didn't allow pets or anything around when Mrs. Montgomery was ali—" He stopped short. "Sorry, I shouldn't have said that." He looked down at his feet and fidgeted in the silence that followed.

We had both done things we shouldn't have in front of each other, though drunkenly admitting to having sex with your boss before staying the night with him in his condo was considerably worse than dander.

"Colin, it's okay. Really. You've seen me at my worst and kept it to yourself. I owe you."

His eyes searched mine for a moment, as if he had forgotten. Maybe he had. "Your secret is safe with me."

Choosing to believe him, I nodded. "I'll let you know when I get a hold of someone."

"Okay." He lingered with an odd expression on his face, then left me for the front doors. I looked at the pile of fur in my arms and sighed.

• • •

I took the furry fugitive outside for a bathroom break, and he seemed to calm down. I sat at the top of the stairs with

Biscuit—the name the veterinarian's office gave me from the rabies record number on his tag—beside my hip.

"You're cute, but you're a little menace. Yes, you are," I said in a chipper tone that made his little tail wag. His head nuzzled against my leg, and he went back to sleep.

There was nothing left for me to do but wait for the vet to call me back. Surely, that would happen soon.

I sat watching the maids complete the precarious task of dusting the grand chandelier. One held the base of a ladder on the steps while the other swiped each strand of crystals from top to bottom with a feather duster.

In the quiet, my mind wandered back to Augustine. Letting him drop was one of the most irresponsible things I had done. I triggered something in him, yes, but not during our scene. He was blissful by the end; he had come down, then somehow, the words flew out of his mouth as easily as a breath.

Lara. I knew her name now. I had started to think she didn't have one, or that I wouldn't maintain my employment long enough to hear him say it. But he had. At the worst possible time.

It would betray my experience and intentions to hurt him in a way he hadn't requested. I wouldn't allow a repeat of what happened, but if I didn't know what caused it, how could I keep from doing it again?

In one night, our arrangement had become more precarious than before.

My phone vibrated, pulling me out of my thoughts. "This is Aubrey."

"Hi! We got in contact with Biscuit's owners. They're relieved to know you found him. If you'd like to bring him to us, they will come pick him up from here."

"Great, thank you. I'll have someone head your way soon."

I ended the call feeling relieved. One less worry. "Looks like you're going home, little—"

I couldn't finish my sentence before realizing the dog was no longer at my side. I looked around frantically.

"Biscuit?" I called out. I went down the hall, peeked into the playroom, leaned over the railing to scan the foyer, but I couldn't find him anywhere. Panic set in. The thought of searching for a puppy in one hundred rooms was a nightmare.

"Biscuit!" I yelled in desperation.

Quiet yips came from my right. I crossed the mezzanine toward the sound and called to him again. The barks echoed from inside the dark expanse of the ballroom.

My heels clicked loudly on the polished wood floors, my eyes tracing the narrow strips of light that shone through the curtains and bounced off the chandeliers and sconces. Being here felt like trespassing, and I didn't know why. I paused to remember what Mildred had told me. *Across there's the ballroom. Behind it's another catering kitchen that connects to the main kitchen on the ground floor. Behind that is . . .*

The Master's Chambers.

The bedroom Augustine hadn't returned to since losing Lara. Remembering did nothing to ease my anxiety.

While I cursed in my head, the distant barks echoed again. I shivered when a chill spread over my skin.

"Biscuit. Come here," I said in the sweetest voice I could manage. "I'm begging you. For the love of god, Biscuit, where are you?" Finally, I heard his bark from the hallway. *Damn it.*

I went to the entrance of the hall and stopped on the old carpet. The air felt colder somehow. Heart pounding, I crossed my cardigan tight over my chest and hugged myself. Like something out of a horror movie, the hall was long and absent of other doors. Only a single window at the end provided enough light to see.

The hall turned onto an entryway; a grand doorway flanked by empty vases. I looked around for the dog, trying to find any corner or crevice in which he could hide, but found nothing. The pair of doors looked much like you would expect to see in a mansion like this. Tall, mahogany wood, a carving of an insignia or a crest, surrounded by a frame of curled leaves and twisted vines. They sat askew, possibly warped from age, a beam of sunlight shining through them. I stepped closer, peering through the gap, seeing only a sliver of what looked to be a vestibule, filled with bright light from windows beyond the threshold.

Curiosity replaced fear in my mind; the instinct to look upon the forbidden while no one was watching. In a moment of weakness, I placed my hand on the doorknob and pressed down.

It didn't move. *Locked.*

There couldn't have been a more glaring sign from the universe that I needed to mind my own business. With a shiver, I turned and made my way back up the creepy hall. When my heels met the hardwood again, I looked back over my shoulder, nibbling my lip with regret. There were no answers a room could give me.

Everything had to come from Augustine.

"Aubrey!"

I felt my soul leave my body for a second before I saw him. "Matthew!" I leaned against the wall with both hands against my chest, my heart pounding against my palms. "Don't scare me like that!"

He laughed. "What are you doing in here?"

I didn't let the guilt touch my face. "Looking for an outlet," I said in jest.

Matthew snorted. "Don't puppies run on batteries?" He moved his hand from behind his back, the fluffy little shit in his grasp.

"You found him!" I knew I could always count on Matthew to help me cover my ass. "Colin is going to take him home. Let's take the twins outside. Let them forget about the dog before they decide to mention it to your dad."

"Good luck with that."

• • •

It was easy to forget Matthew and I were the same height when I didn't have heels on. Strolling with him through the gardens felt like a scene from *Jane Eyre*. Bushes trimmed and proper, flowers swaying under the hazy sun, the ambient trickle of the fountain accompanied by the ruffling of the breeze through the trees. The twins held hands as they ran through the flowers with abandon, the tops of them shedding petals into the air behind them.

I sat on the stairs at the crest of the hill, looking down as they ran around, listening to their playful shouts as they ran along the pathway that led to the docks. The greenhouse I hit when I first arrived was back to its former glory. My dad's boat, however, looked about the same as before, though it was now safely secured in the docks. The boat wasn't what mattered to me. The memories did.

Matthew sat next to me on the steps, bringing me back to reality. Before coming here, I never met someone with whom I could compare my losses. Matthew was a glimpse into my past. I wished I could do more to help him the way Crystal's family helped me, but he was still in the in-between of his grief, struggling the way I had when I couldn't get my dad to connect with me the way I needed.

"What's that face for?" he asked.

I smiled at him. "I'm just thinking."

"About what?"

"My dad. That's his boat down there. The broken one." I pointed.

"That old piece of shit?"

I blinked slowly. "Yep, that's the one."

"Why did you even keep that thing?"

"Because of something you won't feel until you are older. Nostalgia." I sighed. "We used to take that boat down this river. I don't know how many times we passed by this island and wondered who could live in a place like this."

"You did?"

"Yes. I don't think you realize how incredible this place is. An island to yourselves."

"It's fine, I guess."

"It's a lot better than fine. I almost regret asking your father if we could spend the summer at the loft instead."

Matthew groaned. "You asked him that? Why?"

"I was trying to give you a chance to spend more time together while you're out of school." The look on Matthew's face told me he didn't agree. "I get the impression you're not happy about that."

"I like it better when he's not around, you know? If he never came home, that would be the best summer ever."

"Do you mean that?"

"Yep." He pulled at tufts of grass next to him and tossed them into the wind.

"I don't understand why you two can't get along. You're so much alike it hurts."

"I'm *nothing* like him," he growled. "No matter how much of a crush you have on him, you don't know him like I do." He pitched the last tuft angrily and watched it float away with a scowl. "I wish it was him who died, not Mom."

I placed my hand over his. "You shouldn't say things like that."

"Well, it's true."

He curled his knees up and rested his arms atop them, holding his downcast glare, but it wasn't low enough for me not to see the tears building in his eyes.

My heart broke for him. The teenage version of me had similar thoughts on occasion, but had I known . . .

"You know, I lost my mom when I was thirteen," I said.

Matthew's eyes widened, then shifted to me.

"That's how old you were when you lost yours, right?"

"Yeah." He rested his chin against his arm to hide its quivering. The familiar ache settled in my chest. I let it hurt, sitting with it the way I always did.

As painful as I knew it would be to continue, I had a point to make. "My mom was sick for a long time. Two years or so before she passed. Knowing it was going to happen didn't make it easier. In some ways, it made it so much worse," I told him. His brow furrowed with sadness. I knew I had struck a chord. "It was the opposite with my dad. One minute he was there and the next . . . he was gone." I remembered how benign the chest pain had seemed until the doctors walked out with frowns on their faces. "I was sixteen when he died. A few months from where you are right now."

His eyes widened with surprise. "You lost *both* of your parents?"

"I did."

The realization made him drop his gaze from me again in shame.

"I don't know the details of what you had to go through with your mom, but I do know a little bit about what you're feeling right now. There are still days when I'm angry at the world and everyone in it because they were taken from me." When he lost his fight with a tear, I rubbed my hand against his arm to soothe him. "I hope you know I am here for you, even if your father can't be—even if you don't want him to be. But I promise you don't want your dad to be gone, Matthew. Not really. And not forever."

He scoffed. His knee bounced nervously beneath his arms. The avoidant gestures spoke loudly to me.

"It isn't your job to mend your relationship. He is the parent. He needs to do the work to repair what he broke between you. But I hope you'll give him a chance to do that."

"He doesn't deserve it," he said just above a whisper. "He can't 'repair' what he did to Mom."

My brow tensed with confusion while trying to understand what he said. "What do you mean?"

His eyes narrowed as he stared ahead of us. "Why don't you ask *him* what I mean."

Before I could look, Tabitha squealed, "Daddy's home!"

Matthew stood and walked back to the house. I watched with dismay as he disappeared through the front doors.

When I turned back, I instantly locked eyes with Augustine. He strolled past me, white shirt unbuttoned to the middle of his chest, sleeves rolled up, a child in each hand. I had to remind myself to breathe.

"Welcome back, Mr. Montgomery."

He looked down at me, a hollowness behind those dark

hazel eyes, and said nothing back. His mood was unreadable, and so I read into it profusely.

Between him and Matthew, I was in a fight where no one spoke the same language, both unaware they were arguing over wanting the same things. A widower and a son betrayed. Every new day brought a new twist to my job, leaving me scrambling to find new ways to help give them what they needed most: each other. On a mountain of healing, I was backsliding while trying to convince them the view from the top was worth it.

But I couldn't give up. After all, I needed the view for myself as much as them.

Nineteen

The next day, my morning yoga session was fruitless. Too many thoughts and worries warred in my head, making it impossible to turn off my brain and relax. I had given up on meditating, settling for some basic stretches with a balcony view, but unexpectedly found my view was Augustine. Coming out of my sun salutation, I caught him again as he finished running his third lap around the island.

He hadn't said a word to me since he returned from his trip. To be fair, he hadn't said much of anything to anyone. This run was the first time I had seen him leave his office.

I had tried not to take it personally or worry that his distance was because of our last time together. I had pushed him, bent him, and now I feared I may have broken him.

The breeze off the water had a chill to it, but as the sun lifted higher, the summer warmth came with it. Augustine stopped running to remove his shirt. He looked up in my direction and turned his body to face me. We were too far away from each other for me to make out any sort of expression, but if I could see him, he could see me.

I placed my hands on the railing and straightened up,

holding my ground. He stared for a moment and then went back to running. The breath I was holding left me like a sigh.

He was being avoidant. If he wouldn't come to me, I would have to go to him.

• • •

Later that day, when the kids were preoccupied, I went to Augustine's office, pausing by the door. I hadn't decided how to approach him yet, how to broach the subject of communication when he was so intent on doing the opposite.

"Come in, Ms. Nielson," he called to me through the door. I froze in place, still completely out of his sight. *How did he know—* "I'd recognize the sound of those heels anywhere." *Oh.*

Timidly, I stepped inside. "I didn't want to interrupt anything."

"I find that hard to believe." His tone had an edge of humor. He stared ahead at his computer screen while he typed with furious speed. "To what do I owe the pleasure?"

I walked closer, practicing my words until my hips and fingers touched the edge of his desk. "I wanted to check in." When he still did not look my way, I elaborated, "We haven't talked since we left the loft."

He hummed, still staring ahead at his screen. "It's as if I've been busy. That seems out of place for me, doesn't it?" His sarcasm grated against my nerves. "I'm glad you've come. I wanted to speak with you about something."

"You do?"

"I do." He slid open his top drawer. The corner of a gold frame caught my eye. *The picture with Lara in Paris.*

"Augustine, you don't have to talk about—"

I stopped short when he pulled out an open envelope and

held it out to me between his first two fingers. I stared at it until he said, "Matthew's final marks."

My anxiety faded for a mere second before I realized I didn't know if his grades were good or not. I took the envelope from him and pulled out the card. When I saw them, I covered my mouth in shock. Tears began to well.

One B, the rest As.

Augustine walked around his desk to stand by my side. I continued staring at the letters as if they would change when I looked away.

"You're surprised he did so well?" he asked.

"*This* well? Yes. But I knew he had it in him." I fanned my tears to regain my composure. "He's been through a lot. You both have. I'm just happy to see him succeed."

Augustine leaned back against the desk, looking at me over his shoulder as I did the same with him. "I apologize if I have been inaccessible since the last we spoke," he said. My eyes widened. *An apology?* "I'm in the middle of a major negotiation that, once finalized, will free up my schedule. If all goes well, I should have more time away from work while we're at the loft over the summer."

His words sucked the air out of my lungs and words from my tongue. "What?"

"Your expertise has proven to be reliable time and time again," he gestured to the report card. "And I trust your intentions. I trust *you*."

My heart threatened to drop from my chest onto the desk. I placed a hand over it to keep it in place. "Augustine . . ."

"My work has kept me very busy, but do not mistake my distance for disinterest." His gaze drifted down to my lips, then back up to my eyes. "There are few things that pique my interest as much as you."

The last time we were alone, he was pulling away. Now, he was pulling me right back in. "I have to say, I'm surprised. Last time we were together, I worried I had pushed you too far."

"No. You were right where I wanted you to be," he said, the timbre of his voice reminiscent of a moan. His double meaning was not lost on me.

I turned away with a coy smile. "I'm glad to hear that. But . . ." I trailed off, not wanting to ruin the moment.

"But?"

I parted my lips to answer, but another voice spoke instead.

"What's going on in here?" Matthew asked from the doorway behind me.

With an almost practiced level of nonchalance, we both turned to look at him. I held up the card and felt teary once again. "Why didn't you tell me about your grades?"

His look of suspicion dropped. He put his hands in the pockets of his hoodie and shrugged. "I don't know. It's not a big deal."

"It is a *huge* deal." I went over and hugged him. He didn't return it with as much gusto as usual, undoubtedly because of who was still in his view.

"I'm proud of you, son," Augustine said. Matthew and I stilled at the same time. I looked at him over my shoulder and was stunned to find a small smile on Augustine's lips, then I turned back to Matthew, whose mouth hung agape. "You've done well this term. I hope you continue to do the same in the next."

Matthew looked to me with a nearly fearful level of bafflement.

"This is where you say 'thanks,'" I whispered.

"Oh, yeah. Thanks . . . Dad." His pause added a grim edge

to their pleasantries. With an awkward backward shuffle, he left us alone again.

That, however uncomfortable it may have been, was a huge win for me.

I stood in disbelief for a moment. "Wow," I cooed. "You gave him a compliment and didn't burst into flames."

Augustine looked at me from the corner of his eye and rounded his desk. "Do you ever grow tired of being cheeky?" he said as he picked up his cell phone.

I knew that was my cue to leave, but I wasn't done. "Augustine. What I was saying before. About checking in . . . I came here to ask if you were all right. Not being able to talk to you since leaving you that night has worried me."

He didn't look my way. "Your concerns are misplaced, Ms. Nielson."

"I don't think they are."

He looked up from his phone but provided no rebuttal.

I lowered my voice. "If you were any of my other partners, I wouldn't have let you be alone that night. But you're . . . you."

"I'm me?" He cocked an eyebrow.

"Yes. Stubborn. Cagey. Brattish."

His signature look of annoyance returned.

"I wasn't comfortable with how I left you that night, then you left me in the dark for another week."

"That isn't—"

"You said you trust me, and for that, I am grateful. But I still need you to communicate with me," I told him. "I will always respect your limits, but I can only do that if you tell me what they are *before* I reach them. Not after."

His eyes stared into mine for a moment too long. As if he had lost a war with his thoughts, he sighed. "I believe I *have* been avoiding you this past week, however inadvertently," he admitted. "You've asked me to be more open with you. I believe, in my own way, that I've done that. However, there are topics I do not wish to discuss. My wife is one."

My gaze fell subconsciously in the drawer's direction. "I understand."

"As you said, what we do in the bedroom ends when we leave it. I think it's best we both honor that agreement."

Hard limits are lines never to be crossed, and with a single slip of his tongue, he had pulled me over that line against my will. What he was feeling on that roof was what he tried to control through kink. He was vulnerable, and he *hated* the way that felt. But he would never admit that.

The phone rang, drawing his attention away from me. Our conversation was over.

"Shall I find you later?" he asked.

His calm demeanor contrasted with his previous warning, but that didn't surprise me. He wanted his sense of control back, and I was the only one who could give that to him completely.

"If that's what you would like, Mr. Montgomery."

His dark eyes looked into mine, driving in his message. "I would very much like that, Ms. Nielson."

He went back to his work, and I left him having more answers than he meant to give me.

Twenty

Later that night, Augustine used me to fuck his demons away, and I could not have been happier.

He had me just how he liked me: naked, collared, wrists cuffed together and tethered from the cross post of the bedframe above us. On my back, my arms were stretched out above me, the strap too short to fully lie down. He had me spread-eagled, legs outstretched to the sides, the tops of my feet touching the mattress. I had missed someone using my hard-earned flexibility, but he took full advantage, forcing me to hold the position on my own, taking away his perfect cock and the delicious vibrations each time he had to correct me. Every time I got close, my legs would curl, and he'd stop completely, edging me, driving me fucking insane.

His hips pumped in perfect time beneath the deep hum of the wand on my clit, his eyes staring into my soul while he watched the intense pleasure unravel me again. It was too much.

My head fell back onto the bed. "*Oh, fuck,*" I cried.

"That's right," he said. "Give into me and I will give you everything you want."

My arms burned as they were pulled taut, my wrists

screamed with the leather's bite, my legs shook while I tried to obey. His strong core flexed as he leaned back to get a better view of his presence inside me. He was the image of pure masculinity and carnality. I was so wet, and so, *so* close.

His free hand pressed down on my inner thigh, helping me stay in the position he demanded. *Maybe he'll let me finish this time.*

"Your body—your pleasure—belongs to *me*," he growled. "Beg for it. Beg for me to let you come." But I couldn't say another word before the orgasm overtook me.

My arms strained from the shackles as my entire body quaked with my orgasm—a rolling, deep surge of pleasure choked me each time my sex gripped and released his rock-hard cock.

As I came down, my vision returned. The scowl on his face made me clench around him again. Air had to fight to enter my lungs, leaving no room for words.

"I'll have to punish you for that." In a calm motion, he pulled out of me and set the wand aside. "But that's exactly what you want, isn't it?"

Before I could answer, Augustine pulled me up and turned me onto my knees at the head of the bed. I fell forward, but the restraints were too short for my hands to reach the mattress. When I tried to sit, he pulled my hips back up and landed a hard spank against my cheek. I yelped with the sting. The best I could do was brace my palms against the headboard, poised to receive anything and everything he did to me.

He moved closer, his chest against my back, lips against my ear, one hand pinning both of mine in their place. With a slow thrust, he pushed inside me again, pulling my hips back against his to take every inch of him.

His hand slid over the dewy skin of my hip and up my back. Then, he tangled it into my hair and yanked my head back against his shoulder. His fingers traced the inside of my leather collar, pulling it tighter around my neck. As he eased himself out and slowly, oh so slowly, slid back in, my scalp and throat burned with pain while my sex quivered in ecstasy.

"So greedy, Ms. Nielson," he said huskily, his lips brushing against my ear with every word. "No one fucks you like I fuck you, do they?"

Unable to gain enough air to speak, I managed nothing more than a moan.

He released his grip on my choker to tease my breasts. Every inch of me vibrated beneath his touch—my body an aura of sensations in his grasp. When his hand slipped between my legs, I wasn't sure where I ended and he began.

"Tell me you love it when that snug cunt's wrapped tight around my cock." His thrust timed perfectly with the last word.

My legs shook with the intensity of his movement against my sensitive walls. "I love it," I moaned.

Without pause, he pushed my head forward and began fucking me hard like before. My legs shook as his hips slammed against mine every time he pulled them back against him. I wailed each time his cock pushed hard against my G-spot with every thrust.

The pleasure was too great, too hot, too painfully good. I cried in ecstasy.

With a growl, he teased me again. "What's wrong, love? Do you want me to stop?"

"No."

Fisting my hair, he yanked my head back again, his tongue sliding up my cheek, licking my tear away. "Then tell me."

"Don't stop."

"Where are your manners?"

"Please," I added. "Please don't stop."

"Good girl."

His grip left my hair and joined the company of his other hand on each of my hips. He groaned as he fucked me harder than before. My moans turned to screams, my body squeezing around him as his delicious assault continued.

When he pulled himself from me suddenly, I collapsed as much as I could with my wrists still fastened above my head. He turned me around and lifted me from my knees, hurling me upward with him as he stood and slammed my back against the wall.

My arms dropped onto his shoulders with the slack allowed by our new elevation. With my legs draped limply over his arms, he pushed into me again without hands. His cock slid deep, so deep, his head massaged against a delicious spot few men ever reached.

Hungrily, I kissed him, our tongues mingling while he eased in and out of my wet center. He thrust hard and I gasped. He continued at that level, harder, faster, nailing me to the wall while he stared into my eyes. His warm breath on my lips teased them while I moaned uncontrollably. The heat building between us covered every inch of my skin in a mist, his hot muscles burning against my palms as the pleasure built deep inside me. Then I felt it.

The orgasm hit me hard and fast. My legs tensed and my arms squeezed his shoulders while the pleasure tore through me. He moaned loudly against my cheek, his muscles shuddering while his warmth flowed in rush after rush inside me.

As we continued to communicate in breathy moans and gasps of pleasure, he pressed his damp forehead against mine. His fingertips dragged down my thighs as he sank back down to his knees. Still pressed against the headboard, my arms above my head, I looked at him in awe.

Augustine was right. No one had ever fucked me the way he did, and I loved every second of it.

He kissed me passionately, his hand sliding over my cheek, then back down to my chin. My pain faded beneath his calming touch. The sultry caress of his tongue, the gentle sucking of my lips. I would have kissed him the rest of the night if I could.

Lost in his touch, I barely noticed him unfasten my wrists until he was laying me back against the mattress.

"Tears mean I did well, I hope," he whispered, stroking a thumb against my cheekbone before lightly pressing his lips against it.

My face split into a smile. I couldn't form words, so I hummed a yes and pulled him into my kiss again. He pacified me until I drifted into blissful sleep.

• • •

I woke up in Augustine's bed. Augustine's *empty* bed.

My arms were jelly, my back and shoulders aching from last night. Gravity was too strong to fight in my ravished condition, so I flopped back onto the pillow with a sigh, blinking away the last of my sleep. The sound of a shower running caught my attention. Then, the suitcase sitting by my feet. My mood instantly went south. *He's leaving again.*

The water stopped a few moments later. Augustine walked out in only his underwear, drying his hair with a towel, body tight and vascular from a morning workout. He had been awake for an hour, and I couldn't even sit up.

"Where are you going now?" I asked.

"I've been called out to Beijing. A bellend of a client is attempting to ruin the deal I've been setting up for months," he spewed with frustration.

"How long will that take? Anything longer than four days and you are going to miss the twins' birthday," I reminded him.

He closed his eyes and cursed under his breath.

"They'll miss you horribly. Tabitha will be heartbroken." I knew he had a soft spot for his only daughter.

"I *must* go to this meeting. If I'm not there, the Chinese will pull their offer, and I will lose my leverage against the Malaysians." He acted as if I knew anything about what he did for work, and, more laughably, that I cared.

"Have you ever considered bringing them with you?"

His brow creased with confusion. "Bring children to Beijing?"

"Believe it or not, children exist all around the world," I said with satirical wonder. "I'm sure you can afford extra tickets and a bigger hotel room. Bring them."

"I am going for business, not pleasure. Neither of which would be suitable for children."

"Sounds like you should hire a nanny or something." I refused to let his excuses ruin Tabitha and Sebastien's special day. "If it helps to pretend I'm standing in your office and not lying naked in your bed when I say this, do so. You have to find a way to step away from work for the twins' birthday, or, bare minimum, find a way to do both. Take the kids. Finish what you need to, then spend the rest of your time with them."

He narrowed his eyes at me, then looked away with a tut. "Fine. I will bring them if you agree to watch them."

As if Augustine would ever agree to be a father for more than two hours at a time.

"Deal."

Twenty-One

I had never been to China before. The only reason I had a passport at all was because of a travel study in Italy I had during college. Work had kept me busy, and my salary had done little more than pay my rent. There was a new world at my fingertips, but I was forced to look upon it from behind a series of windows.

We had barely left the room since we arrived. Even if the city wasn't densely populated and difficult for a foreigner to navigate alone, jet lag was brutal on kids. All three were cranky from being denied sleep when they wanted and told to wake before they were ready.

We stayed in a swanky suite on the top floor of a hotel whose name I couldn't pronounce. The room was the size of a house, fitted with four bedrooms, three bathrooms, a sprawling living space, and a full kitchen. The hotel had a pool, restaurants, and every other amenity we could need to occupy our time, but with Sebastien anxious at the mere thought of going into a crowd, Tabitha and Matthew more interested in sleeping than anything else, and Augustine focused on his upcoming deal, I could barely broach the subject of taking an outing to unwind. It seemed all of us had yet to enjoy this vacation.

The twins' birthday arrived. I was able to get us a reservation at one of the restaurants, hating that it felt pieced together in the last minute.

In the curved booth, Matthew slumped beside me with fatigue, the twins sandwiched between me and their father. The elegant restaurant was filled with crimson accents and gold fixtures, the lights dim enough to enjoy the glow from the city view. The ambience was better suited for adults, but so was the hotel.

"Happy birthday, Tabby and Bastien. Happy birthday to you!" I sang to them. Together, they blew out the candle on a small tart decorated with glistening candied fruits. They probably wouldn't like it, but Augustine did not seem to notice. His eyes had barely left his phone the whole night.

I wasn't sure why I had expected anything less. All his talk of finishing work so he could be more available to them, and yet nothing felt different. We had traveled here together just for Augustine to remain a world away.

The check came, and Augustine hardly batted an eye as he tucked in his black card. I peeked before he closed it, almost choking on my drink when I saw the amount.

He spoke with the waiter effortlessly. I had yet to pick up on any words or phrases except hello, goodbye, thank you, and yes. His intelligence both attracted and annoyed me.

"Do you know how amazing it is that your father is fluent in Mandarin?" I asked Sebastien as he shoved an oversized bite of the tart into his mouth, leaving a portion of it on his cheek.

He nodded.

"You should ask him to teach you."

Sebastien looked up to him, but Augustine didn't take notice.

"I'm not fluent in Mandarin," he said as if he were scolding me. "After Sebastien has worked with Chinese businessmen for nearly twenty years, he'll have learnt it himself."

If he had set down his phone, he would have seen the death glare I was sending his way.

He cleared his throat and tucked his phone into the breast pocket of his suit. "Happy birthday, my love," he said to Tabitha, placing a kiss on the crown of her head. "And happy birthday, darling." He did the same to Sebastien. "I can't believe you are seven already."

"Thank you, Daddy!" Tabitha gave him a hug around the neck.

A smile perked at his lips ever so slightly.

He stood and left the booth. "Be good."

"You're leaving already?" I asked. "When will you be back?"

He peered down his nose at me with a look of annoyance I wanted to slap off his face. "I don't pay you to babysit me, Ms. Nielson. I will return when I return."

He would pay for that later.

• • •

Hours passed like days in the hotel room. The twins had gone to bed, leaving Matthew and me on the couch. He had caught his second wind after dessert, providing me with some much-needed companionship. We attempted to watch TV from beneath the plethora of Chinese captions and dubs. Eventually, he gave up and played his game, and when he decided we were done with that, he retired to his bedroom without a word.

"Goodnight," I said to him sarcastically. He gave me a wave, then shut the door behind him.

I turned off the TV, enjoying the silence for a moment

while I stared through the window again. Beijing was noisy, dense, tall—not so different from New York City until I tried to speak to someone. Only Augustine could manage that. At this rate, we would be lucky to see him at all while we were here. This was business for him, not a vacation. I couldn't convince him otherwise. With that thought, I made my way to my bedroom as well.

I had been asleep for either minutes or hours when I was awoken by a crash, and "*Shit!*" followed by laughter. *He's back.*

I got up and walked into the main room, finding Augustine tilting back a bottle of wine in the kitchen, and a smashed vase on the floor near the entry.

"You're back," I said. The smell of alcohol radiated from him. "And you're drunk."

"Surprisingly so," he slurred before taking another swig from the bottle. "They drank me under the table! Half my size with twice my tolerance? Who'd have thought?" He smiled at me drunkenly and lifted the bottle to his lips again.

"Yeah, you should stop drinking." I pried the bottle from his hand.

He wrapped his arm around my shoulders and leaned too far, almost toppling over. I stood him upright. His hand on my cheek made me still.

"My god, you are beautiful, Aubrey," he mused, dilated eyes taking in the features of my face like a painting in the Louvre. My breath stuttered. He took my face in both of his hands and pressed a kiss on the corner of my mouth. "Should I tell you more often, love? That you're breathtaking? Or do you feel most adored when I spank you?"

Moment ruined. I closed my eyes with a sigh. "You need to go to bed."

"Yes. Bed." He glanced around the room. "Where is that exactly?"

The two of us were far more similar than I cared to admit. He was as messy while drunk as I had been after my date that night in the city. The night before everything changed.

I led him across the suite to his room, opened it for him, and made a grand gesture with my hands to direct him inside it.

"What? You're not going to join me?" he joked. Laughing at himself, he stumbled inside. "Can you at least help me undress?"

"I'm not paid to babysit *you*, Mr. Montgomery," I used his words against him. "But if it will get you to go to sleep, fine."

I helped him unlace his expensive Louboutins. He laid back on the bed, chuckling to himself. "They took me to a strip club," he said as if I had asked. "These women—if you can call them that—were upside down on poles, spinning around like tops. Completely nude. Which would have been lovely if they didn't look like teenagers." He gasped. "*Were* they teenagers?"

I shook my head at him. "Do society a favor and never get drunk again," I said. With a groan, I pulled off his second shoe.

"Should I feel bad that I let one give me a lap dance? Daddy issues and all?"

I unfastened his belt and pulled it from the belt loops beneath him. "When have daddy issues ever stopped you?"

He looked off into the distance. "Maybe I helped her pay for college." He pondered his statement for a moment, then he tossed his head back and laughed.

"Go to sleep, white devil," I murmured.

He grabbed me by the waist and pulled me between his legs. "Don't leave yet. Not before a little fun." He gripped my ass with both hands and ran his tongue slowly up the side of my neck. Even drunk, he was a brat. "I've been bad," he growled. "Sit on my face as punishment, mistress?"

I pushed him to his back. He grinned at me as if he were receiving some reward. "Get. Some. Sleep." I made my way toward the door.

"Lara always found me charming whilst we were drinking," he murmured, stopping me from leaving. "Until I had too much. Then she said I was an arsehole."

I agreed, but the mention of her name put me at a loss for words. I turned back to look at him. He was still lying on his back.

"That's what made me fall for her. Nothing could stop her humor or keep her from smiling. Not me, not the pain, not her illness. Nothing."

The room was eerily silent after his words. For a moment, I wasn't sure if he said something or if I just imagined it.

Finally, he took a deep breath. I thought I had lost him to sleep before he said, "I miss her." The light coming through the window traced the lines of his furrowed brow and made the tear sparkle as it rolled down the side of his face.

The sight of his unmasked emotion made my heart wrench. "I know you do," I whispered.

"Do you know why I like you, Aubrey?" he asked without wanting an answer. He turned his head to look at me. "It's because you're nothing like her."

I stared at him, trying to figure out whether I had more contempt for him or pity.

"Goodnight, Augustine," I said, but he was already asleep.

Twenty-Two

My sleep that night was restless, and the next morning, I couldn't seem to get up. Having Augustine compare me to his late wife hurt more than I expected. Seeing him display an emotion other than anger hurt more than expected, too. Toeing the line between pleasure and pain was usually easy for me, but with him, there was no line. It was both at once, all the time.

When the sun was high in the sky, I knew I had to get up, regardless of my lack of desire to see Augustine again. A desperate need for caffeine finally pried me from the sheets.

In the main room, Matthew had his siblings organized with towels, ready to leave. "Oh, hey," he said. "We're going to grab food from downstairs, then go to the pool. After we wait thirty minutes, of course."

"That's not a real thing, but you shouldn't take the twins to the pool on your own," I told him. "Just give me a minute to get dressed and I'll go with you."

"We're kind of tired of waiting on you so . . . I think we'll just go. You should get more sleep. You look like you need it." He smirked proudly over his cutting remark.

"Do you have the room key?"

"Yes." He showed it to me.

"And money for breakfast?"

"*Yes,*" he insisted with a hiss. "We've been here for five days, Aubrey, we know how this works."

"Okay," I gave in. "Be careful and don't let the twins out of your sight or in the pool until I get there."

"I know."

"Did you bring sunscreen?"

"Oh my god, goodbye!" Matthew walked out with the twins, the little ones giggling as they did.

I closed the door behind them, happy to know they would be spending time together. Watching them be carefree—opposite to the way I felt the night before—reminded me why I loved this job. They had become my happy place, making me feel like I was finally part of a family again. Caring for them, despite the constant obstacles their father provided, brought me a sense of healing. I wished Augustine could feel that as well.

The smell of coffee caught my attention. With my tiredness nagging, I was thankful to have a pot that brewed itself each morning. After a few sips, I meant to finish getting dressed for the pool, but I stopped myself. I poured a second cup, grabbed some items from the cabinets, and made my way to Augustine's room.

I knocked timidly on the door but heard no reply. After letting myself in, I was surprised to find him awake, sitting up while working on his laptop. His hair was damp from a shower, his chest was bare, as was the bent leg that protruded from beneath the sheets. Augustine naked in the morning was one of my favorite treats, but I wasn't sure I had the taste for him after last night.

Anxiety crawled over my skin while he continued to ignore my presence in the doorway. "I brought you some coffee."

He looked up at me, giving me a once-over as if he hadn't known I was there. "Lovely. Thank you."

I went to his side. He smiled when the cup met his hand, humming his pleasure over the first sip. "You're less hungover than I expected after last night," I said.

He smirked. "Don't trust me to hold my liquor?"

I dropped the saucer onto the nightstand with a loud clang, making him wince and clutch at his temple. Just as I thought. "I brought you aspirin too."

His glare was betrayed by the twitch at the corner of his mouth. "Thank you again."

I handed him the pills, and he took them with a swig of water. A ping called his attention back to his computer.

"The kids went to breakfast," I said when he set down his coffee and began typing. "They plan to go to the pool afterward if you want to get ready and join them." I leaned a hip against the bed and sipped my coffee, waiting for him to respond.

He paused his typing but didn't look my way. "Did they take a room key?"

"Yes, and money for breakfast," I said, answering the question I had also asked.

"Good." He moved his laptop to the sheets beside him and picked up the coffee as a replacement, drinking it as quickly as the temperature allowed.

There, I waited for any sign that he was hiding shame or remorse for what he had said last night. The circles beneath his eyes were barely noticeable—he rarely slept more than a few hours anyway—and his brow was not marred by the usual indiscernible perturbances. As he sipped, the handsome angles of his face looked bright in the sunlight and against the added darkness the water gave his hair.

He was his normal self. Somehow, that was more upsetting to me than the version he had been a few hours prior.

His eyes locked with mine, and an eyebrow raised in question, prompting me to explain my hovering. "Do you remember anything that happened last night?" I asked.

"I remember making a tremendous amount of money," he bragged. No guilt hid behind his sly grin.

"You already had a tremendous amount of money."

"Well, now I have more. I closed the deal."

"At the strip club?" I prodded.

"Over dinner. The club was merely a celebration." He eyed me over his cup, then leaned back against the headboard. "I feel as if you want me to apologize for something," he prompted me with a tinge of humor.

The playful look on his face saddened me. He wouldn't behave like this if he knew what he said—if he remembered he had cried in front of me while thinking about *her*. It appeared I was alone with the burden of that memory.

Setting his coffee aside, he grabbed my hip and pulled me closer, inviting me onto the bed with him. Reluctantly, I did so but refused to look his way. "What have I done, love?"

Not wanting to answer, I hid the full story behind a double entendre. "You made a mess," I said.

"How so?"

He wouldn't drop it. So, I told him a white lie. "You smashed a vase."

A laugh burst from him. "I'll buy the hotel a new one."

"Of course you will." Disdain flattened my tone.

Augustine hummed with a similar sentiment. "Come here."

He turned me toward him with a commanding grasp on

my waist and thigh. My body fed off his touch, reacting with instinctive obedience. I climbed up, just as he wanted, straddled him, and sat on his lap. His hands slid up and down my waist, mine against the nape of his neck, but still, I couldn't look him in the eye. I couldn't face the mask hiding the real Augustine I saw last night.

"You're pouting. The vase upset you this much?" he asked. There was no response I wanted to give him. "I quite like it when you're upset with me." His hard morning erection twitched beneath me. "Right now, I would enjoy that anger very,"—he rolled me to my back—"*very* much."

I gasped a split second before he placed a sumptuous kiss on my lips. Beneath him, chest to chest, cradled in the cloud of an expensive hotel comforter, he pulled me in, consumed me. The feel of his hand sliding slowly down my lower back matched the slow suck of my bottom lip. As torn as I was, I melted back together with him.

The way he touched me set me on fire, burning off all sense of reality and pain. In so many ways, we were designed to do this with each other. Our power balance was unmatched by anything I had had in the past. That balance existed *everywhere* between us, whether I admitted it or not.

With his mouth on mine, he tugged down my shorts, and before I could protest, pulled them off completely. When he broke the kiss to get the consent he needed to fuck me, he didn't find what he wanted.

"Do you not want my apology?" he asked.

"Your apology?" I repeated sardonically. "You're trying to fuck me vanilla."

"What's wrong with that? I remember enjoying ourselves the last time we tried."

"Oh, yes," I feigned agreement. "So much so, you never wanted to do it again until you were dry humped by a teenager."

Dismissively, he chuckled. "The look on your face . . ." he said to the scowl that hadn't faded. "I so love it when you hate me."

He pulled my shirt up and his mouth found my nipple, tongue sliding over it slowly before his lips closed around it and sucked. Pleasure tugged in my belly, making my sex warm with desire. His mouth moved to my other breast, his fingers teasing where his mouth had just left before sliding downward. His hand grazed over my seam, then disappeared to smack hard against my inner thigh. I gasped with the pain. His teeth sank into my nipple while he repeated the exhilarating torment a second and third time.

His mouth and fingers continued to tease me, the warmth growing to a needy ache. When his fingers slid inside me and found that special spot, I hid a moan beneath a sigh.

As much as I wanted to give in to him, to fuck away the tension and discomfort still lingering between us, I couldn't rid myself of the mental block telling me this was unfair to him.

"I think you should see a grief counselor," I blurted out.

His eyes found mine. "What?"

"I think it would be good for you." His brow tensed with confusion.

I ran my fingers through his hair. "I can find one for you when we get back to the city."

"Have you gone mad?" he asked. He pulled his fingers from me. "Do you believe *this* is the best time for this conversation?"

"Yes. You told me not to worry about you, but I can't do that and keep doing *this*."

He shook his head with a tut and got up to sit on his heels.

"I do not need to go to *therapy*." He overaccentuated the word as if I had made it up.

I leaned up to my elbows, breasts still exposed, and legs spread wide. I watched his eyes take a quick, appreciative look. "Why not?"

"I'm English, Aubrey. I keep calm, repress, and carry on," he said. I sank back to the bed, rolling my eyes. He fell forward onto his hands and laid his erection against my seam. "Americans always have to make such a fuss of everything." He flexed his hips to rub himself against me. "Sex is the best therapy there is."

He leaned down and kissed my neck. The head of his cock grew slick as it slid against me. When he changed the angle to slide himself inside, I reached down and stopped him from doing so.

I knew he could fuck me to orgasm in less than ten minutes, but then what? He was palliating the pain of his grief—avoiding the fact that it would kill him if he let it. Even after witnessing it firsthand, I was guilty of doing the same. The only difference was, I ended up in bed with someone who exploited it for their benefit. I refused to do that to him.

"Do you like fucking me?" I whispered into his ear, tangling my fingers into his hair.

He moved his hips to stroke himself in my grasp. "Yes."

"Do you like the way I make you come?"

A growl rumbled in his chest. "Yes."

I let go of his cock. With his next, slow thrust, he found his way inside me. I moaned as I stretched around him, pulling him closer. "Do I satisfy you? Do I give you everything you desire?"

His lips nipped my cheek. Just as expected, he said, "Always."

I gripped the hair laced between my fingers and pulled it hard. He hissed with the pain. "Then why do you still not listen?" I asked. Though it seemed like a tease, I meant it. "Look at me." When he kept his eyes closed, I smacked my hand against his cheek. His expression strained, much like his cock inside me. "Look at me!"

His eyes found mine, and behind them burned the familiar, brattish desire. This Augustine I could handle. This was the version of him I could reach.

The uninterrupted eye contact made every touch feel more profound, heightening my senses. His cock slickened inside me, becoming audible when he pulled out to just the head. A quiet moan slipped from us both when he pushed in again.

"You think you are in control, but you're not. In this bed, you are mine. Out of this bed, you are mine." The furrow in his brow turned upward as his anger faded to desire. "You do what I tell you." He breathed a heavy breath, his hips still moving between my thighs, his cock still stroking slow and steady inside me. "Do you understand me?"

"Yes."

I slapped him again. "Look at me." He groaned as his eyes found mine again. "Yes, what?"

"Yes, mistress."

"Good." I tangled the fingers of my other hand into his hair and pulled his head down to mine. I traced my tongue over his lips but denied him the kiss he wanted. "Now fuck me. Hard," I whispered to him. "And don't you dare look away."

He tasted his lips where my tongue had been and did exactly what I asked.

His hips pumped between my thighs, stroking it just right, his breath quickening. I held his stare, even when I felt myself unraveling, even when watching him do the same made my sex

181

quiver around him. When his eyes closed and an anguished "fuck" left his lips, I slapped him again, pulled his hair hard, twisting his head to the side. Our lips brushed against each other's before I allowed him a single kiss, following it with another slap.

My hips shivered with the pleasure that rippled through me. It seemed to affect him in the same way. He breathed in each gasp I made, every cry of pleasure he would otherwise try to hide. When I clenched around him, he moaned.

"*Fuck*, Aubrey." A shuddering breath, a look of yearning on his face. "I—"

The sound of a door closing caught our attention. Augustine slowed while I listened for the sound again.

"Aubrey?" Matthew's voice called from the front room.

"*Shit*," we whispered at the same time. He pulled out, and I shoved him off me. Scrambling, he helped me gather my clothes from the bed.

"Bathroom." Augustine gestured toward the door just as a knock sounded on the other. I ducked inside, pulling the door behind me without closing it completely. The two cups of coffee sitting on the nightstand made my eyes widen.

"Dad?" I heard the door open. The sound of the twins' laughter carried in from the distance. Adrenaline left my heart pounding so hard in my chest, I feared it was audible.

"Matthew. I'm glad you felt entitled to let yourself into my room."

"I can't find Aubrey, so I assumed you two were in here fucking each other."

I covered my mouth with a silent groan. His suspicions were correct, and it was shameful.

"You're a tactless one, aren't you?" Augustine said.

"Learned it from the best."

"Well, she's not here, I'm afraid. You must have just missed her."

"Oh," Matthew said as if he believed it. "Cool. Well, sorry to bother you with my presence." Those words fell over me like cold water.

Matthew shut the door behind him. Augustine glanced my way, but we waited for the sound of the front door closing as well.

He came to me, pulling me against him, his kiss hungry. I pushed him away.

"This isn't happening," I said.

"Why? I'll be quick," he begged.

"I should be with them. *You* should be with them, not hiding up here, using me to ignore the reason it hurts you to be around them."

He leaned away from me, eyes narrowing at my words. "Don't," he warned me when I verged too close to a conversation he deemed off-limits.

"I didn't, Augustine. You did. But until you're willing to face that, we'll both be waiting patiently for the other to give us what we want."

His glare burned into my back when I left the room.

Twenty-Three

At the pool, the sun was bright and the heat oppressive as it bounced against the pale concrete deck. We had come down separately, leaving Augustine no time for breakfast before the twins begged to get in the pool. It was the perfect combination for a horrendous hangover. I enjoyed the thought of Augustine's head killing him while his blue balls ached.

The twins held my shoulders as I glided through the water. Yet another problem on my list to remedy: the twins didn't know how to swim. Not well, at least.

Augustine lounged in a poolside chair, the sunscreen making his skin glisten in the sun. As I swam in his direction, I couldn't decipher his mood beneath the dark lenses of his aviators. He was mad. Frustrated at least. His towel was conveniently draped over his lap and those short, short swim trunks.

"Again!" Tabitha yelled.

I pulled my eyes from Augustine and smiled at her over my shoulder. "Okay, keep kicking! We're gonna go fast!"

They wriggled their legs, splashing without knowing my feet were against the wall. I pushed off and smiled when they both squealed with delight.

Matthew sat at the edge of the pool with his feet in the water. He hadn't set his phone down since his father joined us. It was no surprise he wanted a distraction from Augustine. Much like life in the mansion, he had locked us away and gifted us with luxuries in lieu of quality time with him. Having him today was a sharp turn away from normal. Even if uncomfortable, this would be good for them all.

"I think it's time to take a break and reapply some sunscreen," I told the twins. They let go of my shoulders and held onto the edge next to their brother. "Can you help get them out?" I asked Matthew.

Surprisingly, he set his phone down without rolling his eyes and pulled the twins from the water one at a time. He seemed closer to them, more caring than he usually was at home. For a moment, I wondered if the trip had been a bonding moment for them after all.

I climbed out of the water, pretending not to notice Matthew watching while I resituated my bottoms. Ahead of me, Augustine's glasses were still firmly in place, but his head was turned toward me.

A lock of hair hung wet against my neck. I brushed it up to gather it with the rest of my bun, looking back to keep Matthew from staring at my ass. He turned away quickly and pushed off the edge into the water.

On the lounge chair next to Augustine's, I dried myself and the twins with a towel, sighing with exasperation at the state of Tabitha's hair. "Come here, wiggle worm. We need to fix your braids."

I pulled the twisted band from her tangles and combed my fingers through them delicately. Sebastien hopped from the lounge and bounced over to Augustine's. He lay next to him, mimicking his pose, arms behind his head, one knee raised.

Augustine ran his hand over his hair in acknowledgment but never managed a smile.

"*You're still upset, I see,*" I said to him in French.

"Oui," he answered curtly.

"*Will that keep us from exploring the city today?*" I continued in our code. He didn't answer. "*Have you at least considered our plans for when we get back? Our extended stay at the loft? Will your schedule free up now that your deal here was successful?*" No response.

"*There are summer courses the kids could attend. Music lessons for your prodigy, a summer ballet intensive for your tiny dancer. Independence for your eldest—*"

"*Is it time you want me to spend with them, or less time you will allow me to tie you down and fuck you into oblivion?*"

My body warmed against my will. Our unplanned edging was not a one-way street. I, too, was suffering from the lack of completion. The best and worst part of edging was that it made you desperate.

I focused on weaving Tabitha's hair together between my fingers. "*We will find ways to make it work. Same as always.*"

He shot a glance at me over the top of his glasses. "*Maybe I'm not interested in more of the same.*"

"What are you talking about?" Tabitha asked while I secured the tie to the end of her braid.

I shook off my haze of desire and smiled down at her. "Our secret plans for where we're going today!"

Her lips formed an O. I pressed a kiss to the middle of her forehead, and she laughed.

"Where are we going today, Daddy?" Sebastien asked.

"Well," he started with more enthusiasm than expected, "first, we'll take a long car ride to see the Great Wall."

"What's that?" Tabitha asked.

"It is a very, very great wall." The twins laughed. "And after that, we'll go to the Forbidden City."

For the first time in a while, he sounded like a real father. An attentive parent of young children. Though I wanted to be upset with him, I loved who he was right now.

"Can we leave now, Daddy?"

"Why not?" he said, suspiciously slow. His eyes found mine. "We've nothing better to do here."

I returned his gaze with a glare. "Go grab your brother so we can get ready to leave," I told them. They bounded away like little lambs. Feeling scorned, I stood to gather our belongings. "You really do not like delayed gratification, do you?"

"I don't like much of anything at the moment. Especially you."

I snapped the towel in the air before folding it. "Yeah, well, that's not what you said last night." Realizing how callous my statement was, the guilt crept over my skin.

"I remember what I said," he told me. "Every word."

The crawling of my skin turned icy. I faced him, feeling the look of regret was marring my face. "You do?"

"Your actions this morning were sobering in more than one way." The stern cadence of his sentence did not imply appreciation.

"Then do you understand why I asked you to talk to someone?"

His snarl answered my question and told me exactly what he would do next. "My children need you for their care and educational development, nothing more." His tone grew more bitter with every word he said. "They are not in need of someone to take their mother's place. I am not in need of someone to 'heal' me of pain they can't possibly imagine."

I was the last person who needed a lecture on irreparable loss and the scars it left behind. "That isn't—"

"You are an obsession—an affliction I unwillingly developed—but you will never, *never* compare to her."

I knew he was speaking from a place of grief, but that never seemed to make it hurt any less. "Why the hell would you think I want to?"

The kids returned. My lips quivered as I forced a smile, but I hoped they couldn't read the pain on my face. We followed them back inside, no further words exchanged. In the elevator, I stared at Augustine's profile beneath a tense brow, trying to pin down which emotion I was feeling. He hurt me, he healed me, and then he hurt me again. At what point would he prove to be correct? How far would we blur the limits of our arrangement before it would have to end?

• • •

I had the twins dressed and a bag ready for snack attacks and sore feet. Once everything was situated, we joined the vengeful widower by the door.

"Let's go or we'll miss our ride," Augustine said.

Tabitha took me by the hand. "Let's go!"

"Ms. Nielson will not be joining us today," he said.

Dejection gripped my throat, but I was not surprised. Augustine wanted nothing to do with me today. At least, I hoped it would only last a day.

"What?" Matthew asked.

"Why not, Daddy?" Tabitha joined him.

"A 'family vacation' includes family, not the nanny, my love," he said to her in a tone that sounded calm but felt like a punch in the gut.

Tabitha looked at me in confusion. I hid my hurt the best I could.

"It's okay. Here." I handed the bag to Matthew, who looked back at me with as much hopelessness as I felt. "I packed some snacks, water bottles, and sunscreen for everyone." The lump in my throat made it harder to speak when I said, "Have fun."

The distress on their faces nearly broke me. I vowed not to let myself cry in front of Augustine, but my eyes stung with tears. He would deride me, he would submit to me, he would run me in confusing circles until we were both exhausted, but I would not have taken this job if I didn't think it would be worth it—if I didn't think those three perfect kids were worth it.

Watching them walk toward the elevator made my knees weak. Suddenly, Sebastien pulled his hand from his father's and ran toward me. I kneeled and pulled him into my arms. He squeezed me tight, burying his head in my shoulder.

"I don't want to go! I don't want to go!" he cried.

My eyes clouded with tears. Changes to his schedule and new experiences were difficult for him. I stroked his hair to comfort him. "It's going to be okay," I told him. He continued to cry. "Look at me, Bastien."

He leaned his head up, and the pitiful expression on his face broke my heart. Tears rolled down his cheeks.

"You are going to go with your brother and your sister and your father, and you are going to see something most people will never get to experience." *Myself included*, I thought. "You are going to have so much fun, you'll see. You just have to be brave for a little while first, okay?"

"Don't make me go, Daddy!" he cried again, laying his head on my shoulder. "I want to stay here with Mommy!"

The air left my lungs and didn't come back.

I blinked a few times, wondering if I had misheard him, but when I looked up and saw Augustine's quiet rage, I knew I had not. "Bastien," I cooed. "You meant to say Aubrey, sweetheart. You know I'm not your mother."

He hugged me closer and said nothing else. *Fuck.*

"Stay if you bloody want," Augustine said through his teeth.

He took the others and left. I gripped Sebastien tighter, fearing it would be my last time to hold him.

Twenty-Four

The flight back home was horrid. I knew Augustine was pissed. Every time I managed to get near him, he found a way to move. Locked away in his room at the hotel, taking a second car to the airport, making call after call from the gate. After nearly twenty-four hours of anxiety, my stomach was in knots. That, on top of my lack of sleep, made the urge to cry harder to ignore.

If we could talk, I would tell him that I knew Sebastien's words hurt him. That they hurt me too. We would have to talk at some point, but I wasn't sure how long he would keep us from doing so.

When we finally made it to JFK, there was only room for Augustine and the little ones in the Rolls, so Matthew volunteered to ride with me in a cab. It was late, the sun bleeding its last bit of color onto the clouds behind the city's skyline, the streetlights flickering on. On our way to the loft, the masses of people on the sidewalk had already shed the workday's business attire.

That was what I loved most about this city: the way it came alive at night. It was the time I got to stop being the Aubrey everyone expected and could start being *me*. That freedom . . .

I hadn't felt it was missing in months. Since I started working with this family, I hadn't wanted to be anywhere but with them. And, on occasion, with *him*.

This family, as odd as it sounded, was my new freedom, my liberation from a lifetime of displacement and isolation. Only when I feared I would lose them did I realize how much peace I had gained.

Matthew pulled me from my thoughts when he nudged my arm with his. "Are you okay?" he asked.

"Yes, I'm fine. Why?"

"You look upset."

I thought I was doing well at hiding my apprehension from him, but when I appraised my current position—slumped down with my feet against the back of the seat in front of me, my arms wrapped tight around me like a hug—I realized my body language was saying exactly how I felt.

"Are you gonna talk to Dad when we get back?"

"That was the plan."

"He was mad after what Sebastien did. Like, *real* mad."

"I figured." I watched Matthew as he avoided looking me in the eyes. "How did you feel about what Bastien said?"

He shrugged. "I don't know."

"You don't know, or you don't want to tell me?" I waited for him to answer, but he didn't. "Did it hurt to hear him call me that?"

His mouth twisted. "Yeah. Kind of."

"I think that's what your dad is feeling, too. Hurt. He just doesn't know that it's okay to express his emotions in any way other than anger."

Matthew snorted. "That's a nice way of saying he's a dick."

I knew I should scold him, but I didn't have the energy. "It was a nice way to say he's a *toxically masculine* dick."

He laughed and I smiled.

I went back to staring out the window at a life I no longer had until Matthew's head leaned onto my shoulder. When I looked over, I found him asleep.

• • •

Traffic gave Matthew a little more time to sleep. I told the driver to circle the block until he stirred awake on his own, then we went inside. We walked off the elevator into quiet darkness. I turned to tell Matthew we should go to sleep when a light caught my eye.

Augustine's phone cast an eerie glow onto his face as he leaned his hip against the dining table. Matthew and I exchanged a knowing look, then he left me for the safety of his bedroom, giving us space.

When I approached, Augustine leaned up as if expecting me to speak first. "Augustine, could we—" I stopped short when I saw he was standing next to a pile of my things. My heart dropped into my stomach. "What is this?"

"Your belongings," he answered matter-of-factly. "I don't need your services any longer. A car will be here to collect you shortly."

Without another glance in my direction, he turned and walked down the hall toward his bedroom. I stood in a stupor, trying to comprehend what had just happened, the blood rushing loudly in my ears.

That motherfucker thinks he fired me. I didn't accept that. I wouldn't. Something inside me snapped.

I ran down the hall after him and caught him as he attempted to close the door. He sighed when I pushed my way into the room, unsurprised and unamused.

"What the hell is wrong with you?" I seethed.

He looked down at me with cold detachment. "I told you I no longer require your services, Ms. Nielson. I'd like you to finish packing and leave."

"Are you fucking serious?"

"Quite." He returned his attention to his goddamn phone.

"Oh my god." I laughed, though I found no part of the situation funny. "I've been with you for months now. You think I can't see through your bullshit?"

"I'm sure you can, as well as I can see through yours." The neutrality of his tone was more cutting than the rage I had expected. "You cannot fuck me well enough to change my mind on this. So, for the third time, I am done with you, and I would like you to leave."

"Fuck you!" I spat. He chuckled, and the floodgates opened. "You are a selfish piece of shit. You're barely capable of being a father, yet you get mad when your own child acknowledges that? Fuck. You."

"This is not the way to—"

"You are twisted. You are *broken*. This self-confidence you pretend to have is nothing more than a mask. Deep under all that kinky bullshit is nothing but a sad pussy bitch."

He smirked. "And what does that make you, love?"

My mind caught up to my mouth, and I composed myself. "You think we're the same, but we're not," I answered. "All of us who hide part of ourselves in the dark do it because we aren't getting something we need in the light. You are broken, just like the rest of us, except *you* don't have the balls to deal with it."

He never looked my way. Rather, he continued typing on his phone. "Are you done?" he asked.

Oh, hell no.

I snatched the phone from his hands. When he reached to take it back, I sent it flying at the wall, relief rushing through me when it hit with a crash.

His eyes widened. "What the—"

"You're running from the real issue, same as always," I continued with his full attention. "You're pushing me away because I'm getting too close, and closeness terrifies you. The same way you hide behind kink because you don't know how to be intimate with anyone but your wife."

The narrowing of his eyes told me I was correct. "Is that so? Then why do *you* do it?"

My chest seized at the mere thought. It was a pain so familiar, so constant, I rarely acknowledged it. But when reminded of it, I remembered the wound was still open, raw, bleeding.

It hurt like a bitch.

"Because people die, Augustine. You love someone, they die, and you don't know who you are without them. So, you find a way to fuck someone without the risk of loving them because the thought of loving someone again—having to *lose* someone again—is too fucking scary," I read him.

He turned to me, his arms crossing in that practiced show of impenetrability.

"You are in pain. You are grieving," I tried to explain. "Believe me, I know how it feels to—"

"You have no bloody idea how this feels!" he yelled. "My wife and the mother of my children is dead. She is never coming back. You cannot begin to fathom the pain I feel."

"That's not what I was saying," I said as calmly as I could manage. "But I know grief. Just like I know hearing Sebastien call me 'Mommy' felt like your worst fear coming to life. The reality that he may not remember her is excruciating, even for me. But taking me away from him is not going to solve that. Talking to him about his mother, however, might."

"What the fuck do you know?" he roared as he pointed angrily in my face. "Who are you to pretend you know anything about what I should or shouldn't do?"

"Because—"

"You have no idea what I've been through—no idea how it feels to be in my position. You know nothing. Nothing!"

"I know how it feels to be *him*!" I shouted back. "I was the kid who had to figure out what it meant to live in a world without her mother!"

His anger faltered. A tepid silence fell between us, tainted by our heavy breaths.

"I was thirteen when I lost her, just like Matthew. Then, the minute I thought I had it figured out, I lost my dad."

Augustine's expression dropped. "I didn't know."

"You didn't ask," I corrected him. "I am not trying to fill the void of their mother's absence—that will never happen. *Never*. When they graduate high school, when they fall in love for the first time, when they're standing in a store and a child looks at them over their mother's shoulder . . . Every moment that passes—significant or insignificant—they will know she isn't there. When they least expect it, they will remember one of the most important people in their lives is missing . . . and it will feel like they are losing her . . . all over again." I barely managed to finish before losing myself to tears.

I covered my mouth with both hands in a feeble attempt to hide the sound of my sob. Augustine turned away from me to hide his emotion, but not before I saw it. That hurt too.

The purpose of my message struggled past the lump in my throat. "I lost my mother, then I had to hear my dad cry in his bedroom every night when he thought I was asleep. He was in pain, and I couldn't help him because I was drowning in my own."

I wiped away a tear with bruising force, a punishment for the memory, but another tear followed right after.

"It doesn't stop hurting. It never stops hurting," I cried. "But you either learn to live with it, or you let it kill you. I don't want your kids to lose their dad like I lost mine."

He tutted, still refusing to look at me. His knuckles were white as he dug his fingers into his hips, an attempt to maintain his composure.

"You are grieving, but so are they, which means they will need someone to be there for them when you can't. That someone, like it or not, is me." I wiped my cheeks and stared into his eyes to drive in my threat. "Push me away all you want, but I will not let you take me away from those kids."

He was silent for a moment after that, but he felt less distant than before. My words were a sorrowful bridge bringing him back to me. Only when I heard his sniffle did I know he was crying.

He wiped his eye and turned back to face me. "I love my children. More than anything in this world. But I can't explain to them what happened. I can't defend what . . ." Emotion stole the last of his sentence. He looked away and gnawed at his lip while he waited for it to pass. "I don't mean to hurt them, Aubrey. I don't mean to be absent when they need me, but I can't look at them and not see her," he said with a shaking voice. He hid his face in his hands and sank to sit on the edge of his bed.

My heart broke for him, but I couldn't find it in me to pity him. "There's no right way to grieve, but grieving isn't an excuse to treat them the way you do."

"I know!" he shouted.

One last burst of anger was his only defense. His shield was down; he was exposed and vulnerable. My goal had not been to hurt him, but there was no way to look inside without cutting yourself open.

I sat next to him on the bed, but I didn't touch him, only listened while his breaths calmed. His muscles were bound tight, as if he was trying to pick up a shield that was now too heavy to hold. After a moment, he raised his head. "Am I beyond repair?"

"No. Not at all." I rested my chin on his shoulder. "You have plenty to work on, but you are far from ruined."

He ran his quivering hands through his hair. "Where do I even begin?"

"Shift your focus, take some time to be with them, be more present when you are," I proposed. "If you get overwhelmed or something triggers you, tell me, and I'll take care of the kids while you work through it. But you *must* work through it. No more running."

Though hesitant, he nodded in agreement.

"You don't have to do this overnight, and you don't have to do this alone. I will be here to help for as long as you let me."

His reddened eyes were still wet as they traced over my face. "Why do you care?"

"About you?"

"Yes."

Though the question was simple, the answer was not. I looked into his eyes, the truth wrenching in my chest. "Because I know when I was hurting the most, I wouldn't be here if someone hadn't stepped in to save me from myself."

His gaze dropped with understanding, and possibly a bit of shame.

"I'm not leaving, Augustine. If the rest is too much—if the sex makes it feel like I'm getting too close—we can end it."

"No," he said simply.

Relief washed over me. With a hand on my cheek, he surprised me when he pulled me into a gentle kiss. We lingered there for a long moment. The slow way his lips left mine was a more believable "thank you" than if he had said it.

He turned away from me again. There was nothing left to discuss. I would stay. He would try.

"I'm going to go unpack my things," I said. "I'll come back later to check on you, okay?"

He nodded.

With that, I left him, closing his door behind me. I wiped my eyes again as I walked up the hall, but stopped when I saw a shadow.

Matthew took one look at my face and assumed the worst. "He didn't. He can't!"

"No, I'm staying. I didn't let him fire me."

Matthew sighed with relief and came over to pull me into a hug. I returned it, accepting the much-needed comfort. His warm embrace breathed life back into me after what felt like a battle.

When I felt close to tears again, I pulled away. "Go to bed. I'll see you in the morning." I pressed my lips against his cheek.

"You promise?" he asked.

"I'm not leaving you. I promise."

"Okay." He headed for his room but stopped. Fidgeting, he looked over his shoulder, but not at me. "Love you, Aubrey."

My heart stopped for a moment. I could barely breathe beneath the wave of emotions washing over me. "Love you too, Matthew." He scurried off into his room, and I lost myself to my tears.

• • •

It was an ungodly hour by the time I was able to unpack my bags. My body was tired but my mind was sharp with a second wind. It would take time to recover from jet lag.

As promised, I tiptoed up the hall and let myself into Augustine's room. I found it empty. The door to the closet was open. On the dresser sat an array of toys, whips, and shackles. Temptation warmed in my core but quickly faded to the cold air of dread. There, in the next room, I found him, naked and on his knees.

He sat there, staring down at the ground, blank-faced, disassociated. I went to him. With my hips level with his eyes, I ran my fingers through his hair and watched his head move just a breath from my sex. He didn't look up at me. It was as if he was waiting for permission, submitting to me completely.

I crouched down to eye level, tilting his chin up to make him look at me. The pain behind his eyes made me feel as if I were looking in a mirror.

"What do you need?" I asked him.

Just above a whisper, he answered, "I need you to hurt me."

Twenty-Five

The leather straps bit against my thighs when I secured the harness around my waist. With Augustine in this condition, I wasn't comfortable leaving him to go change, but staying in casual underwear didn't put me in character without something extra. I was still hurting from before, coming down from hours of anxiety, the last of my anger cooling beneath the hope I had for the future. Feeling the full spectrum of emotions in a short time was overwhelming. I needed to work it out, same as Augustine. Mixing desperation with sadistic behaviors was a dangerous combination, but that seemed to be his intention.

I knew what he wanted, and I knew why he wanted it. Physical pain was tangible, controllable. It was a release, if only for a moment. To say I didn't want to hurt him would be a lie.

Accessories in hand, I went into the room where I had left him and closed the door, locking us away in our quiet isolation. The ends of the long flogger dragged against the floor with my slow steps. His eyes stayed glued to it, a bit of life returning to his face.

He needs this.

"Hands up there." I pointed above us.

He stood, reached above his head, and wrapped his hands

around the metal cross rail. The muscles of his strong arms and core flexed, and his cock hung swollen between his legs. He was too tall to be overextended by the reach. A simple kick against his foot widened his stance and stretched his arms out straight.

"Good."

I tossed the satin ribbon over the rail, wrapped it around his wrists. He avoided my gaze, that same look of dissociation lingering on his face.

"Your safe word is what?"

"Red." His voice was low, tone flat.

"Say it when you need to—*before* you need to," I instructed him. He tried to shake his head no, but I stopped him with a hand on his chin and a press of my lips against his. When I pulled away, I insisted, "I need to know you'll say it."

"If I need to," he paraphrased, "I will." A brat through and through.

I stared into his eyes as I ran my hand down his chest, over his abs, and between his legs. My hand wrapped around his length, my lips catching his again.

He gave in to my kiss, even accepting my attempt to breathe life into him with another. His kisses were hesitant at first, but as I stroked him, he gave in to me. I teased my tongue against his between each taste of his lips. In the quiet, echoless room, the sounds of our kisses seemed louder, more intimate. It was as if we were two bodies in a void with no ability or desire to exist beyond these walls.

Breaking the kiss, I sank slowly toward the floor. My tongue teased over one nipple, then the other, my lips feathering kisses down his abs, and lower still. Then, I took him into my mouth. As I moved up and down his length, I sucked him hard, feeling him swell between my lips. When I looked up, I found the pain behind his eyes was muted by desire. That was what I needed to see before what came next.

"Remember, baby. I am here to please you. But I am going to hurt you." I picked up the hood and stood, then yanked it over his head. "Badly."

Taking the flogger in one hand, I ran it through the other, feeling its weight and testing its edges. It was good quality— unsurprising coming from a leather fan like Augustine. I stretched my arms and shoulders, watching him stand ready. Every breath he took was calm yet expectant. A quick inhale followed by a slow, quiet exhale. A perfect pet, ready and willing to accept anything I wanted to do to him. As thrilling as the possibilities were, I reminded myself to only give him as much as he needed, rather than what he thought he wanted.

From its position above my head, I swung the flogger hard, catching his ass and legs with my downward motion. He grunted with the impact but wouldn't give me the satisfaction of letting me know it hurt. I swung it again in the opposite direction, then flipped my arm to repeat the path of the first, his skin reddening in an X as perfect as the position in which he was tied. His quiet moan was muffled by the hood.

Like a dance, I traced the strands against my palm to angle my strike, lashed it against his skin, circled my arm to its original position, and caught it by dragging the tendrils against my palm once more. I walked around him slowly, the sound of every strike titillating me, teasing me, the pull of desire in my sex bringing me back to life. His body was a canvas onto which I painted my pain, my regret, and my desire for power over both.

The lashes hit his chest, his thighs, his upper back, his ass—every safe location I could find until he was pink and shying away. His breath was quicker in the wake of my assault, but it wasn't enough. I whipped him straight against the strong muscles of his upper back. He growled quietly, his arms quivering in response. I did the same against his chest, his core flexing and jumping with his stuttered breaths.

I stopped the flogger in my hand and noticed my excited breaths came in too short, too heavy, the ache in my sex unignorable. I wasn't in control anymore.

"Say it," I commanded him.

He shook his head.

Swirling the flogger over my head, I whipped it hard against his front. His body shivered with pain. "Say it," I repeated.

"No," he growled.

I whipped his ass once, twice. The third time, he groaned. "Say it!" I yelled, my final thrash loud in the quiet room.

"Agh!" He went slack, leaving him hanging by just his wrists. He stood back up on shaking legs. His skin was red, the lashes raised.

As beautiful as it was, I knew better. I was going too far.

I dropped the flogger and went to him. He flinched in fear when I pulled the hood from his head.

His eyes focused on me when my hand touched his face. The pain I had inflicted was apparent in the deep stitch of his brow and the shakiness of his breath. I brushed his hair from his face as he panted. When he leaned forward and caught my lips between his, I pushed him away by the throat.

"You didn't say it." My voice quivered slightly, ruining the force I intended.

"I didn't want to."

"But I told you to say it. I told you to stop me."

"I didn't want to!" he bit out through gritted teeth.

I slapped him, then kissed him passionately.

His kisses were desperate, hungry. His shoulders flexed as

he fought against the restraints. Every time his tongue licked mine, my body begged for more. I couldn't deny him or myself any longer.

I released one of his arms, and he wrapped it around me, pulling me against him with emphatic velocity. When I freed the other, he stumbled forward until he pinned me back against the wall.

He pulled my leg up by the strap on my thigh and ripped my panties to the side. Without pause, he pushed inside me, staring at me while my mouth dropped open. He moved closer, pushing deeper. Our lips a breath apart, we let out the same quiet, trembling moan.

His hips moved against me while he stroked himself slow and deep. With my hands, I traced his jaw, his neck, but the second I touched his chest, he winced with pain. I had done enough to hurt him.

"Lay me down and take me," I whispered. "However you want."

In a swift move, he lifted me from my feet, never leaving me while he laid me on the couch beneath him. Face to face with my hands in his hair, we met where we left off in Beijing. What we had wanted since that day—the heat, the passion, the perfect balance between our pleasure and our pain—was back in our grasp.

No talking, no questions, no answers, only intertwining bodies and wild passion. I moaned after every groan that escaped him, my brow twisting as hard as his. We were right there, and yet, we lingered, dancing on the edge until my sex gripped him and my nails dug into his swollen back. I watched his pupils dilate, his mouth open, and with that, the feeling exploded within me so hard I nearly screamed.

With the first clench and release of my orgasm around

him, he filled me with his heat. My head fell back, my skin prickled beneath a mist of sweat, and the pleasure covered me in a heat that flowed hard and heavy through every inch of my body. The tears streamed down the sides of my face.

His strength left him, his body growing heavier on top of mine. I wrapped my legs around him, holding him still while the last of my orgasm fluttered around him. In our calming embrace, our fire settled into a warm, comfortable glow.

"Thank you," he whispered against my cheek.

Twenty-Six

The freestanding tub sat opposite the shower like an expensive decorative bowl on a saucer, the Epsom salt bath so hot Augustine hissed when he climbed in. Once fully submerged, he sighed with relief.

Had he not seemed more level than he was when we started, I would have worried I had gone too far. But he communicated his needs, trusted I would meet them, and . . . I had. It never crossed his mind that I wouldn't. If anything, he tested the trust I had in myself.

"Will you join me?" he asked, bringing me out of my thoughts. Given what I had just put him through, it would have been wrong for me to deny him what he needed to come down.

While I untied my robe, he moved forward for me. Carefully, I climbed in behind him. The water sloshed toward the rim, but I managed to keep it all inside.

I poured palmfuls of water over the red marks on his back, but it wasn't enough. He needed to soak. I pulled him between my legs, his back against my chest. He slid down into a comfortable position and laid his head back onto my shoulder. Even in the oversized bowl, both of our knees protruded from the water, but in our lounged position, with him cradled in my arms, I could think of only a few moments when I had been more comfortable.

He stared ahead as if in a daze. "I'm sorry I never thought to ask about your family," he said.

"It's okay."

"I worry I may not know anything about you."

"You know more than most people," I said.

"But I want to know everything. Your life outside of my needs. Who you were before we met."

Augustine thought there were chapters of my life he was missing, but if I were to summarize the basis of my identity, it would be my loss, my education, and my kinks. His access to my CV and my body made him intimately familiar with two of the three.

"Before I met you, I was unemployed and afraid I would have to move back home," I said.

"To Maine?" He remembered more than he let on.

"Yes."

"Do you have people there?"

"I do. Crystal, my best friend, who I consider my sister. We've known each other since we were six; grew up right down the street from each other. When my father died, her parents took guardianship of me. They were both in psychiatry and were probably the only people around who were equipped to help me. Help me learn how to help myself." I couldn't appreciate everything they did for me until years later, but I would never forget it. "Therapy was one of the reasons I started exploring kink, by the way. There are benefits to it, I promise."

I meant to be humorous, but he seemed solemn in his desire to fill in the blanks.

"May I . . . May I ask how you lost your parents?"

His question gave me pause, but it was far from the most intimate thing we had done that night. "I lost my mom after a long battle with metastatic breast cancer. And my dad . . . I lost him to a heart attack." The memories made my chest hurt. Sympathy pain, perhaps. "I still believe it was heartbreak syndrome. It was almost three years to the day after my mom passed away."

"I'm sorry."

"Don't be." Though I couldn't manage to say it outright, I hoped he saw where my worry for him originated. I ran my fingers through his hair, using the water to keep it out of his face. His expression hadn't changed.

After a moment, he asked, "Did you have a good relationship with them?"

My mother was a teacher, strict yet loving, much like I strove to be. My father, the rugged deep-sea fisher, was a softy through and through. They met in elementary school. As they were two of only a handful of Black kids in their small town, my mother was adverse to the assumption they would end up together, but my father never let her get too far from him, following her to college, asking her to marry him the day after she landed her dream job. They carried that love into their parenting as well.

"I did," I answered. "A very good one."

"I can only imagine that."

"You didn't?"

"No." He sighed and shifted his weight. The water lapped against the side of the tub's walls. "I believe I was born out of duty and not love or desire for a child. I was raised by my nanny. A few, actually. My parents and I only speak during dutiful holiday check-ins."

"I'm sorry to hear that."

"All I've wanted is to give the children the best life I could possibly give them. To have them want for nothing." The fingers of his left hand brushed back and forth against the top of my knee. "I'm too far gone with Matthew. All I can do is give him the tools to leave me and create a happy life for himself."

"He can have a relationship with you and a happy life, you know."

"I don't know that he wants that. Or that I deserve it."

I ran my fingers through his hair and pressed a kiss to his temple. "You *do* deserve that."

He disagreed with a quiet sigh.

We simmered there in comfortable silence until the water got cold.

• • •

After the bath, I laid him in the bed. The lashes on his back and legs were still red, but no longer raised. I smoothed aloe vera over his skin, massaging his sore muscles at the same time. He looked as tired as I felt. I wanted nothing more than to curl up right there on his back and pass out.

When his muscles felt pliant beneath my palms, I thought he had drifted off to sleep. I rolled onto my back next to him and found his eyes open.

"Are you feeling any better?" I asked him. He contemplated it for a moment, then nodded. "Do you want me to stay?"

"Yes," he muttered half into his pillow.

"Will you be able to wake me before the kids do?"

"Of course." His accent made his words seem warmer than they were.

I nuzzled into the pillow, exhaustion settling its heaviness over my body. Just as I began to drift, I felt his arm around my waist. A moment later, he pressed his chest against my back. His warmth was soothing, the tickle of his breath against my neck calming.

"I am yours, Aubrey," he whispered against my nape. "In this bed and out. I won't fight it any longer."

I stroked my fingers over the top of his as I fell asleep.

• • •

I woke up at what I thought was an early hour. The midday sun glaring through the windows showed I was wrong. I cursed under my breath and turned to Augustine, but he wasn't there. I wasn't in his room. He must have carried me back to mine at some point. Had I slept that heavily?

I searched under my pillow to find my phone where I had left it. My screen was full of missed calls and two text messages.

Crystal: Guess who's coming to the Big Apple!

Crystal: Can you get away to meet us?

What a terrible friend I had been, so concerned with the trip and Augustine, I couldn't even spare ten minutes to give her a call. I pressed the video call button, not bothering to sit up or get out of bed.

"Hey, babe!" she said. Her energetic smile warmed me like sunshine. "Looks like someone's been too busy getting her brains fucked out to call me."

I laughed and wiped my hair from my face. "I'm really sorry. Things have been crazy this week."

"Still getting your rocks off with the ineligible bachelor?"

"Yes and no. I mean, yes, with him, but . . . I don't know. It's gotten complicated."

"Oh, because it was easy before?"

I sighed. "Good point, as always."

"What's going on now?"

"Something happened in Beijing. Sebastien called me 'Mommy' and it pushed Augustine over the edge. When we got back, he tried to fire me, and we got in a huge fight."

"But you're still sitting in his house with sex hair, so I assume things went well after that?"

"Yeah. I mean, after a while. I blew up, told him off, and I think we came to an understanding. He opened up to me."

"Oh, wow. Shit, I was starting to think that would never happen."

"I know. It feels like we're on the same page—that he understands how I can help him and why I would want to."

"You told him about your parents?"

"Yes."

Her brow furrowed with concern. She knew that wasn't a conversation I had with just anyone. "Are you okay? Do you need a session?" she asked.

"No, I'm fine."

She frowned the way she always did when she couldn't decide whether to scold me or accept my poor choices.

"I was actually hoping you could help me get one for the kids."

"Of course. I'll get some contacts and a referral for you."

"You are amazing. Thank you."

Her smile returned, but with an edge of sorrow. "Aub, you love me, right?"

"Of course I do."

"Then why are you not telling me the full story?"

I raised an eyebrow in question.

"You got in a fight. You talked to him about the thing you never want to talk about, and it sounds like he did the same."

"Yeah. That's everything that happened."

"So you're not playing stupid, you are actually *being* stupid," she said.

My brow tensed with confusion.

"You don't open up for people who fuck you right, and if you're kindred spirits like you say, neither does he. He cares about you. I think he might have real feelings for you."

"That's not . . ." The rest of my rebuttal never appeared.

"Do you have feelings for *him*?"

I blinked. The thought had never crossed my mind. My heart ached in my chest. "I . . . I don't know."

"Well, while you figure that out, let's figure out these appointments."

I let out a nervous chuckle. "Yeah, sounds good."

I could feel the smile on my face, but I knew it wasn't real. The rest of the day, all I would be able to do was wonder if I had gotten tripped up for a night, or if I was truly falling.

Twenty-Seven

The next day, we were back at the mansion. Crystal came through for me the way she always did. It took her less than twelve hours to match us with a child psychologist, though it helped that money was no object. The twins had an initial assessment the following week in an Alexandria office with follow-ups as needed at a partnering Manhattan practice. Matthew's appointment would come after we moved to the loft for the rest of the summer, and Augustine's . . .

We'd call his appointment *To Be Determined*.

The other thing Crystal managed to do was get into my head. She often proved she knew me better than I knew myself, and for that reason, her words stuck with me. It wasn't my intention for Augustine to develop feelings for me. It wasn't my intention to gain feelings for any of the members of this family, but the twins and Matthew had my heart long ago. I couldn't tell how much of my desire for him stemmed from my love for them, and how much, if anything, existed on its own. In the rush of traveling home and getting everyone back on schedule, I hadn't had time to figure out anything else, and to be completely honest, I wasn't sure I wanted to.

Tabitha spun on her toes and leaped with the song Sebastien

practiced in the adjoining room with his piano instructor. I watched him through the doorway, his smile spreading the more the song went on. What it must be like to find your passion so young.

As complicated as our relationship was, nothing could tear me from my need to protect them and provide for their emotional and mental stability. Though their father seemed to be on board, I was timid to broach the subject of repairing what had set all of this into motion.

Sebastien couldn't possibly think I was his mother. Right?

He was overstimulated and likely lacked the words to describe what we meant to each other. At my grown age, I found myself in a similar situation with Augustine.

The song ended and I clapped for both twins emphatically. Tabitha ran to my chair and leaned her hands onto my knees.

"When do our classes start?" she asked with sparkling eyes.

"I still have to ask your daddy if it's okay."

Her face melted into a pout. "But my teachers said if I work real hard this summer, they'll move me up to level two."

"I don't doubt that one bit. Look how quickly you've improved."

"Please, Aubrey. *Please* tell Daddy to let us go."

"I will later today, don't worry." Peeking into the other room, I could see Sebastien's instructor packing his things away. "Ready to go?" I asked Tabitha.

She nodded. I took her by the hand and gestured for Sebastien to join us. As he ran toward me, Augustine appeared. He caught Sebastien in his hands and kneeled.

I watched as he took a knee in front of his son, placing himself at eye level. I realized I hadn't moved when Tabitha tugged on my hand.

"Go find your brother in the lounge," I told her. "I'll be

there soon." She looked toward her twin with a frown, but did as she was told.

Augustine held Sebastien by his sides as he spoke. I stepped closer to the doorway and listened in on their conversation.

"Daddy gets very sad when he thinks about how Mummy is no longer with us." Augustine's tone was as gentle as it was sincere. "Sometimes when we're sad, it makes it seem as if we're angry at those around us. But I was never upset with you. I am sorry if I ever made you feel as if I were."

Sebastien nodded in understanding.

"Can you forgive me?" Augustine asked. Sebastien leaned forward and hugged his father around the neck. Augustine hugged his son to his chest. "Thank you, my darling." He pressed a kiss to his cheek, letting him go right after. Sebastien ran to me like the carefree child he was, but I was frozen by emotion.

I hadn't told Augustine to do that. He hadn't asked for the right words to say. This was all him. This was the man I knew he could be if he allowed himself to be vulnerable for his kids.

Augustine stood. His head turned when he spotted me in the doorway. We locked eyes, my heart beating hard yet slow.

"Aubrey, let's go." Sebastien pulled me by the hand and away from my thoughts.

• • •

With the twins down for a nap and Matthew engrossed in his video game, I slipped away to grab the gift from my room. I made my way down the grand stairwell, my nerves kicking up again.

Downstairs, I peered through the open door. Augustine stood near the lounge in his office with the butler and some other staff, staring down at the phone in his hand, the shattered screen slowing the usual speed of his typing. The sight was comical at first, but the package hidden behind my back reminded me that I was the one who caused the damage, and the guilt returned.

Augustine didn't look my way when he said, "Something you need, Ms. Nielson?"

His formality, while being intimately aware of my presence near him, was interesting. "Yes, but it can wait."

"Please," he gestured for me to come closer. "We are ironing out the details of our summer relocation, but I believe we're finished here, no?" He looked at the company in question.

The men agreed, exchanged a few more words, and then left the room. Warren eyed me while he closed the door behind them.

I walked closer to Augustine, gripping the box. "You didn't have to do that."

"I was praying for an interruption. What was it you needed?"

"A few things. But first, I wanted to say I'm sorry I broke your phone."

He smirked. "You're not."

I allowed myself a sheepish grin but dropped it before holding the new phone box out to him. He looked at it, then his gaze lifted to mine.

"I'm sure you've already ordered a replacement, but we passed by the store on the way back and I figured . . ." I trailed off, feeling awkward stammering out an excuse for my gift.

The surprise on his face was replaced by one of the softest smiles I had ever seen him make. He lifted it from my hand. "Thank you, love."

His unwitting nickname made my heart squeeze. "You're welcome."

We stared at one another, an odd sense of fear hidden beneath the discomfort of our vocalized appreciation for one another. When his dark eyes dropped from mine, I could finally breathe again.

He took the phone box to the front of his desk and set his old one down. The dreaded pair of scissors made their reappearance to cut the taped sides. "You said there were a *few* things."

"Yes. I also need to talk to you about the appointments," I said, remaining vague to avoid upsetting him.

"Right."

There was no discernible shift in his mood at the mention of therapy, which was uncharacteristic but appreciated. I crossed my arms over my chest and returned to his side, watching him begin the new phone's setup as I talked. "The office I selected has a location here and an associated office in the city. There are sessions available next week if that works for your schedule."

"I will make it work," he said. "When do the summer arts programs begin?"

"The second of next month." He would *make* it work, *and* he remembered the twins' classes. Who was this man standing before me? He was being so . . . *daddy*.

"We'll have the children's appointments, then we can travel to the loft the following weekend. How does that sound?"

"That sounds perfect. Thank you for being so accommodating."

"Of course." He pulled me toward him by the waist until I came to stand with my feet between his, our hips lightly pressed against one another's. With him leaned back against his desk, we were eye to eye. "You've made it easy to be."

He brushed a kiss against my cheek, his hand leaving my waist to sink down and grip my ass. My body warmed with his touch, an erotic pull in my core. His hand disappeared and returned with a hard slap. I let out a soft moan with the pain. If this was his version of a hug, I wasn't complaining.

As I pressed my hands against his chest, a faint red mark became visible beneath his shirt. My mind went back to Crystal's accusation, and more so, that night, the last words he said before we fell asleep together. *I'm yours.*

"When will I see you tonight?" he asked.

I took a breath while my eyes remained fixed on his chest. "I think it would be best if we take a little more time," I said with reluctance. "Our last scene was very intense for me, and I don't know if I'm in the best headspace to give you what you need right now. Taking a little more time would let me . . . process it."

He hummed his disagreement. "I could help you process it." His voice was low, taunting. My heart pounded nervously when his thumb ran over my lips, testing my resolve. "Naked." His hand dropped, and his fingers traced the swell of my breasts visible behind the buttons of my shirt. The teasing caress made my skin prickle. "Bound and breathless whilst I make you come over . . . and over."

His hand lifted again and gripped my throat, instantly turning me to putty in his hands. My teeth sank into my lower lip.

"Do you need time to process *that?*" he asked.

I knew desire was painted on my face when I fought myself not to give in. The corner of his mouth twitched into a smirk. He leaned closer, his lips stealing mine in a delicious kiss.

Giving myself to him would end exactly as he said: mind-numbing orgasms, blissful distractions. The issue was that I needed time to think. The line between professional and pleasurable had all but disappeared in one night, and though I was thankful to know he would make himself more available to his kids with my support, that, in practice, was foreign territory.

I wanted this job, I wanted to help them—*all* of them—but I didn't plan for this to become so much more. An open horizon was laid out before me, and yet, all I wanted to do was stay beneath the familiar rain cloud of my own creation.

Happiness didn't exist for people like us. There was no "easy" in lives shaped by grief.

He broke the kiss, his heavy gaze staying on my lips, waiting for them to say what they couldn't.

"I need some time," I whispered.

His eyes searched mine, hands drifting from my skin. Attempting to hide his disappointment, he leaned his hands onto the edge of the desk behind him, his knuckles whitening with his grip.

"Whatever you need." He looked me up and down, desire still etched on his face. "I'll be here. Waiting."

Reluctantly, I left his gravity, making my way to the door. "I won't be long," I told him.

"Do you swear it?" He sounded as enamored as he was bereft.

It was a struggle not to run back to him. All I needed was time for this feeling to pass.

"Enjoy your new phone, Mr. Montgomery." I closed the door, leaving him and my confusion behind it.

Twenty-Eight

"Who is this friend you're staying with?" I asked Matthew while we sorted through his clothes.

"Maxwell," he whined. "I've told you this five times."

Volunteering to help him pack was a bad idea, but I wanted to spend more time with him before he left me for his friends. It was our last few days in the mansion before we headed off for our extended stay at the loft. I was looking forward to our move. Matthew, not so much.

He tossed a shirt into his bag, which I immediately picked up to fold when he turned to grab another. "I just don't understand how you haven't mentioned him before now."

"Maxwell is a 'her.'"

What an interesting tidbit of information you didn't think to tell me. The expression on my face would have said it all, but he never looked my way. "You're staying with a girl for three days?"

"And two other friends, yeah."

"Did you ask your father about this?"

He looked at me as if I was stupid. "Why would I do that?"

"Because he might have an opinion on whether that's appropriate."

He laughed at me. "Okay, one, he's European. Two, he's Dad. Trust me, he doesn't care." The little shit had a point.

"Okay, well . . ." I toed the line between educator formality and parental compassion. "Has anyone taught you how to use condoms?"

His eyes went wide and cheeks pink. "Aubrey!"

"If you are planning to have sex, you need to know how to do it safely." A lesson his father did not seem concerned with during our first time together. "You can either have this conversation with me, or you can have it with your dad."

"I don't want to have it with either of you!" He crossed his arms and looked away. "Besides . . . it's probably not gonna happen anyway," he finished under his breath. A teenage boy's way of saying he wished it would.

"Well, before it does, you need to be prepared."

"Aubrey, I don't want to talk about this."

"Yeah, well, neither do I."

"I know how to use condoms. I've done stuff," he said with reddened cheeks. He hugged himself tighter. "I mean, I haven't done *that* . . . I've done other things, just . . ." Matthew fidgeted and avoided looking in my direction.

I grew nervous that he had something worse to admit. "Just what?"

He looked at me under a furrowed brow. "Just . . . not with a *girl*. Yet."

His sentence took a moment to click. A smile threatened as I looked at him, feeling both surprised and happy that he trusted me enough to tell me. I fought back my grin and remained stern.

"You need to know how to protect yourself during *all* types of sex. Condoms are only part of it. Oral, vaginal, and anal sex all have different intricacies to them, which means you'll need to know how to—" I stopped short when I saw tears building in his eyes. "What's wrong?"

"I haven't told anyone that before." The tear slipped from his eye a split second before he wiped it away and pretended it had never been there.

My heart ached for him. "Oh, Matthew. Come here."

I pulled him to me and wrapped my arms around his shoulders. He hugged me back around my middle and sniffled against my shoulder. I held him tight and swayed us back and forth gently, silently telling him he was safe with me. Always.

"You know how much I love you, don't you?" I asked him. He shrugged beneath my arms. "Well, it's a whole lot."

"Yeah?"

"Yeah," I said. He squeezed me a little tighter. "My love for you isn't contingent upon anything. All I want is for you to be happy and healthy. And to do your homework," I joked. He laughed through his tears. "Thank you for telling me, Matthew. I hope you know you can always talk to me about anything."

"I know." He pulled away and wiped his eyes. "Thanks for being cool about it."

"Of course." I pulled his head toward me and pressed a kiss to his temple. "But you still need to wear condoms."

He pushed me away with a groan. We shared a laugh while he dried his face.

"I miss my mom in times like this," he said quietly. I ignored the pang in my chest. "I'm really glad you're here to talk to about this stuff."

"I am too." That much was true. "But, you know . . . even though it may not feel like it sometimes, you do still have your dad to talk to as well."

"He wouldn't understand."

I smirked. "I think your father is more open-minded

than you might think." He didn't believe me, and I would not elaborate. "Finish packing so I can take you to the store for condoms before you leave."

"Aubrey," he groaned. "I am not going to do it with anyone."

I laughed at his expense. "Then I'm grabbing you one from my room."

"Ew! You have some here?"

"Yes. Just because I have them doesn't mean I'll use them, but if I need to use them, I'll have them. See how that works?"

He threw up his hands. "I am so done with this conversation."

"You and me both," I said with a laugh. "Finish up. I'll check on you later."

He grunted in lieu of a goodbye.

I left him and went down the long hall to my room. I couldn't remember the last time I used a condom, but I still had the ones I bought for my date. *They must be in my dresser.* I pushed my clothes to the side and leaned down to search through my things. Still finding nothing, I straightened back up, then jumped with surprise when I saw him.

Augustine stood in my doorway with his shoulder leaning against the frame. In a rare sight, he was dressed casually. Camel-colored pants, an untucked linen Oxford rolled up to the biceps and unbuttoned one too far, revealing the delicious veins of his forearms and the deep seam of his chest.

He was sex personified—the air of someone who just had it, but the look of someone who wanted it. My body was hoping for the latter.

The more open he allowed himself to be, the more attractive I found him. Having one less layer of toxicity made him more palatable, more delicious. Even with the awkwardness of our interactions the past few days, the hesitation to dive in deep while feeling so raw, I still found myself wanting a taste.

"Mr. Montgomery, I'm starting to think you like seeing me bent over," I teased him. He managed a small laugh. "What are you—?"

"Aubrey! Aubrey!" Tabitha shouted to me, running into my room while dragging Sebastien with her. "Daddy is going to take us outside."

"Oh, is he?"

"Will you come with us?"

I had a feeling it wasn't Tabitha who came up with the idea to invite me. I looked at Augustine, fighting the smile that pulled at my cheeks. "Let me give something to your brother, then yes. Of course I can."

• • •

The four of us strolled along the waterfront, the breeze coming in over the water barely cool enough to keep me from breaking a sweat.

The twins ran ahead of us. "Don't go far! And stay away from the water's edge!" Augustine called after them as they scurried away.

Seeing him act like a father made my heart sing. Though he still had layers to shed, there was a good parent hidden inside.

"Some shade and a cold beverage would be lovely, don't you think?" he asked me.

His attempt at nonchalance was not lost on me. "Definitely."

The gardeners scurried away, the same way all the staff ran away any time Augustine approached. Beneath a wisteria tree sat a blanket, some pillows, and a tray with two overturned glasses and two sweating cannisters, the neck of a wine bottle extending from inside one.

The look I shot him landed on his cheek. Was he really going to keep pretending he hadn't set up a romantic picnic for us?

I sat at a casual distance from him and got distracted by the beauty of the canopy above us. The tendrils of the branches fluttered in the wind, the last of its purple petals falling into a colorful tapestry on the ground around us.

Augustine handed one of the glasses to me. Inside it was muddled fruits: oranges, peaches, lemons. He removed the bottle of wine from the ice. "I know you prefer reds, but do you like sangria?" he asked.

It was no surprise he knew my preferences, but everything else about this scenario was *very* surprising. "I love it." He poured the wine into my glass, and my mouth watered at the smell. "I can't believe you're not working," I mused.

"Don't I often take time for guilty pleasures?" he teased. "Cigarettes, good wine, great sex." His accent gave his final word a lustful lilt.

I took a sip to hide my smile. The fragrant wine and citrus danced deliciously against my tongue. "Mildred used to have tea with me every afternoon. I think I prefer this instead." He seemed unfazed by the mention of her name, sipping his drink while he looked out toward the water. "May I ask you something?"

"You want to know why I let Mildred go," he clairvoyantly finished my question. He took a slow drink, then cleared his throat. "Besides the fact she wouldn't retire from working for me unless forced to do so . . . she said something I didn't appreciate at the time."

"What did she say?"

He didn't look my way as he swirled his glass. "She said you'd be good for me."

My jaw dropped, but I regained my composure and looked down at my glass. "Oh." I wasn't sure what to think about his words, or about him saying he didn't appreciate it *at the time.* "She worked for you for over ten years, though. That's a lot of time."

"It can feel that way. Or it can feel like a mere moment." He tilted his glass back for a sip and said nothing else.

The twins sped by, Tabitha yelling when Sebastien ran ahead. "Careful!" we yelled simultaneously. We shared a glance and a laugh, the solemness of our previous exchange waning.

With another sip, I took advantage of the lighter mood. "Tell me something about you," I said. "Something I don't know."

His dark hazels studied me, reading into the subliminal intent of my open-ended question. There was so much he could tell me, but only one subject I wanted him to divulge on his own.

"Do you want to know why I bought this place?" he asked.

"I assumed because you could."

"Yes, but also no. I bought it for Lara." He read me quite well and left me without words in the process. "This place was everything she wanted but would never ask for."

Hearing him talk about her, seeing that the memories seemed to bring him comfort rather than the usual unease, made me so happy.

"She wanted a *castle?*" I asked to keep him going.

"Yes, actually. It was similar to the estate my grandmother, Tabitha, owned in Yorkshire. We lived there until Matthew was three, but Lara had always planned to come back to America— before I interrupted her plans."

"Interrupted?"

"She was meant to be enjoying a gap year traveling Europe, but in nine months, we had met, made Matthew, and eloped in Paris."

Paris. I remembered the photograph in his desk, the Arc de Triomphe behind them. It began to make sense. "You eloped?"

"Yes. We knew her parents would be furious, but she insisted after we found out about Matthew."

My smile widened. "She was pregnant *before* you got married? How blasphemous," I teased with a laugh. He joined me.

"We received our punishment. Matthew was a horrid baby," he said. "Colic for months, screaming throughout the night. It felt as if I didn't sleep until he turned two." Hearing him talk about parenthood brought me inexplicable joy. "The twins were also a surprise."

"That explains the snip."

"I couldn't be trusted," he joked back. "Twins are difficult, but they were much less temperamental than their brother."

"Not much has changed," I said.

"No, not much."

We both sipped for a moment, then he poured us another glass.

"How did you meet her?" I asked carefully. I wasn't sure if the classic line would upset him or not.

He lounged back against the tree trunk, draping an arm atop his knee. Looking off in the distance, a little laugh escaped him.

"I was at uni, living the true bachelor life, and one day, I saw this American girl attempting to ride a bicycle, nearly tumbling off the side of it each time she took off," he said. "So, like any horny young man, I went to her and offered my help. She told me—and I quote—to fuck off, and that if she needed help from a British cuck like me, she'd have asked for it."

My head fell back with the laughter that burst from me. "Oh my god, that's amazing."

"I got quite the laugh from that as well. When she wobbled away, I was completely smitten," he said. "As clichéd as it sounds, I turned right around and told my mates, 'I'm going to marry that girl.'"

I groaned. "Did you really?"

"I did." He glanced over at me and saw my sneer. "What? You don't believe in love?"

My mood dipped a touch. "Of course I believe in it. My parents were a shining example of the best kind. I just don't trust it."

"A bad experience?"

"Something like that."

All my shame and lessons wrapped up in one curse of a man. Such a shame he had to be my first. It felt selfish not to give Augustine the same openness he showed me, especially when I knew his truth likely hurt as much as mine.

"I dated a much older man when I started college. I had just decided to explore kink, and he brought me to a fetish club. It was like a light came on. I could work out my pain, safely, pleasurably, with people who understood me, then I could go on having a normal life the next morning. I became his submissive, and I loved it. I loved *him*."

"But?" he prompted me to continue.

"But, slowly, his true colors came out. He didn't subscribe to rules or limits that didn't serve him. He used the lifestyle to cover his true Machiavellian personality. The more I discovered my true self, the more he manipulated me back into what he wanted me to be. When I asked to try switching, he . . ." I detached from any lingering emotions before saying, "He hurt me without my consent, so I left him as soon as it was safe to do so."

There was a look of horror on Augustine's face. "I'm so sorry."

"It's . . ." *Fine*, I almost said, but it wasn't. I stroked my thumb over the condensation on my glass and watched it drip onto my leg. "I haven't crossed a kink relationship with a romantic one since."

His eyes assessed me as if he was trying to read the intent behind my words. He brushed the backs of his fingers against my chin, his eyes dropping to my lips. "Would you?" he asked.

Before I could even fathom an answer to that question, a scream drew our attention. We looked to where the kids had been, finding Sebastien standing alone on the edge.

My heart stopped when he screamed, "Daddy, help!"

Twenty-Nine

We scrambled to our feet and ran down the hill to Sebastien. Augustine's speed left me trailing lengths behind him in seconds. "Tabitha?" he called. "Tabitha!"

A muffled scream came from my left, and I looked just in time to see Tabitha's hand disappear into the water. Fear rose into my throat like bile.

"Augustine!" I shouted. He looked to me, and I pointed to the water. "She's there!"

He spotted her and changed his course. My heart seized when he dove off the dock into the water.

Sebastien tried to follow him. "No!" I ran after him, caught him in my arms, and skidded to a stop. As much as I wanted to, as much as every shred of me was screaming to do so, I couldn't go after her without risking Sebastien falling in as well. I had to have faith that Augustine would save her.

We waited silently. My heartbeat was hard in my chest, Sebastien's doing the same against my palms. I wanted to cry when Augustine resurfaced alone.

He paddled quickly downstream, then went under again. I took Sebastien with me, treading as carefully as I could while keeping up with the river's current. My heart pounded in my ears while I scanned the water for signs of them.

Nothing. No ripple, no shadow. Every second felt like a minute. *It's been too long.*

Not a moment later, Augustine returned to the surface. I didn't breathe until I saw Tabitha's head on his shoulder.

"Oh, thank god."

Sebastien ran with me toward them, Augustine climbing out of the water onto the shore, Tabitha's arms clinging to him. I helped him onto the grass and he laid her down gently.

"Tabby?" I cried.

She coughed and gripped my hand—a great sign. I rolled her onto her side and brushed the wet hair from her face. She coughed up water, then inhaled deeply and opened her eyes to look at me.

"She's okay. You're okay, sweetheart." I pulled her into my arms, hugging her shivering body against me.

It took me a moment to realize she wasn't the only one shaking. The adrenaline pumping through my veins left me vibrating.

Augustine, still panting and dripping wet, looked at me with relief. On his knees, bracing himself with his hands against his thighs while he tried to catch his breath, his wet clothes clung against his skin while his chest and stomach heaved. He combed his fingers through his wet hair and dropped his head back with a sigh of relief.

Nothing, no fear, not even a second of hesitation to remove his shoes, could stop him from going in to save her. And he had done just that. She was okay because of him.

My love for him had never been stronger than it was at that moment.

• • •

A few hours later, once the doctor had checked her out and verified she was fine, I helped Tabitha take a hot shower, washing the river—and the trauma that threatened to come with it—down the drain in a lavender-scented foam. After a terrifying day, both she and Sebastien were exhausted. He refused to leave her side, even choosing to sleep in her bed with her. They hugged each other as I tucked the covers tightly around them.

I stayed with them longer than usual, not wanting to leave until I knew both felt safe and sound enough to sleep. Sebastien drifted off after the first two pages of *Le Petit Prince*, but Tabitha hung on until the end for her favorite story, eyelids growing heavy in the last stretch.

When I tucked the book away, her eyes closed above a smile.

"Get some rest, sweetheart." I kissed her forehead, finding her eyes open when I leaned away.

"You were right," she whispered.

"Right about what?"

"Daddy didn't let me drown."

I had nearly forgotten about her dream. Empathetic tears welled in my eyes again. "Of course not, sweetheart. Your daddy loves you more than anything. He will always be there for you." She smiled and nodded in agreement. "Sweet dreams, baby girl."

Tabitha snuggled up to her twin and shut her eyes. Not a minute later, she was sound asleep.

I left the room, going up the hall and tucking myself around the corner. There, safe from view, I closed my eyes and leaned back against the wall, letting the emotions I had been suppressing come to the surface. The immensity of my fear, and eventually, relief, all came out in the form of tears. This day could have gone in a very different direction had it not been for Augustine. For that, I was thankful beyond measure.

I looked over the banister, down in the direction of his bedroom. Every moment that passed showed me a different side to him, providing proof that, as complicated as he was, he had always been the man I knew he could be. That, possibly, the blurred line between our days and our nights might not be as scary as it seemed.

As I wiped my tears away, the desire to be near him grew more intense. I needed comfort, and he provided that better than anyone or anything. So, I went to him.

Inside his office, I found him at his desk spewing frustrated Italian into the phone, his hair damp and his shirt unbuttoned from a shower. He spotted me and invited me in with a flick of his hand. I locked the door behind me and walked to him timidly, gauging his conversation for importance, wondering how long he would make me wait—how long I *could* wait—to feel him. I found out the answer immediately.

My body crashed onto his like a magnet, my arms wrapping around him, head cradled in his neck. His sentence stammered to a stop. Warmth seeped from his skin into mine, the anxious chill burning away with every second.

He asked the person on the phone to hold on. "Are you all right?" he whispered to me.

"I am now," I said into his neck before pressing a kiss to it.

Even when I closed my eyes, he overwhelmed my senses. The fresh smell of his cologne healed my lungs, the feel of his skin under my palms brought life back into my body. I held his neck and kissed it again, allowing myself a little taste. He choked back a moan with a shaking breath.

"*I have to go*," he said, and set down his phone. He tilted my face up in his hands, an amused grin on his face. "Are you sure you're—" He stopped short when my lips crashed against his.

The fervor of my kiss caused him to stumble back until he was stopped by the wall. What was meant to be a "thank you" quickly turned into a grand gesture of my adoration for him. Days of keeping him at arm's length helped me avoid what? This feeling? Admitting the place I wanted to be most was with him?

Each kiss he gave me burned from passion to desire. The previous warmth he gave me burned hotter the more he took over. He kissed me back with the same intensity, his hands exploring my body for just a moment before I started tearing his shirt from his shoulders.

He flipped us around and pushed my back against the wall. I moved my focus from removing his shirt to undoing his belt. He helped me, never stopping our passionate kisses and only encouraging our excited breaths. With deft fingers, he reached through the seam of my shirt and ripped it open. A couple of my poor buttons pinged against the floor.

I unzipped his fly and pulled him close. He took me by the wrists and pinned them to the wall beside my head. His lips left mine, but stayed just a breath away.

"What are you doing?" he asked with a grin.

"I'll do anything you want," I breathed.

"*Anything?*"

I nodded. "You deserve it. So, take it." Even in the low light, I could see his eyes dilate with desire.

His hand slid down my arm and gripped my breast, moving his kiss to my neck. Dragging the lace of my bra down my shoulders, he ran his tongue over my nipple, sucking it into his mouth while he teased the other with the pad of his thumb.

He stepped to the side and flung me forward onto the desk. I caught myself with my hands, but when I tried to push myself up, he pressed his hands onto my back and my head, pinning me down with my face against the wood. My excitement heightened.

"Do you remember the first time you were bent over my desk?" he asked. He yanked up my skirt, caring little for the tightness of the material as he moved to expose my ass. "You looked just like this, ass calling to me, that beautiful cunt begging to be fucked."

His fingers looped into my panties and pulled them to the side. The pressure of his hand left my back, and a second later, I felt his tongue against my seam. A teasing circle of my clit and a dip of his tongue inside me was enough to make me moan. His mouth disappeared, then returned in the form of a hard bite on my ass. I gasped with the pain, hoping he would give me more.

"The number of times I made myself come to the image . . ." He stood. The clinking of his belt buckle made my knees weak. "The number of times I imagined fucking you, right here, just like this."

He spanked me hard, the sting of his swift hit making me wince. Another spank hit me harder and made me yelp with pain. With my cheek still against the desk, I looked back and watched him focus on his work, making sure it was exactly how I liked it. The heat in my core built hotter than before.

Every smack against my ass made me more desperate to feel him inside me. The next spank hit me hard against my sex. A loud moan slipped from me, and it broke him.

The sound of his fly unzipping was barely audible beneath his heavy breathing. I braced myself for what I knew would come next.

His cock was rock hard when he rammed it inside me in a single, painful thrust, fulfilling my need while making my craving more intense. He fucked me hard, gripping the bunched skirt at my waist like a handle. My hips crashed against the hard edge of the desk each time his slammed against my stinging ass.

My vision blurred as the pleasure built inside me. Pressed against the cold wood, my body was aflame. My sex quivered while he stroked deep, hitting every spot I needed him to. Then—

"Ah!" The orgasm hit me sudden and hard. When I arched back, he pressed me down with both hands, leaving me shaking when he didn't slow or stop his menacing pace.

As the pleasure rolled through me, his grunts turned into moans, and my moans turned into screams. "Fuck," he said and pulled out.

In an animalistic rush, he shoved everything on his desk to the floor and turned me onto my back. I crawled back, and he climbed up, spreading my legs wide before shoving himself into me once again.

My body welcomed him, my muscles pliable, my skin misted in sweat. I couldn't come down from my high. Every touch kept me right there. I looked at him, feeling the tears leaving my eyes. His head fell back with a moan.

He fucked me hard and fast, his hips pumping between my thighs, his ass flexing beneath my palms. Hungrily, he leaned down, pulled my head to him, and kissed me.

His tongue licked mine, our breaths heavy and hot, our grips tight and unforgiving as we fucked like animals right there on his desk.

The knock on the door made us freeze.

"Mr. Montgomery?" a woman's voice called from the hall. Augustine looked toward it with fear.

"I locked it," I assured him.

"Mr. Montgomery, is everything all right? I have your tea here."

He relaxed and rested his forehead against mine. We shared a hushed laugh.

We were getting careless, brazen in our moments together, but I didn't want it to stop. I was losing my ability to put anything above giving him the pleasure he wanted and deserved.

"Mr. Montgomery?" the voice called again.

Augustine moved off the desk and back onto his feet. He held his hand out to me. "Shall we take this to a more appropriate location?" he asked rhetorically.

I smiled, took his hand, and he pulled me to my feet.

• • •

Early the next morning, when I was done getting dressed, I limped until I found a gait that felt manageable. The ache of my backside—inside and out—made me whimper, but so did the memory. After two rounds, Augustine was done for, and I was just getting started. The only way I could get him to wake up and give it to me again was to literally milk it out of him. He paid me back in kind. I was sure neither of us would be sitting comfortably at the breakfast table this morning.

I went to get the twins and found Augustine inside their room, giving them a kiss while gripping his travel bag in his hand. My mood dipped.

"You're leaving?" I asked him when he came out of the doorway.

He didn't miss a step. "Yes. I'm off to catch my flight."

"Your flight?" I scurried after him as fast as my ass would let me. "How did I not know about this?"

"Because it was decided an hour ago."

I sighed with frustration. "Well, there's a lot happening in the next few days, remember? Matthew is staying with his friends tonight. He will go to the city with them and join us at the loft on Sunday."

"All right."

"The twins have their first therapy session the day after tomorrow, then my friend will be in the city mid-week. If you are still away, my friend's sons are six and eight. The twins might enjoy spending some time with them, if you're okay with that."

"I am."

"And where will you be?"

"Italy. Briefly."

"Briefly?"

"Yes. I'm not going on holiday."

He started down the steps, but I stopped him. "How long is 'briefly?' Do you know what day you'll be back?"

"When do I ever?" he said. I crossed my arms with a huff, which only seemed to amuse him. With a grin, he teased, "Why the upset? Will you miss me?"

I hesitated for a reason I didn't quite understand. "No, but I know your kids will."

He appraised me with his dark eyes, a quiet chuckle sounding from him. Then, with his hand on my waist, he leaned in and kissed me.

It caught me off guard so much, I didn't close my eyes. His lips left mine with a sound that made my heart flutter and my sex ache with need. "You are a terrible liar," he said.

Frozen with surprise, I hadn't even uncrossed my arms. That wasn't a thing we did—gentle kisses and *I'll miss yous*—but at that moment, it felt like it was.

"Wait." I followed him down to the third step. When he turned, I took his face in my hands and pulled him to me.

I kissed him the way I wanted, the way that felt more like a proper goodbye. He hummed quietly against my lips, his hand on my back pressing me tighter against him. I slowly pulled myself from him, but he caught my lips with his for just one more.

My eyes opened, and I caught his gaze. "Bye," I said, feeling more flustered than expected.

He looked me over again, a grin lingering on his lips. "See you soon, love."

He turned and left down the stairs, two staff members meeting him at the bottom and following him toward the front doors. He looked back at me before walking through them.

My breath left me in a rush. I pressed my hands against my cheeks and found them warm. *What the hell was wrong with me?*

I climbed back up the steps to go to the twins' room, but stopped short. Matthew stood by the railing as if waiting for me.

My skin turned to ice. "Good morning."

"What was that?" he asked me when I took a step closer.

My heart raced, but I kept the fear from reaching my face. "What was what?"

"You. That face you made while watching him leave." *Watching him.* My fear calmed ever so slightly.

"I'm flustered that he's leaving in the middle of everything going on this week." That was true.

"And that makes you blush? You don't blush," he said.

My eyes narrowed. I wasn't sure if that was a jab at my personality or my melanin.

"I knew it! You want to be with him. I called it day one."

"No, Matthew."

"Really? Because it kinda looks like it."

I let out a heavy sigh. Fighting hormones with fire achieved nothing. "Yesterday was terrifying, and the last thing I want is for him to leave again. That's what you saw."

"But do you?" he said, his voice a little too loud for my liking.

"Do I what?"

"Do you love him?!" he yelled.

I was taken aback by his anger. "I said no. Why are you so upset?"

"I told you I don't need a stepmom! I told you I don't want you to be with him!"

"Matthew . . ." He stormed back into his room, and I followed him. "Matthew, don't leave. Talk to me."

"You cannot fall in love with him. Please, Aubrey, you can't." When he started to cry, I was baffled.

"Honey, what is going on?" I brushed my hand over his hair. He pushed it away. My eyes widened with shock.

"You don't understand!"

This wasn't like him. He had reverted to the kid he was when I first met him, and I desperately hoped he was overreacting and was not actually triggered.

I spoke softly, trying to calm him down. "I'm *trying* to understand, but you aren't telling me what's wrong."

Matthew paced back and forth. "He's going to turn you into Mom and you can't let him."

It was just as I had feared. I took a breath to maintain my composure. "Your mother is irreplaceable, Matthew. There is nothing anyone can do to change that," I assured him. "She was sick and left you far too soon. I know how painful that is. But, if and when your father decides to be with someone else, you have to be able to accept—"

"Mom didn't die because she was sick, Aubrey," Matthew cried. "Dad killed her."

The air left my lungs and didn't come back. I stared at him and waited for the words to make sense, but they never did.

"I—I'm sorry, *what?*"

Thirty

Matthew's statement didn't make sense to me, but it scared me all the same. "Matthew, what do you mean he killed her?"

"He did, Aubrey," Matthew said with tears in his eyes.

"But . . . Wait." I pressed my palm against my forehead to slow my mind from racing. "Do you mean some kind of accident or—?"

"No! I mean . . . maybe. I don't know for sure," he said while wiping his cheek. "Mildred made me think I had made it all up, that it was a bad dream, but it wasn't. It was real. I know what I saw the night she died."

My blood was ice in my veins. "What did you see? Start from the beginning."

He took some deep breaths and collected himself, his eyes looking off into the distance as if he were watching it happen. "Mom almost died when she had the twins, and she was really sick for a long time after. She'd get tired easily, she'd still have days when she wouldn't be able to get out of bed, and some weeks, the doctors would have to stay at the house to treat her. A couple of times, they had to take her to the hospital."

His words brought up memories of my own. Painful ones I wish he never had to feel. "I'm so sorry."

"But then she got better. For the first time in months, it was like I had my mom back. Before she died, she was able to spend the whole day with us and have fun with the twins. We were all so happy. Except Dad. He was like he is now, mad for no reason. He would barely talk to anyone the whole day, didn't want to do anything with us at all. And that night, I saw them."

His brow furrowed again. His eyes filled with tears. I rubbed my palms against his arms to comfort him.

"They never fought. Ever. He couldn't be upset at her for anything until she got better," he said. "I couldn't hear what they were saying, but he was angry, yelling at her, not letting her walk away. And then the next morning . . . she was dead."

He started sobbing. Pulling him against my chest, my heart aching, I let him cry against my shoulder.

"They took her out of the house in a body bag and he didn't even cry. He just stood there and watched her leave, then he went downstairs to his office to work."

My skin crawled. None of it made sense to me, but I owed it to him to listen without judgment. "Why didn't you tell me this before?"

"Because when I told Mildred, she said that's not what happened. She said I was too young to understand what was going on," he cried. "She didn't believe me."

I felt sick.

"We took pictures that day. Mildred framed one, but Dad didn't want it, so she hid it somewhere," he said. "If you could find it, you'd see what I'm talking about. Please, Aubrey. You have to believe me."

I didn't know what to think, but I knew what he needed me to say. "I believe you."

He hugged me again. "If you love him . . . if he falls for

you . . . I'm afraid he won't fire you if you make him mad. He'll hurt you. Or worse."

What could be worse than this?

• • •

I was able to calm Matthew down before he left with his friends, but he wasn't in a good headspace. I was worried for him *and* myself.

It was too much conflicting information, too much to process. Augustine, the man I knew him to be, was complicated, yet in many ways, predictable. He was like reading a book that appeared to be written in a different language, but upon closer inspection, was just a complicated font. As much as it bothered me that no one would speak about what happened to Lara, nothing Augustine did made me think he would harm her in any way. I had a hard time believing he would have even hurt her the way he hurt me; mercilessly but consensually.

On the other hand, Matthew had never lied to me. He omitted the truth, yes, but never outright lied to my face. Whether I wanted to believe Matthew or not, I couldn't brush off his story before I knew more.

"You can watch from here," the therapy administrator told me.

I forced myself out of my stupor and back into the psychiatry office. She took me inside a room with glass walls that looked into where Tabitha and Sebastien's sessions would take place.

"This is just the initial assessment, but listening may give you a new perspective on some of the topics you were concerned about."

"Okay, great. Thank you." She left to give me privacy.

The twins were in separate rooms that were both filled with similar décor and toys. Sebastien chose a coloring set. Tabitha assembled blocks into a towering castle. They were rarely separated, but when they were, the differences in their personalities were stark. Tabitha was already blabbing away while Sebastien had yet to warm up to the new stranger.

"Who told you that you'd be spending time with me today?" the therapist asked Sebastien.

"My Daddy and my Aubrey."

"Is your Aubrey not your mommy?" Sebastien didn't respond. "Where *is* your mommy?"

"She's not here anymore."

"What do you mean by that? Where is she if she's not here?"

"She's in heaven."

"I'm sorry to hear that. Can you tell me about her?" Sebastien shrugged. "You can tell me anything. Big or small," she encouraged him. "What did she used to do with you? What did she look like? Or even, what did she smell like?"

Sebastien kept coloring and didn't look up. "I loved her a whole lot. I love Aubrey too. Is that okay?"

"Of course that's okay. We love many people in our life, don't we?"

"Yeah."

Tears blurred my vision. I was equally touched to know how he felt about me and pained that he couldn't remember his own mother.

I wiped my cheek and turned to Tabitha's room, bracing myself for my heart to be broken all over again.

"What is your favorite subject in school?" the other therapist asked Tabitha.

"I like Spanish class," she answered. "It's fun."

"What is so fun about it?"

"My Aubrey speaks other languages with Daddy all the time. It's fun when they do that. I want to do that too."

"Your Aubrey? Who is that?"

"The lady who brought me today. She's supposed to be my nanny, but I like her way more than that. I think my Daddy does too. Which is good."

"Why is that good?"

"Because she makes Daddy love us more," she said with a smile. My brow tensed.

"What makes you say that?"

"He got sad when Mommy died, and he didn't want to see us as much. He comes home a lot and spends more time with us now that she's here. He even saved me yesterday!"

"Saved you?"

"Yeah! When I jumped in the water."

Jumped? The word hit me like a slap in the face.

"Aubrey said he would save me if he loved me, and he did."

My mind spun in circles until I felt dizzy. I sat down and hung my head in my hands, trying to make sense of the senselessness. *She jumped? She was willing to drown herself for his attention?* The pounding in my chest was so loud, I couldn't hear the rest of her conversation. I wasn't sure I wanted to, anyway.

Matthew believed his father caused his mother's death, Tabitha wouldn't believe her father loved her without risking her life to prove it, and Sebastien couldn't remember the person whose loss caused his father unimaginable pain.

This was what happened when they were together, their grief swirling like a cyclone, pulling them in four different directions, and I had volunteered to be in the middle of it all. This is what I signed up for. I couldn't give up on them the moment it was all coming to a head. I couldn't help them heal from their loss, but I could help them mend their relationships. But how?

As I sat, the fog of shock cleared, and the truth became easier to see. The string between all the kids' emotional stability was Augustine, and now I had reason to suspect he was the cause of their frayed knot.

Only when the administrator came to gather me a few minutes later was I able to compose myself. I stood with her as she went over her notes.

"So, things went really well today, but I think it would be great to have them come in again for another assessment," she said. "While they don't seem to be showing signs of trauma, they don't seem to have a good understanding of what death means, especially when it comes to their mother, which isn't abnormal for children their age."

I swallowed hard past the knot in my throat. "What is the best way to help them with that?"

"The best way is open communication from a parent or trusted adult in their lives. Allow them to ask questions and give them truthful answers. Avoid euphemisms that might confuse them. Phrases like 'passed' or 'not with us' may make children imagine death as something imaginary or impermanent," she explained. "What caused their mother's death?"

Anxiety crawled up my spine. After months with the family, no one would tell me. Now, I couldn't help but worry why. "I'm not sure, actually."

"Oh? Well, if you can get their father to come with you next time, that should help us discern the best way to broach the subject with them."

"Absolutely," I agreed, wishing they could teach me the best way to broach the subject with *him*. "I'll do that."

• • •

Augustine had danced on the edge of telling me what was wrong with Lara, but never did. Whatever happened hurt him deeply, but my promise to Matthew put me on the edge of opening that wound for the sake of his kids. There had to be a way to avoid hurting anyone in the process. Finding the truth without their help was my best option.

I approached Warren when he was done directing some of the staff.

"Hello, Ms. Nielson." His formal tone barely hid his tinge of distaste for me. "Did you need something?"

"I was wondering if Mildred kept any family keepsakes when she left. Matthew mentioned something she had of his."

"Do you think she took something that didn't belong to her?"

"No, nothing like that. It was a picture."

Warren's chin lifted as if he caught my underlying message. "All the family's belongings should have been returned to them. The master prefers all photos and keepsakes to remain in his quarters. His *true* quarters, not the room where you spend your nights together."

Of course he knew about us. At this point, we were lucky most of the staff hadn't caught on.

He walked away, leaving me to stew in my discomfort.

Colin appeared beside me. "Don't listen to him," he whispered. "He's an asshole."

"I've noticed," I grumbled.

"What do you need?" The question people rarely asked me.

"It's not about me. The kids need to be able to ask about their mother. I don't know the answers, and I don't think

Mr. Montgomery is in a place to be able to answer them either. I just need to know how she passed."

"I don't know. Mr. Montgomery sent everyone home the night it happened. She was sick the whole time I worked here, but I don't know the details. Only Mildred, Warren, and the doctors knew. Everyone else was told not to ask questions."

"I was told the same thing. I wouldn't ask if the kids didn't need it."

"I wish I could help you more."

"It's okay. I'll figure something out."

We left each other, but I didn't get far. "Ms. Nielson," Warren's voice behind me made me flinch. I turned to face him. "You'll need the key."

"The key?"

"To the room," he said. He held out his hand, the skeleton key resting flat on his palm. "All the family's photos are in the console just inside the door."

I stared in shock. "Why are you giving this to me?" I asked, not understanding why he would push me further into Augustine's private life after judging me for being in his bed.

"I may not agree with how you got together, but for what it's worth, I can tell you've helped him. Most of us can." That touched me. Deeply. "If you believe this will help him, too, so be it."

After today, I wasn't sure of anything.

• • •

I stared at the doors for what seemed like minutes, wondering if this was the right thing to do. Augustine couldn't be happy about this, but everyone else was pointing me here, asking me to see what was behind the mahogany barrier in front of me.

The key was heavy, and it wasn't clear which way it fit into the lock. When it finally slipped in, I turned it carefully until . . . *click*.

The door cracked open on its own. As I looked inside, I expected to feel ashamed for encroaching on something meant to be private, but the reality was worse.

A small foyer led to the main room. Inside it was nothing but a bed. A light layer of dust covered everything, tufts of it floating through the air in the sunlight peeping through the tall windows' heavy drapes. The gold-color sheets were disheveled and pulled down from the top corner as if someone had just gotten out of bed. It looked as if nothing had moved in years, as if time froze the moment her body left the room.

Augustine hadn't been avoiding the place he used to sleep next to his wife, but the place where he said goodbye to her. The memories were undoubtedly too painful for him to spend time here, but when three years had passed . . . for it to remain in this state was unnerving.

I swung the door open further, revealing the shallow entryway table sitting beneath the window. A collection of gold frames, much like the one in Augustine's desk, sat atop it, familiar faces smiling back at me.

The twins were babies, Matthew just a kid, as they sat in the living room with their parents. Mrs. Montgomery, beautiful, smiling while the sunlight lit up her blonde hair. She looked different than she did in the Paris photo. Her hair was pulled up in a similar, carefree style, but her face was hollower, her eyes dimmer. Her smile was the same; natural and infectious. I tore myself away from the image to continue looking for the photo Matthew described.

The console's drawer was well camouflaged by the skilled craftsmanship and slid open smoothly. Inside it were stacks of papers and pictures, with a journal. I lifted it from its home and opened it gingerly, only for photos to spill out. I tried to catch them as they fluttered onto the table and the floor.

There were five polaroids, each one a different picture of Augustine and Lara together. She was beautiful without trying. They were always smiling, one of them always looking at the other. In the last one, they were lying together in a bed, Augustine covering his eyes while displaying a wide, laughing smile.

I realized that I didn't know either of the people in these pictures.

Augustine didn't smile like that anymore, uninhibited and gleeful. Even though he smiled more now than when I first met him, it was nothing like this. This was a smile free of guilt, free of grief.

I placed the photos back in the drawer and opened the journal again. Each page was a scrapbook of sorts, one dedicated to an event, one to each child. Matthew as a toddler, sitting on a grassy hill in front of a stone mansion. The twins swaddled together side by side in their newborn portraits. Then . . .

A family portrait on the front steps of the mansion, the twins around three, and Matthew at the cusp of his teens. Augustine sat to the side, scowling, almost leering at Lara.

Just as Matthew said, in no other picture had Augustine looked at his wife with anything but affection. So why was this day different?

It didn't make sense. Or, maybe I didn't want it to.

I sat there on the floor, studying every detail of the image, taking a moment to see the oxygen tank hidden behind Lara, and the clear tube draped like a necklace against her blouse. She was sick, like Augustine said, but she was also happy while

Augustine was not, exactly the way Matthew remembered. *That* was the Augustine I had met when I arrived: cold and apathetic. To know he was this way before he had to lose her . . . I didn't know what to think.

The stories of two of the people I cared for most were at odds, and the "evidence" had confirmed each of their versions of the story.

The truth was somewhere in between, lost in a chasm of morbid secrets. Only one person knew what happened that night, and there was only one way to get the answer from him.

Ask.

• • •

I couldn't sleep that night or eat at all the following day. My stomach was in knots, my body sore from constant anxiety. The family portrait sat in a protective envelope amongst the items I needed to pack for our relocation. Was I going to move into smaller quarters, not knowing whether the person I was growing closer to had harmed the last person he loved? I had been through that before, falling for the man who satisfied me so well, only for him to show his true colors when I was in the firm grasp of love. And here I was again, falling for a man who could trap me and hurt me all over again.

That night, Sebastien read his book aloud to me. I sat curled up next to him in his little bed, stroking my hand over his soft locks of hair while he sounded out the harder words without asking for help. Tabitha had already passed out in her bed a half hour before and hadn't stirred since. It was painful to know the playful little girl had been hiding such dark thoughts, but she was young and misguided. The last thing she needed was for someone else to leave her life while she was in the middle of figuring out what life meant.

Sebastien's words slowed, then paused. I glanced down and found his eyes closed. When I sat up to put the book away, he wouldn't let it go. "It's time for you to go to sleep," I whispered, then pressed a kiss to his crown. His pout was his only form of protest. I climbed off the bed, tucked him in, and turned off the lamp. "Goodnight, Bastien."

"Goodnight." His eyes fluttered closed.

The dark walk to my room was eerier than ever, the house full of more secrets than the day I arrived. A figure stopped me in my tracks.

Augustine.

His dark suit made him look sinister in the shadows cast by the moonlight. He stepped further into the light, and I could see his grin. He walked toward me, my nausea returning.

"You're back," I said.

"I am." He pulled my face to his and pressed a kiss onto my lips.

In an instant, my anxiety lessened with the flutter of my heart beneath his touch. I pulled him closer, making the kiss linger, letting him deepen it with a sigh. I tried to remind myself of the man he was—tried to convince myself he wasn't the monster I was led to believe.

Our lips separated, and I could barely look at him, my eyes staying on my hand as he took it in his, our fingers interlacing. "Let's go downstairs," he spoke in a whisper.

He guided me with him, and I followed without question, my body moving on its own desire to be near him. That was the problem. Physically, we were perfect for each other. Emotionally, we were opposites in a way that balanced beneficially. But now a chasm had appeared between us, and I didn't know if it was too wide to jump across.

"I need to talk to you about something," I said.

He grinned. "All right," he agreed with a seductive tone. He didn't have the slightest idea.

He pulled me with him in the direction of his office. A shiver crept up my spine. My stomach turned when I thought of the words I needed to say to him, the way I might have to betray his trust to confirm my own.

Once we were inside the room, he closed the door and pushed my back against it. He lifted my wrists and pinned them above my head. My breath became choppy as my body danced between the fear and excitement he gave me.

"I've missed you," he whispered into my ear before nipping it with his teeth. "And I want you. Right now."

He kissed me hungrily, his hands sliding from my wrists down my sides. He pulled up the hem of my dress to reach under it, looping his fingers into the sides of my panties. I shivered when he kneeled to drag them down my legs. Tears burned my eyes.

"Augustine, wait—" He turned me around, my palms catching me against the door. "I need to talk to you."

He flung up my skirt and held it against my waist. "I need to feel you come first. We'll talk after."

The clinking sound of his belt turned me into ice. "Stop," I whispered. He ignored the word the way he always did. With my forehead pressed against the door in shame, I uttered the word I hated most. "Red."

Augustine dropped his hands from me immediately and stepped away. "What's wrong? What did I do?"

I turned to face him, words failing me. "It's—I need to talk to you."

His brow furrowed with a mix of confusion and worry. "So you used your safe word?" he asked incredulously. "What is it you need to discuss so badly?"

I hugged myself, subconsciously putting up a shield against him. "Matthew told me something."

"And what might that be?"

Tears clouded my vision when I tried to look at him. "He thinks he saw . . . He thinks you did something." I watched as his eyes narrowed into a glare and felt my brow stitch. "I don't want to believe him—I want him to be wrong—but I can't know for sure unless you tell me what happened, and if I ask you, I'm afraid you'll hate me," I rambled with fear.

"Spit it out!"

A tear fell down my cheek. "He thinks you killed Lara," I said, my voice pinched and shaky. His expression faded from confusion to something unreadable. His eyes dropped from mine. "But I know you didn't. You loved her. You would never do anything to hurt her, ever." A painful silence settled between us. ". . . Right?"

Augustine wouldn't look my way. He only stared ahead of him with a furrowed brow and shook his head. Not in denial, but in disbelief. His lips parted, but he never answered.

My heart dropped to my feet.

"Oh my god," I cried. He looked at me again, but still, he was unable to find his words. "What did you do?"

Thirty-One

Warring between fight and flight, I froze. I stood against the door, trapped by my fear. And still, Augustine denied nothing.

"If you didn't do it, just say no!" I cried. "Why are you not saying no?"

"It's . . . not as simple as that."

The air left me in a rush and refused to return to my lungs. "It's a yes or no question. Did you kill your wife?" I asked him directly, as if that would somehow help him. Somehow help *us*. "Just say no! Please, say no."

"I did not murder my wife!" he yelled.

"Then why can't you say no?" I asked, my heart still lodged in my throat. "Why can't you say no?"

His face twisted with rage. "Do you know what it's like to love someone unconditionally?" he asked, his tone harsh and threatening. "To love someone so much you would do anything for them?"

I stared at him. "Yes."

"Anything?" he asked again. "Even if that meant helping them die?"

I blinked a few times, the pieces falling into place after his words settled in my ears. My pounding heart slowed to a guilty thud. "Augustine, I'm so sor—"

"Get out."

"I didn't mean to—"

"*Get out!*" he roared. The fear and pain behind his expression—so much like Matthew's—shattered my heart into pieces.

He stepped toward me, and I scrambled through the door to escape his anger. He slammed it loudly behind me.

Behind the door, I heard things crashing and things shattering against the walls. Frightened and ashamed, I fled back to my room, leaving him alone, knowing that was the last thing I should have done. Inside the safety of my room, I slid down the wall to the floor and covered my mouth to muffle my sobs.

● ● ●

Hours later, unable to sleep or be alone with my thoughts, I busied myself by packing my bags for tomorrow's move. My hands shook. I wiped my tears with the back of my hand and tried to calm myself enough to fasten the buckle together.

I wasn't sure if we should still go, or if Augustine could. The only thing keeping me sane was knowing I would get to see Crystal once we got there. I needed her—needed to hear someone tell me I wasn't the monster I felt I was. More than that, I needed Augustine to know that I was sorry I had forced him to relive his pain, that I understood why he couldn't talk about it, and that I cared for him deeply. But I didn't know if he'd even talk to me. All I knew was that if I didn't try, it was going to wreck me.

It was four thirty in the morning, around the time the staff would arrive, and a bit shy of when Augustine usually woke. I made my journey down to the ground floor, my pace slowing to a creep the closer I came to the office door. When I found it cracked open, I warmed with optimism, but all that changed when I went inside.

The floor was covered in strewn items and bits of broken glass. His bedroom door sat ajar as well. I tiptoed over and peeked inside, only to find it empty. He wasn't here. My anxiety worsened.

I left the room, careful to avoid stepping on glass. In the room down the hall, Colin stood with Warren and some of the other staff. He saw me approaching and looked at me with a worried expression. Warren turned around, gaining a similar look when he saw me. I had forgotten I'd been crying for hours, and my face likely showed it.

"Sorry. I was looking for Mr. Montgomery," I said. I didn't have the energy to deflect their assumptions. "Have you seen him?"

"No, ma'am. Not recently."

"When was the last time you did?"

"Not since last night," he answered. A chill prickled my skin when I realized that I knew where he was. I looked over my shoulder up the grand staircase.

"Did you need help looking for him?"

"No," I said. "I'll find him. Thank you."

With nervous energy, I ran up the stairs and through the ballroom, hoping I was wrong. But I wasn't. I could hear him before I made it down the hall.

I froze in the doorway when I saw him. He sat on the floor, leaned against the side of the bed where the sheets were undone, folded over with his head hanging between his knees. His body wracked with sobs.

"Augustine . . ."

I ran and dropped to my knees in front of him. His fingers were tangled in his hair so tightly his knuckles were white. His quick, ragged breaths continued. He was going to hyperventilate if he continued like this.

"I need you to breathe. Please," I begged him. "Look at me." Tilting his chin up in my hand, his eyes lifted to mine in a glare. "I know you hate me right now, but you have to breathe."

I inhaled and exhaled audibly. His hiccupping slowed as he tried to follow my breathing the best he could. After a few moments, his breaths, while still choppy, calmed to discernible inhales and exhales.

"I'm sorry," I whispered. "I didn't mean to hurt you."

"She was ill," he seethed. "And in pain—so much pain. I would never have—" A sob kept him from finishing his sentence.

"I know. I'm so sorry."

After a few more breaths, he leaned up, letting his arms relax atop his knees. He closed his eyes and let his next breath leave slowly through his lips.

His hair was disheveled from his grip, his brow stitched in pain, his face red and wet. Broken open and raw, I was finally witnessing the version of himself he had barricaded beneath layers of detachment, locked as deep down as he could. This was what I thought I wanted to see. Now, all I wanted to do was put his walls back together.

"She was ill," he repeated. "And not the sort of ill where there's hope."

"What did she have?" I asked as gently as I could.

His brow furrowed. "Cystic fibrosis."

I had heard of it before, but I wasn't sure of the details. Something to do with malfunctioning glands and chronic respiratory issues. What I knew for sure was that it was incurable, it was hereditary, and that most with the condition were lucky to see forty. My heart sank with the realization.

"So, you knew before . . ."

"We had children?" he completed my question with a self-deprecating tone. "Yes."

I didn't know what to say. Was there anything to be said in response to that?

"She didn't tell me. Not until we knew about Matthew, and by then it was too late. We were too in love. With each other and with him." His voice was low, his eyes welling with tears. "I should have known. She was always ill, said she couldn't be around too many people at once, we never went anywhere really . . . but I thought nothing of it. All I wanted in the world was to be with her."

I wasn't sure if he was telling me or if he was ruminating. His guilt was so palpable, I felt it too.

He sniffled. "So, yes. I brought children into this world knowing it could shorten her life—knowing if it didn't, they'd lose her young, all the same," he said. He looked me in the eye, his face still twisted between guilt and disgust. "How dare you tell me to be a better father when all I've done is hurt them from the start."

My brow tensed. "Don't say that."

"And Matthew thinks I—" The word choked him. He started to cry again and hid his face in his hand.

"He was young and didn't know what was happening." I tried to soothe his worries, finding I used the same words Mildred chose as well.

"You don't understand." Augustine shook his head. "He didn't know what she had. We never told him."

"You . . . He didn't know at all?"

Another shake of his head confirmed the worst. "She never let on. Most people wouldn't have noticed, until the twins put her in such a bad state. At the end . . . she was in horrible pain without medication, and when she did take it, she could barely spend time with the children without drifting off under the sedation it caused. She couldn't bear either. It tore her apart that she couldn't be with them," he explained. "The doctors said she could survive another six months. Maybe a year. I would have done anything to help her, to take away her pain. But she believed there was only one way to do that."

"No . . ." I whimpered, remembering my mother saying something similar just before the cancer took her. I wiped my cheeks with my sleeves, unable to speak past the clenching pain in my chest, but not able to look away from him either.

"She begged me, but I pleaded with her to give us just a little more time. She told me there would be no right time to go. She'd rather it be on her terms, when she felt it would be the least painful for them," his voice quivered. "So, I did it. I got her the pills." He cried, hiding his face behind his hands. "She took them, and it was so slow, and yet so fast. The way she relaxed in my arms . . ." His hands trembled like his gasp for air. "I couldn't believe . . . she was gone."

He doubled over and wept.

I stared at him and could do nothing but feel myself shatter. The tears streamed down my face faster than I could wipe them away.

There's something about the way someone goes while medicated. The slow slip, like drifting off to sleep. It doesn't register at first—at least it didn't for me. They're still there, still warm. They had been there in that vulnerable, feeble position for so long, it had become their new normal. Then, everyone around you was saying they're gone, but that didn't make sense.

They're right there. But they're not.

His cries were the most heartbreaking sound of my life. I wrapped myself around him to give him any comfort I could, holding him as tight as my strength allowed, trying to ground him and keep him from slipping back into his panic. On his shoulder fell my own tears. Beneath the sound of his sobs were my own.

"I'm so sorry," I cried. "I'm so, so sorry."

His crying continued, his body wracking against mine. "How . . . do I tell them?" he asked through his hiccupping. "How . . . do I tell them . . . what I did?"

I ran my hands over his hair, pulling him closer by the back of his neck. A silent way of telling him it would be okay. His breathing started to become erratic again. Finally, he gripped onto me and his fingers dug into my skin. I knew he needed help, but I couldn't give it to him like this.

I brushed his hair out of his face. His grasp on me tightened. "I'm here. I'm not leaving," I assured him. His eyes opened and his breathing slowed. I covered my hands with my sleeves and wiped them over his cheeks. "But I need to get you out of here, okay?"

"Okay."

I stood and helped him to his feet. I wrapped my arm around his middle to brace him. When he looked back at the bed, I pulled him away faster.

• • •

Only when I had him back in his room and a hefty dose of antianxiety medication in him did he calm down. I left him only for a few minutes to make sure the twins were still settled in bed and to refill his glass of water. When I came back, he was exactly where I had left him.

Laid on his back, arms splayed out, he stared blankly at the ceiling with glassy eyes.

"Come here," I said. "You can't sleep with all your clothes on."

He looked over slowly, his gaze vacant. This must have been the state he was in the morning they took Lara's body away. The indifference Matthew saw was simply a blanket of heavy sedatives covering a chasm of pain.

I held my hands out to him, and he took them, allowing me to sit him upright. I plucked each button of his shirt and pulled it from him, then did the same with his belt. His hand smoothed over my hair and pulled my head to his. He pressed his lips to my cheek and lingered. A silent thank you.

"Lie down," I told him softly. He did so, and I rid him of his pants and helped him move into a better sleeping position.

"How was it?" he asked, his voice quiet and hoarse. "The children's therapy."

This wasn't the time to pile more onto him. "We don't need to talk about that right now."

"Does Sebastien remember her?"

I hesitated, not wanting to answer, but after what I put him through, I owed him an open, truthful response to anything he asked me. "Not much. I'm sorry."

His brow furrowed ever so slightly. "And Tabitha?"

"She does, mostly. But . . ." I didn't want to tell him the rest. His eyes shifted to mine, waiting for me to continue. "She said she jumped into the river on purpose, to see if you loved her enough to save her."

He said nothing when he looked away, but I could see the

tears welling in his eyes. I lay down next to him and stroked my hand over his hair.

"Tabitha may not fully grasp what she did. They are old enough to understand what death means, but the therapist said if we don't speak openly and honestly about it, and allow them to ask questions, they will try to fill in the blanks for themselves."

"How am I supposed to talk to them when I . . ." He trailed off, his sentence as muted as his emotion.

I told him I would be there to help him when the hurt was too much, but I couldn't answer their questions before today. Now, I understood why Augustine couldn't either. For him, the guilt didn't come from her loss, but the life they chose for their kids from the start.

"You don't have to be strong for them all the time, Augustine," I told him. "It's okay for you to break down. And it's okay if they see that."

"Is it?"

"Yes. They need to know more about her, and know how much you loved her, to understand why it hurts that she can't come back."

He lay there for a long while, blinking, sorting through his thoughts in the air. Finally, he held his left hand up in front of his face.

"I know she is no longer here, and I need to move on, but . . . I still can't seem to take this off."

His wedding ring. I laced my fingers through his. "Then don't." I gripped his hand tight, laying it on his chest. "She will always have been your wife; she will always be the mother of those amazing kids," I told him.

Augustine's eyes stayed fixed on mine, unblinking.

"The best thing my therapist ever told me was that healing

doesn't mean letting go or moving on. It's knowing you can hold onto what you had and still allow yourself to be happy for what comes next."

He studied me for a moment. Then, he leaned over and kissed me. As gentle as it was, I could feel the emotion he hid behind it.

After a moment, his lips left mine, and he laid his head on my chest, his arm settling around my waist, his leg lying atop mine as if to keep me from running away.

Sleep took him quickly, his breaths growing slow and even against my skin. I found him beautiful when *I* brought him to this point of placidity, but I hated seeing him brought there by grief. I wanted nothing more than to care for him and bring him back to the man he knew himself to be.

Quietly, I reached for my phone, then typed and sent only one message.

Me: I need your help again.

Thirty-Two

"I can't thank you enough for this," I told Crystal. We had made our move to the loft, Augustine staying behind us by a few hours for more time to recover. Crystal had come out a day early to take the twins and give me time to get the house, and their father, in a better condition for them. "I swear I will be a better friend after this."

"A better friend? Please," she tutted. "You're my family. You know that." She pulled me into a tight hug. "Do what you need to do. I'll be here when you're done."

"Love you," I said into her shoulder.

"Love you too."

I pried myself from her comforting embrace with reluctance. "Are you excited about your sleepover at the hotel?" I asked the twins.

Tabitha, of course, looked thrilled. The promise of pizza and candy was enough to distract her from almost anything. Shy Sebastien lacked the same enthusiasm. I leaned down to offer him reassurance. "Crystal is my sister. She's just like me, but is much more likely to give you candy and let you stay up late," I told him.

"Sister?" Tabitha cut in. "You don't look alike."

"Well, that's because she's not my twin, silly," I teased her. Sebastien gripped my hand and didn't seem to want to let go. "It will be okay, sweetheart," I whispered to him. "Just a few hours of fun, then we will be together again. Sound good?"

A smile spread across his face. "Yeah."

"Have fun, little ones." They kissed me goodbye, took Crystal's hands, and left.

They would only be two streets away, but I wished I could keep them closer. Augustine needed to be in a good place for them, and right now, he very much was not.

Once they had disappeared through the front doors, I took the elevator back to the loft, taking deep breaths to calm myself and refocus on my goal. Inside the loft, I found Augustine hadn't moved from the couch. He sat slouched with his head leaning against the back. As he lounged in the sun, the emerald green of the velvet cushions framed his black and white clothes in a dark luster. His languid posture conveyed the melancholia of a Romantic-era painting. He was impossibly handsome despite it all.

I went around the couch and sat next to him. A glimmer of life returned to him when he looked at me.

"The kids are with Crystal now," I said. "She'll keep them until tomorrow morning or afternoon—whenever you're ready—and Matthew will be back tomorrow night."

"Thank you, love. I will rally soon, I swear."

"Take your time."

He continued to stare ahead at nothing. Less than a day had passed since I threw him into the depths of his grief. I didn't expect him to be able to pull himself together anytime soon, and I welcomed whatever emotions would come.

"How are you feeling?" I asked.

"Lost," he admitted. "To know my firstborn thinks me a

murderer, my daughter feels the need to put herself in danger to test my utter adoration for her, and my son can't remember his mother at all . . . What am I to think?" he asked before looking me in the eyes. "What am I to do?"

I sighed and crossed my fingers in my lap. "You have to talk to them. Talk about Lara as often as possible," I said. His gaze dropped from mine. "Tell Tabitha how much you care, even when you think you've already shown her. Tell Sebastien the memories you have of her, show him the pictures rather than hiding them away. And . . ." My sentence trailed off with hesitation. "As uncomfortable or painful as it may be, you have to tell Matthew what happened. And soon."

Augustine sighed. "He will hate me more than he does already."

"Maybe, for a while, but he deserves the truth." My heart ached with memories that flooded back. "When I was his age, I resented my father for not telling me he was hurting. In a way, I *still* resent that he hid his pain until it took him from me. I'll never stop wondering if, had he shared his pain with me, maybe he would still be here with me today."

Augustine gripped my hand in his. I took comfort in his touch, letting it ground me in the present.

"Matthew can either get the truth from you, or he can continue to believe the version he made for himself—the version where you took her from him and don't care," I said. "The truth will give you back to him. He needs his dad."

Augustine nodded, a flicker of sadness crossing his face before he soothed it away with a deep breath. He sat up straight, facing me, and took my other hand in his.

"I don't tell you what you mean to me enough, do I?" he asked. His gaze lifted to mine. "How thankful I am to have you with me. That I count myself lucky you stumbled into my life."

My heart skipped a few too many beats. He often showed his appreciation, but rarely in such direct words. I diluted his intensity with a joke. "Stumbled? You mean crashed into your greenhouse built in 1904?"

His lips twitched toward a grin, but didn't quite make it there. "Not a shed."

"Definitely not a shed." The return of his humor brought me hope, however small. "I'm happy I'm here, too."

His thumbs brushed over my knuckles. "Lara used to tease me about my 'next chapter,' as she called it. She'd joke about all the bad dates I would go on, talk about the big wedding I'd finally get to have with my next wife. It would infuriate me, but she did it so often in our last few years together. I think, because she knew."

"Knew what?"

"That I needed her to tell me it was all right to keep living without her. So that when I found you, I would let you in, and let you stay."

The flutter in my chest brought tears to my eyes. In so many ways, it felt there was an outside force that had brought us together. Crashing onto his island the day he happened to come home. My trauma and connection to the kids. Our commonalities in both the day and the night. If Lara had sent me to him, I wondered if she knew she was giving me everything I needed as well.

"*Will* you stay?" he asked.

My brow tensed with confusion. His question seemed to ask for more than the words it contained. "Yes," I answered. "Why wouldn't I?"

The way he looked at me made it harder to breathe. "After everything I've said and done . . . you'll stay?"

I couldn't quite pin down the ache in my chest. He wasn't

the only one who had behaved badly in grief. After spending time with him, learning about him, getting him to open up to me, I still didn't believe he would have harmed the person he cared about most. I projected my fear onto him as an excuse to push him away. For that, I felt shame too.

"After everything *I've* said and done, do you still want me to?"

"Yes," he said simply. "I've never wanted anything more."

I stared into his eyes, and the words came without a thought. "Then I'm yours."

His hand dropped from mine and moved to my cheek. He pulled me closer and kissed me.

With his lips against mine, it felt as if I were breathing for the first time in days. The pressure on my lungs lifted, my muscles relaxed. As his kiss deepened, breathing started to seem unimportant. Every slow kiss came with the promise of more. I welcomed them, craved them. His lips felt like an apology. His tongue like forgiveness. His hands desire.

I sighed when he tilted my head back to trace his tongue against my neck. A wave of heat washed over me when he sucked my sensitive skin. I floated in the feeling; the only gravity was his hand cradling my head, the other tickling up my waist under my shirt.

"I want you," he said against my neck between luscious kisses. "I need you. Please, Aubrey."

My body vibrated to life with his words. If I wasn't desperate for him before, I was now. I needed him, too, because having him made everything else fade away. "Take me."

In a quick move, he dropped me onto my back. His hands slid under the hem of my shirt. I broke the kiss only to help him pull it over my head, then did the same with my bra. His tongue circled my nipple as the garment cleared my hair, his lips sucking as I dropped the bit of lace onto the floor.

The pleasure he gave me bloomed hot and heavy in my core. I watched in adoration as his mouth moved from one breast to the other.

He tugged my shorts over my ass and dragged them off my legs. Taking a knee, he pulled my hips to the edge of the cushion and pushed my legs apart. Not a second later, his mouth was on me.

Augustine's worshipping tongue tasted me, teased me, his hands sliding up my thighs to spread me wider for him. The quick, deep pleasure made me shiver. When his tongue slipped inside me and licked up to circle my clit, I moaned, "*Yes.*"

Hungrily, he continued, his quiet hums of enjoyment making it almost impossible to hold on. I ran my fingers through his hair, gaining his attention. He looked up but didn't stop. Instead, he flickered his tongue against my sensitive clit, his hand reaching up to grab my breast. I whimpered.

"Baby, I can't—" My head fell back with a moan.

I was right there, but trying to hold on while he pushed me furiously into my climax. His hand massaging my tender breast, his fingers pushing inside me to stroke against my G-spot, his tongue . . . I lost my grip, falling headfirst into my orgasm.

"Ah! Fuck!" My body shuddered against his tongue, my legs clenching together around his head. But he didn't stop. He devoured my pleasure, his hands spreading my thighs to allow him to lick deeper.

The feeling washed over me, settling in my head like heavy fog. As good as it felt, it wasn't enough. I needed to be closer to him. I needed to feel him inside me.

I panted and ran my hand over his hair. "Please," I begged. No other words formed, but he understood me.

He let me go and pulled his shirt over his head. His strong core flexed with his change in posture. My eyes traced the ridges of his stomach and the trail of hair leading to what I longed for most. He watched me watch him unfasten his fly, then pulled his pants just low enough to free his impressive erection. My sex ached at the sight, my legs spreading to welcome him.

With a sigh, he pushed in, both of us moaning when he slid deep, filling me. He pulled out slowly, dragging the head of his cock against my walls until the cusp teased my entrance, then pushed back in. The wet sounds added a hedonistic accompaniment to his torturous movements.

He fucked me brilliantly. His hips pumped hard and fast, stroking himself in just the right place and just the right tempo. The deep, blinding pleasure made me moan each time. I happily gave in to it.

His hands left my hips and pressed onto my lower stomach. My pleasure heightened instantly when I felt his cock stroking hard under the pressure of his hands. I cried out, loving how he put me right on the line between pleasure and pain.

Every muscle in his body flexed as he moved between my thighs, his veins popping beneath his heated skin. My fingers dug into his arms, my moans like muffled screams. I wanted it to last forever, to live in this feeling for the rest of my life.

"Don't fight it, love," he said breathlessly. "Come for me." His voice was all it took to unravel me.

The orgasm hit me so hard, I arched back, my hips lifting from the couch with the first clench of my sex around him. Again and again, it happened, and each time, it tore me apart. I gripped the velvet in my hands and buried my face in the pillow to muffle my cries.

Augustine grew harder, fucked me faster, then he groaned deep and guttural. His hips shuddered, and his heat spread inside me. I watched the orgasm overtake him, the sweat glistening against his skin as his muscles shivered.

When he had nothing left to give, he eased out and looked down at me with heavy eyes. I stared up at him, my body on fire, my sex filled with his heat yet aching for more. He sat beside me, combing his fingers through his hair while he tried to catch his breath.

But I wasn't done with him. I climbed off the couch and lowered to my knees. His eyes found mine when I tugged his pants from his legs.

His cock was still hard in my hand. I slid my tongue up his length and traced my tongue against his slit, tasting the last of his pleasure mixed with my own. He inhaled sharply but relaxed back with a quiet moan. A teasing trail of his semen ran down my inner thigh while I sucked the last drop of it from his head.

He sighed when I slipped him through my lips and pushed him to the back of my throat. As I moved up and down, my favorite word slipped from his lips in a groan. "*Fuck.*"

I licked him downward, drawing my tongue against the vein down to his balls. I sucked each one for a few moments until they pulled tighter, and his cock grew harder. I lingered until his breath quickened and he moaned.

"Come here," he said. "I need you wrapped around me again."

Needing the same, I crawled up, pulling his face to mine for a kiss. Our tongues mingled for a few blissful moments, then I pushed him to his back on the cushions and straddled him. Unable to wait any longer, I placed him at my entrance and lowered myself onto him. I sobbed when I felt him inside me again. Every inch of him against my sensitive walls pained me, devastated me, all in the best possible way.

He stared up at me, his hands gripping my hips as I swirled them against him, his teeth catching his lip after a groan. I rode him hard, feeding off his heat between my thighs and beneath my palms. Sweat misted my skin. My sex fluttered around him as I started to climax once again.

Frantic and passionate, I barely noticed the roughness of my pace until he stopped me. Leaning up on a hand, he came face to face with me, his dark eyes staring into mine.

My breath stuttered as I looked at him. Handsome beyond all sense, perfect in every way. In his gaze was the desire and desperation I felt, the deep longing I hadn't been able to decipher or label. It was there, written on his face, and spoken by his wordless lips.

We stared into each other's eyes as we moved together. His arm around my waist kept me in time with his movements. Our position brushed my clit against him while he stroked against that deep, pleasurable spot inside me.

His brow tensed, his fingers clawing across my skin. My sex quivered around him. I pulled him into a kiss, our lips meeting briefly between sighs of pleasure. His mouth dropped open in a moan, the pressure built, and I felt it.

Our heads fell back, and we found our release together.

A deep rolling orgasm washed over me in waves as he spilled himself inside me again. Lost in an all-consuming euphoria, we were perfectly connected, emotionally, physically, and, for a few moments, it felt like it had been that way all along.

His hand cradled my back and held me against him. My hands shook when I ran my fingers over the stubble on his cheeks and his soft lips, feeling the warmth of his breath slipping through them as he panted.

"I don't want you to leave," he breathed. "I *never* want you to leave."

"I won't," I assured him. "I'm yours."

Thirty-Three

A tickle against my back woke me up. My eyes opened to soft sunlight spilling through the curtains. Morning already? Augustine's strong chest moved beneath mine. My head was nuzzled in his neck, and my arms wrapped around him. I barely remembered falling asleep, let alone falling asleep like this.

"It's morning," I said groggily.

He grinned, still brushing his fingertips up and down my spine. "It is."

I untangled my legs from his, surprised by how wrapped around him I had been. "I only meant to nap, not sleep through the night."

He smirked. "We were both in need of rest after yesterday."

Memories rushed back warm and lovely. Hours of wordless passion. But what we did yesterday hadn't felt like sex. It felt like more. I wanted to taint it into something carnal, but I couldn't.

When he rolled to his side to face me, his morose expression wasn't what I expected. "What's wrong?"

The trepidation in his gaze made my heart race. "You mean so much to me, Aubrey. And I see how much you mean to the children." His eyes drifted over my face. "I want to see what a future with you could be, but . . ."

It was the same push and pull we always had. The instinct to leave when you've started to want what you fear most. "But it scares you," I finished for him.

The sunlight brightened the muddy emerald of his pupils while he stayed quiet. Then, his head moved ever so slightly in a nod. I understood him better than he knew.

His fingers laced with mine against his chest. I could feel his heart beating strongly beneath them. "You were right."

"I know," I said to lighten the mood. "About what exactly?"

"Why I do what we do," he said. "After Lara passed, I didn't want to—couldn't *allow* myself to be intimate with anyone else. Physically or emotionally." He looked over at me. "Until you."

My brow tensed in disbelief. It was a shock to know I was his first. I always assumed he had been going to the club to get what real sex couldn't give him. His dismissive attitude after our first time came from disappointment in himself rather than me. Last night was stripped down, raw, intimate. It was just *us*. That wasn't something I enjoyed before meeting him. In some ways, he was a first for me, too.

I ran the back of my fingers against the scruff on his jaw. "What changed?" I asked him.

He brushed my hair back, his thumb running across my cheekbone in a similar position to my own. His gaze dropped to my lips. "I'm afraid I've fallen in love with you."

The words landed heavily on my chest, stealing the air from my lungs.

I hid my fear because I knew he was struggling with his own. As frightening as it was to hear, putting it in words didn't alter the truth; it only exposed it. That vulnerability, for people still bleeding from what had wounded them, was the hardest part.

With my heart pounding, I admitted my greatest fear in a whisper. "I'm afraid I've fallen in love with you, too."

We stared at each other without another word, astonishment and relief mixing in the most complicated of ways, spreading smiles across both our faces. Finally, he pulled me into a kiss.

I welcomed the comfort only he could give me. He stripped the covers from between us and rolled me to my back beneath him. His weight grounded me. His touch soothed me. With his skin against mine, my mind quieted.

"What the fuck?!" Matthew yelled. We looked his way in shock and scrambled to cover ourselves. A look of disgust twisted his face. "Are you serious?!" He slammed the door behind him when he ran out.

"Matthew!" Augustine called after him. "Fuck." He scurried off the bed and grabbed his pants from the floor. "Matthew, stop!" he yelled as he left the bedroom.

I rushed to put my clothes back on, but realized they were still in the living room. Guilt and embarrassment settled cold on my skin.

The sound of their yelling flooded in from the front room. There was no conversation, only both of them talking over one another, both upset for different reasons, and it was clear that Matthew was not in a place to receive an explanation. In only a robe, I couldn't get myself to leave the room and upset Matthew any further.

Their voices came closer. "It's been three years!" Matthew shouted. "You can't wait a little longer before you ruin my fucking life?"

He slammed the door to his room. Then, it was quiet. Too quiet.

Augustine walked back into the bedroom, shaking his head in defeat. "There's no talking to him right now. We'll have to let this pass."

"Will it?" I asked. "Do you think if you give him a few hours, he'll accept it and move on?"

"I don't care if Matthew has qualms about this. It's none of his business."

"And what is 'this' exactly?" I asked him. He remained silent and made no move other than to cross his arms. "If you can't explain what we are to each other, how do you expect him to understand?"

Augustine's scowl was enough of an answer. I left him in the room and went up the hall.

I tapped on the door. "Matthew, please let me in."

"No! Fuck no! I can't even look at you right now." His voice was tight, like he was crying.

"I know. But, please. If you let me explain, it might help."

"Explain? What I saw was pretty straightforward!"

"Matthew . . ." I glanced back up the hall to find Augustine's unamused glare.

"I trusted you and you lied to me! Just like he does!"

"I didn't—" My sentence died with my resolve. I had lied to him. "I did not lie to you in the way you think. You know I would never do anything to hurt you."

"No, I don't know that! I don't know anything about you!" Now I knew he was crying. "Leave me alone!"

"Matthew, please. Come out and talk to me."

"No!" he screamed.

Shame fell over me. In the living room, our clothes were strewn about on the couch and floor. The door to Augustine's bedroom hadn't been closed. We were alone, why would it need to be? Even though we didn't expect him for hours, it looked as if we wanted to be caught. Maybe, subconsciously, we did.

With a sigh, I left him, grabbing the clothes from the front room and returning up the hall. Augustine stepped to the side to let me back in. "He will be fine," he said.

"This isn't over," I warned him. They had gotten away with avoiding one extremely necessary conversation for too long. "Far from it."

Thirty-Four

The sun had gone down hours before, the night beginning as harshly as the morning. With the twins back, everything in the loft should have felt complete, but the splintering wedge between Augustine and Matthew was threatening to explode if not removed.

I sat with the twins in their room long past when they fell asleep, hesitant to return to the discomfort waiting for me on the other side of their door. After another minute and with a kiss on each of their foreheads, I decided it was time to be brave.

Augustine leaned back against the kitchen counter. The harsh white of the undercabinet lights framed his perfect body. The similar light from his phone's screen illuminated the handsome lines of his face. His thumbs were going at full force against the keyboard. Two days of missed work had caught up with him, or so he said. There was no doubt in my mind that he was hiding behind his comfortable shield once again.

Two glasses of wine stood beside him. He didn't look up as I approached, but his hand still managed to find my waist and pull me close to him. He tore his eyes from his screen just long enough to kiss me. When our lips separated, he looked down at me with a grin, then returned his gaze to his phone, his hand settling on my hip to remind me I was still part of his focus.

His touch comforted me, but it wasn't enough to ease my guilt. It had been hours, and Matthew still hadn't come out of his room. I lifted my glass from the counter and stared at its ruby color.

"I'm worried about Matthew," I said.

"Don't be. He'll come out when he's hungry."

"It's been over twelve hours. I should bring him something."

"No. You shouldn't."

"You really plan to starve him out?" A hum was his only response. "You do realize he's *your* child, right?"

Reading into my jab, he cocked an eyebrow. "Your point?"

"He will go on a hunger strike if that's what it takes to prove you wrong."

A chuckle rumbled from his chest. "That's what you think of me?"

"Please. He is ninety percent you, ten percent Lara." It felt odd to say her name so casually. I stared at Augustine's profile, watching his eyes flicker over his screen as he read. He didn't seem bothered. "When you talk to him tonight—"

"*If* I talk to him tonight."

"*When* you talk to him," I said sternly, "remember to be open and honest, especially about her illness."

He shifted his weight with a heavy sigh. He let me go and picked up his glass. It was obvious he had no intention of responding.

"Augustine . . ." I didn't want to say it, but I had no choice. "He's either having sex or he will be soon. He needs to know he's a carrier and that he—"

"I understand," he cut me off. "If he—*when* he comes out

of his room, I will talk to him." He finished his glass and set it back on the counter.

"Don't tell me you're leaving."

"I have a call." *As always.* "You can punish me for it later." He pulled me close and caught my lips with his, then left me for the stairs.

• • •

I gave it another hour and a second glass of wine, but still, Matthew hadn't come out. My mind filled the silence with unwanted thoughts until they became too loud to bear. I got up with a huff and went down the hall.

I tapped on the door. "Matthew?" He didn't answer. "Honey, you need to eat something."

"I'm not hungry."

"Yes, you are. Your father is busy. Come out and let me make you something."

After a stretch of silence, the sound of the lock lifted my hopes. He stood in the doorway but didn't leave the safety of his room. Though he refused to look my way, I could still see his eyes were red and puffy. He wiped the back of his hand over one, breaking my heart all over again.

"I'm sorry I didn't tell you," I said.

"No, you're not."

"Yes. I am." The guilt made my skin ache. "I may have lied by omission, but I did not betray you, Matthew. I was doing my best to protect you, like I always have, and I always will."

Finally, he looked at me, tears welling in his eyes. "You asked him about Mom?"

"I did."

"And he denied it, I'm sure. What was his excuse this time?"

"He didn't have an excuse. He told me the truth."

"Yeah, sure. What was it?"

"That's not for me to share. That needs to come from him."

He rolled his eyes. "Well, that will never happen, so I guess I'm good."

Waiting for their talk, knowing the healing they would both gain from it, was torture. "Just come eat something, please."

He hesitated for a moment, then took his first slow steps out. A huge win for me. As he walked with me up the hall, I draped my arm over his shoulder and pulled him into a hug he didn't return.

In the kitchen, I gave him a pastry leftover from breakfast. He tore into it quicker than I could turn around to pour him a glass of water.

When he suddenly stilled, I followed his gaze and saw why. Augustine was halfway down the stairs. The two of them stared at each other like cats waiting to fight.

"No." Matthew set down his food and tried to leave for his room again. I stood in his way. He struggled to escape from my grasp. "I don't want to talk to him."

"I know you don't, but you'll have to at some point," I told him. "Please give him a chance to explain."

Augustine finished his descent, his eyes shifting between the two of us. Matthew stopped his struggle when I gave him a warning glare. I had too much experience putting Montgomery men in their place for him to win this game.

"Matthew, I love you, but this has to end. Please, *please* talk to your father."

He crossed his arms and dedicated himself to his scowl. He looked over my shoulder and said to his father, "You're an asshole."

His father laughed. "And you're a little shit. What of it?"

"I want to leave! I'd rather live on the streets than stay here with you!"

"Bloody well do it then."

"Enough!" I stopped them with a yell. "Oh my god, you are arguing with a *child*, Augustine." Matthew opened his mouth to say something smart. "Don't you start with me either."

I pulled them both by their arms and forced them into the living space and onto the couch. Augustine and Mini Augustine both sneered.

"You two are the same person, and it is so frustrating. You think the same, you act the same. You're even *feeling* the same way right now. You. Just. Need. To. Talk," I said, clapping with every word.

"I don't have anything to say to him," Matthew said.

I placed my hands on my hips. "You don't have to say anything. Just listen."

"Well, I don't care what he has to say either. I already know enough."

With a sigh, I sat between them, creating a barrier and a bridge. "You do care, Matthew. More than that, you deserve the truth," I said. Augustine's apprehension was palpable in the way he avoided my gaze yet clung to my waist.

"Why are you two ganging up on me? Because you're together now or something?"

I glanced at Augustine, finding him already looking at me. "Something, yes," I answered to the best of my ability.

"That's so messed up."

"Why do you feel it's wrong for us to be together?" I asked, prompting him to clarify his discomfort in black and white language.

"Because . . . Because it's too soon." He looked over

my shoulder. "And Aubrey deserves way better than you," he seethed.

"She does," Augustine agreed. "But that isn't how love works."

"*Love?* You think you *love* her?"

Augustine straightened up defensively, but I placed my hand on his to tell him not to respond.

"She shouldn't be with someone who leaves all the time, who doesn't give a shit about his own family. Someone who—" Matthew stopped short when his voice cracked. "Someone who'll hurt her the way you hurt Mom."

"I never hurt your mother," Augustine said, his tone deep and threatening. Taking his hand in both of mine helped him regain his composure. He took a breath. "I loved your mother more than anything. I wish you could have seen that."

"Then why were you fighting the day she died? I know you did something to her."

I nodded to Augustine. *Tell him.* His hand gripped mine tightly while he struggled to fight back his emotion, making me do the same. He looked into my eyes as if to find strength before looking back at his son.

"What you saw that day wasn't anger; it was fear. I was scared because I knew we would lose her that night, and I wasn't ready to be without her."

"You knew?" Matthew's brow stitched with confusion. "What does that mean?"

Augustine brushed a hand over my back, making me look his way. He squeezed my hand as if to say *I'll be all right*, then let it go.

I left them, but not completely, giving them space but lingering a few steps up the hall, tucked behind the staircase just out of sight. "Your mother was ill, Matthew," he said.

"Yeah, I know."

"*Terminally* ill," he clarified. "She knew from birth she wouldn't live a full life."

Matthew's eyes widened, his animosity draining from his face. "What?" He looked toward his father with a quivering chin. It pained me to witness a young adult losing the last of his childhood innocence.

"We planned to tell you when you were old enough to understand, but things happened quicker than either of us expected." Augustine took in a shaky breath. "I would have done anything to keep her with us. I would have taken her place in a second if I had the chance, but I didn't. I'm sorry."

Matthew stared at him with teary eyes, his face twisted in shock at his father's show of emotion. "But . . . But she was fine," he cried.

"She wasn't. She hid it well, but she had been in constant pain for years," Augustine said, his voice shaky. "It was wrong of us not to tell you, but she . . . She didn't want you to be sad."

"You didn't tell me? On purpose?"

"Yes. And I'm sorry." Remorse was etched deeply into his voice. "The last thing your mother wanted was for you to live your life worrying about when hers would end."

Matthew searched for meaning in the ether. "She was . . . And I . . . That's not fair! That's not—" Matthew covered his face with his hands and wept.

Augustine gripped his shoulder to pull him closer, then rested his cheek on the top of Matthew's head. That was the first time they had held each other since I arrived; a bond mended. I shed tears of empathy and relief.

Knowing their walls had finally come down, I left for the bedroom, giving them privacy.

"I miss her so much," I heard Matthew cry on my way up the hall.

"I do as well."

•••

Hours later, I jolted awake, not realizing I had fallen asleep. The clock showed it was just past two in the morning, and I was still alone in Augustine's bed. Unsure where he was, I grew nervous and got up to check on him.

I walked back into the main room, and when I found them, my mouth dropped open. Matthew and Augustine were sitting at the dining table together, smiling over a box of pizza, Matthew talking, Augustine listening. They shared a laugh and I stood in shock, trying to decide if I was still dreaming.

"We figured out we *all* kind of had a crush on Maxwell, so it got awkward. That's why I left early."

"You have a crush on her?" Augustine asked in a teasing tone.

"Yeah. And our other friend."

"Which one?"

". . . Julian."

Augustine paused for a moment. "Julian is the one whose father owns the apartment buildings?"

Matthew's worry melted into a smile at his father's acceptance. He would learn to trust that his father's love was unconditional. "Hotels, yeah," he said.

"God, that's right. His father is a right knob. Are you sure you like his son?"

"Yeah. Plus, I'm pretty sure that's what they say about us, too." Augustine laughed and Matthew joined him.

They both spotted me, the smiles lingering on their faces. "Hi," I said.

"Hi. Do you want some pizza?" Matthew offered.

"No, I'm okay. Thank you, though." I crossed my ankle over the other and hugged myself. "It's late. I was just checking to make sure you two were doing okay."

Augustine's gaze flickered from me toward Matthew. "I think we're all right."

Matthew nodded. "Yeah. We're good."

I grinned at them, but inside, I was beaming. "Okay, then. Goodnight."

"Goodnight," they said in tandem.

Back in bed, I buzzed with energy. I couldn't remember the last time I was this happy.

• • •

A hectic night was followed by an energetic morning. On the roof deck, the breeze was brisk and cool, causing my hair to tickle my neck. I pulled it up, then leaned against the railing to watch the kids as they played.

Augustine appeared in my peripheral. He handed me a cup of coffee without a word.

"Thank you," I said.

He grinned. "I should be thanking *you*," he said.

"Oh yeah? How did it go last night?"

"Far better than expected," he said, his eyes trained on the kids. "I'm certain Matthew still hates me, but being able to talk to him—really talk to him for the first time in years . . ." He didn't need to finish his thought for me to know how he felt.

"I'm proud of you," I said.

"*Proud* of me? Whatever for?"

"What you did last night took a lot of strength. Being open with him about your pain, allowing him to be open with you," I told him. "Last night was only the start, but . . . I'm very proud of how far you've come."

He tried to hide his grin as much as possible. "*You* give me strength, love. *You* make me a better man."

"You were a good man long before I met you, but I will take the credit, if you insist."

His eyes studied me above a smirk. "I do."

I closed my eyes and enjoyed the sun warming my skin as it lifted above the tops of the buildings beyond. The sound of metal on metal chimed in my ear. I looked over as Augustine's fingers left his platinum band atop the railing. He continued to stare ahead, his elbows resting casually on the railing as if his gesture hadn't spoken multitudes. Words escaped me completely.

"I'm going to marry you," he said.

My eyes snapped to him. "What?"

"I'm going to marry you," he repeated. "Not today. Not tomorrow. But soon."

I stared at him in shock, and he looked at me with his dark eyes, as calm as the breeze. The fear I would have felt before wasn't there. Instead, the pounding in my chest was for something much better.

"Nothing cheeky to say?" he asked with amusement, a smile tugging on his lips.

My cheeks were warm, but I hoped it didn't show. "Not this time."

With a smile, he pulled me to him and placed a slow kiss on my lips. I knew the kids would see, but I wasn't afraid they would. He was mine. They all were.

Without another word, we turned and watched as Matthew chased the twins, making them squeal with glee.

"I've never asked," he mused. "Do you want children of your own?"

I smiled to myself. "I already have three."

Epilogue

When life was full of stress, changes, and new arrangements, I found solace in the one place I could always let my stress go: Augustine's arms.

Our free afternoon ended the way they always did, with us wrapped up in each other. Naked and cuffed, I rode him, sliding myself up and down his length in our lotus position, overtaken by the stimulation of peering into his eyes while he held me at the edge of my orgasm. He was still fully dressed, his pants only down enough to give me what I needed. His fingers tugged the chain hanging between the clamps on my nipples, then traced up the center of my chest to my neck. Desire crackled within me.

"I want it," I begged.

"Do you?" he teased.

"Yes."

"How badly?"

"Very."

He lifted me and dropped me onto my back, edging me again, but I stayed high knowing I would get what I asked.

He unfastened my wrists. "I want your hand and eyes at

all times," he instructed. My hand ran down his hard chest and stomach, and my attention stayed trained on the muscles of his lower core flexing as he moved inside me. His hand smacked my cheek. I looked at him. "Eyes. Don't give me a reason to leave you unsatisfied."

His hand wrapped around my throat and pushed up on the base of my jaw, choking me. I gripped his wrist the way I had shown him; the pressure would only exist as long as I had the strength to make it stay. He fucked me hard, his deliberate pace pushing me closer to the edge with every crash of his hips. The edge of fear heightened my lust. My eyes rolled with pleasure. When the pressure of his hand loosened, I clawed at his forearm, pleading for him to give me just a few more seconds.

He did so, staring down at me until my eyes watered and my lungs burned. I dropped my hand, and he released me.

My breath came in a rush, and with it, the pleasure. I wanted to touch myself, wanted to end my torture and push myself over the edge, but when I tried to reach down, he pinned my wrist to the bed. He was in control. Just the way I wanted.

When my cries returned to panting, his hand slid down my face and gripped my throat again. My eyes snapped to his, and my hand returned to his wrist. There, I saw the fire in his gaze. He saw only me, submitting to any and every desire he could want. The power he had over me made me melt around him. A smile curved my lips.

His other hand came down against my neck, choking me completely. I lost my smile to the pleasure that flooded through me, his face twisted in ecstasy, his mouth dropping open with a moan. He fucked me harder, nailing me to the mattress. The pressure built. A tear slid down the side of my face.

I felt helpless in the best possible way. His cock stroked

every sensitive place inside me, his desperate groans of desire filling my ears as he hardened. I was right there, and I didn't want to leave.

My strength left me. He let me go, and with a breath, we both exploded. My knees snapped together, his fingers clawed hard against my skin. My sex squeezed around him so hard, my vision went out. He gripped me tightly and he returned to his punishing pace, his heat filling me, then spilling from me with every thrust. Still shaking, my legs fell open, and I stared down, watching his speed taper as he stroked out the last of his orgasm.

Finally, he slipped from me and wiped the residue onto my thigh. He stood up with a sigh and tucked himself back into his pants as if he had done nothing but use the restroom. He combed his fingers through his hair and then checked his watch, still catching his breath. I loved it when he used me like a toy.

He went into the bathroom. I realized I was shivering; a mix of cold air against my skin and the adrenaline leaving my veins. When he came back, he cleaned me, removed the clamps, then lifted my hands to remove the cuffs. He noticed my shaking.

"Breathe, love," he cooed. "I'm not leaving you just yet."

He was catching a flight to take care of some last-minute business, leaving me for a day before the kids and I would fly out to meet him in London for our Oxford tour.

"You're really going to fuck me like that and then leave?" I whined.

He smirked. "Yes. But I'll fuck you harder when I see you again."

"You are intolerable."

"Am I?" He brushed my hair from my damp forehead and

lay atop me. He placed slow kisses against my neck, cheek, and then my lips. I wrapped my arms around his neck, enjoying his weight and his warmth, hoping he would stay longer if I refused to let him go.

"Was that good for you?" he asked.

"It was better than good." I kissed him again, still drunk off my orgasm and the delicious taste of his lips. He had been hesitant to do breath play with me for months, and now he had nearly mastered it. "How was it for *you*?"

His eyes traced his thumb as he ran it over my lips. "Rather enjoyable, I must admit."

"Really?"

He nodded, his nose brushing against mine. "There are few things I wouldn't do for you."

Giving me a few more luscious kisses to help me come down, he leaned away, took something from the drawer, then held it in my view.

I stared at the ring between his fingers and felt my mouth grow dry. "What is that?"

"An engagement ring," Augustine answered, doing nothing to lessen my anxiety. "It's only proper."

The emerald was dark but shimmered in the light, and small diamonds framed the massive oval-shaped stone in a floral frame. I looked up at him, tracing the masculine features of his face. The dark hazel of his eyes was much more enchanting than the jewelry. Little could rival the allure of Augustine.

"I said I didn't want a ring."

"You said you didn't want a *diamond* ring," he corrected me.

Though he was right, he wasn't fully listening. Adopting the kids before Matthew turned eighteen was a given. Augustine had eloped with Lara, so he wanted the wedding he never had. The combination gave me a short timeline and an ambitious request.

I wanted to marry him, but I didn't want all the traditional fussiness and anxiety-inducing planning that went with it. Massive, expensive jewelry while living and walking in Manhattan was the epitome of fuss.

"Well, I can't wear that. I'll get mugged."

He laughed. "Why the excuses, love? If you don't like it, just say—"

"I love it. Really. I just don't need it." I took it from his hand and slid it into the front pocket of his shirt. "I only need you."

"And you have me. But I would like it if others knew that as well."

I chuckled. "You don't want another eligible bachelor vying for my attention? Or, do you just not want someone to call you my boyfriend again?"

He tutted with a roll of his eyes. "Such a ridiculous term for adults to use."

"You don't want people to think I'm your mistress." I brushed my lips against his, then took his bottom lip between my teeth. He let out a quiet moan. "But I am, aren't I?" I said against his lips, my hand sinking between his legs to grip him. His tongue wet his lips, his eyes heavy when he throbbed against my palm. "Just not the kind people think."

I kissed him. A quick taste of his tongue before my lips closed over his. He slid his hands against my jaw and pulled me closer.

"I love you," he said intently, the way he always did.

I smiled. "I love you too." With another taste of his lips, I sat up to make my trip to the bathroom.

His hand grabbed mine and he pulled me back to him. He

took the ring from his pocket and slowly slid it onto my finger. It looked bigger when it was on, taking up most of the space between my knuckles, and it was heavy. I hated to admit the color looked fabulous against the undertone of my skin.

"The ring is just a ring," he said, "but it would make me happy to see you wear it."

I stared him in the eyes and felt my resolve break. "Anything for you."

• • •

On the way to pick up Matthew in Harlem, the light sprinkle made traffic a nightmare. Picking him up from school reminded me time was running out. He was always open and honest with me, which was how I knew he was excited for a weekend that would inevitably break my heart.

When we moved from the mansion to the loft halfway through high school, I expected him to throw a fit, but it turned out to be better for both him and his father. We were closer to La Guardia, able to see more of Augustine between his trips. The mansion, now mostly a vacation home, allowed us to live a simpler, more intimate life as a family.

Matthew refused to attend a private school in the city and instead opted for an academically excelling public school. He loved the diversity, the culture, having more people who would understand the complicated nature of losing his mother and his father's new relationship with someone who looked like me. Seeing him enjoy school was rewarding enough, but knowing he enjoyed it because of those reasons was special to me.

"Here is perfect," I told Colin. He pulled to the curb, leaving me with the three-block walk to the school. As comfortable as Matthew was with his classmates, he still tried to hide his wealth from them.

I stood at the corner, watching the teenagers slowly drift away from their groups as their rides arrived. The handsome boy with the crooked tie spotted me and said goodbye to his friends. He jogged over and joined me beneath the umbrella. I pressed a kiss to his temple—something I could no longer do without wearing heels.

"How was school?" I asked him as we started to walk.

"It was school," he said in his vague, teenage way. The mist of rain perched atop his dark hair and refused to melt. He brushed his fingers through it and tossed a smile at a classmate as she passed by, making her blush. I sneered.

Matthew was too handsome for his own good. Seventeen going on eighteen, and he looked about twenty-two. He had his father's strong frame, though it was still sinewy from youth. Time had given him the face of his father—angled jaw, plump lips, too much scruff on a jaw too strong for his age—but he had the wide, charming eyes of his mother. He could be a model, but I would never plant that seed in his head.

"Are you excited about Oxford yet?" he asked.

I let out a heavy sigh. "No."

"Aubrey, why?" he whined.

"I'm not exactly thrilled over the idea, because . . ." The wave of emotion hit me suddenly. The thought of him leaving my side and going to a different continent for school was gut-wrenching. "I don't think I want you to go."

"Are you gonna cry?"

My eyes clouded and I was sure he could see. I turned to face him. "Columbia is right here. It's an amazing school, just like Oxford, but you would be closer to home. To me." I blinked back my tears.

His brow furrowed when he pulled me into a hug. I squeezed him tight against me, trying to stave off my desire to start sobbing in front of hundreds of strangers.

"I don't know if I want to go for sure, I just want to see it," he said into my shoulder. He leaned away. "Most people go to school away from home. I just want to see if it's something I want to do, too."

"I want you to do whatever is best for *you*," I told him. "But I won't promise I'll be happy about it."

He hugged me to his side. "You'll have a good time when we go there this weekend. Just wait and see."

A few blocks later, the twins ran down the grand staircase from their school, Tabitha holding a dance bag that was nearly the same size as her, Sebastien trailing behind her, unable to keep up with her energy and speed. Colin helped me take their bags while they climbed into the car. I got in and sat by Matthew, shaking the water droplets from the umbrella.

"What's that?" Tabitha asked me, pointing to my hand. I didn't know what to say. "Did Daddy give you that?"

"He did."

"Because you're getting married, right?"

I paused. Children never seemed to get stuck on how complicated life can be. "Yes, eventually."

"But I thought—"

"Eventually," Matthew cut in. "But eventually *could* be soon. We don't know."

I gave him a look. It was all so simple to them. Fall in love, get married, but Augustine and I were still settling into one another, ironing out the transition from employer to lover to husband.

Everything had happened quickly between him and Lara,

and there was so much guilt and pain he had because of that. Taking our time was healthy for both of us.

"A wedding is not a marriage, and a marriage does not change how much we love each other," I told them.

Tabitha *and* Sebastien's brows creased in confusion.

"When your daddy married your mommy, their wedding was very small, and they loved each other *so* much—enough to make the three best kids in the whole world." That got them to smile again. "Your daddy and I will love each other just as much as we do now, even if we never have a wedding. We have plenty of more important things to worry about right now. Like, whether you will be abandoning us for England or not," I took a playful jab at Matthew.

His lips pursed. "Whatever you say."

I'd focus on getting through the weekend first before worrying about the rest of forever.

• • •

The flight was easier than expected, though it helped that we were in first class. The twin slept most of the flight, both falling victim to the white noise and their usual bedtimes. Arriving in the morning was a perfect way to avoid jet lag, though we had another day to get settled before our campus tour the following morning.

The car ride to the hotel took longer than anticipated, the view through the window changing from a cityscape to the countryside. I wasn't sure where we were staying and hadn't asked questions. I was doing well to keep my emotions in check.

We pulled up a gravel driveway to a sprawling castle with a grand staircase leading up to the entrance. White peonies and eucalyptus stems sat in tall concrete vases on the balcony railings.

"Is this the hotel?" I asked. When no one answered, I looked to Matthew, who wore a conniving smile. "What's going on?"

Augustine walked out of the front doors, looking suspiciously handsome in his usual business attire, this time, a dark blue suit and white shirt.

I walked up the last set of stairs to him, wrapping him in a hug I had waited days to feel. "This hotel is a bit much, don't you think?"

"Where else would you prefer to have our wedding?"

Time paused for a moment. I stared at him, trying to figure out what he'd just said. "What?"

Crystal appeared from behind him, her boys holding each of her hands. Then, a familiar smiling face appeared behind her.

"*Mildred?*" I went to her, giving her a hug.

"Hello, darling." She squeezed me back, her familiar warm embrace bringing back memories. The twins ran to her, taking my place. Matthew wrapped them all together in his arms.

"Crystal?" I hugged her, too. "What are you all—Wait." I turned back to Augustine. "Our wedding . . . will be *here*," I said.

"Yes. Tomorrow."

"*Tomorrow?*" I looked around for answers and found them in the decorations, the perfect setting, and the presence of every person I loved. "Wait. You planned it all?"

"Yes."

"So I wouldn't have to?"

He chuckled. "Yes, love. You don't have to say what you need for me to still know."

I felt short of breath, the scene looking like a fantasy even I couldn't dream up. "What am I supposed to wear?"

"I found a dress for you," Crystal said. "You're going to love it."

"There's a tailor on site ready to make any adjustments you may need."

I nodded, the tears clouding my eyes. We had found everything we needed in each other. A bond that was so often unspoken but never unheard. Two broken pieces that, when placed together, made both of us whole.

"Are you happy?" he asked with an edge of worry.

"I am," I said in a pinched voice, a tear rolling down my cheek. "I really am."

Augustine

One

Ms. Nielson, Ms. Nielson. Whatever shall I do with you?

This person, who was a stranger not long ago, was now everyone's favorite person, it seemed—except mine. I had to admit the presence she created so quickly was fascinating. The way the children fixated on her. Even Matthew seemed unable to pry his eyes off her, though it was obvious his penchant for her was heightened by her physical appeal. She was fit; intelligent. She had a brash attitude and a coy demeanor she used to compensate for it. As often as she made me want to get rid of her, she did something to impress me and make me eat my words.

Aubrey was a source of frustration. I despised her as much as I admired her—how she could be so qualified and talented whilst being so utterly maddening.

Finding her bent over my desk with her backside exposed, the thin material wedged between the lips of her cunt, brought dangerous thoughts to my mind. At night, I pleasured myself to the thought of her bent over my desk again, begging me to bury myself inside her. I imagine her bound in leather, gagged, her eyes as wide as that night whilst I fucked her harder than she'd ever been fucked be—

"Agh! *Fuck*." The quickness of my climax surprised me. My hand continued to massage my balls, the other stroking against my sensitive head as my pleasure spilled over my hands and dripped onto the sheets. I leaned my head back against the wall with a sigh.

It wasn't my attraction to her that twisted me up this way. It was the torment of knowing I would never allow myself to touch her.

• • •

"Mr. Montgomery!"

Without looking, I slowed my pace to allow Mildred to catch up with me. Her trotting gait hobbled to one side. Her body was giving out more each day. The children running her in circles did nothing to help that.

"I heard you've taken Aubrey—erm, Ms. Nielson on permanently."

"I have." I rounded my desk, my eyes tracing the location of last night's fantasy, but dropped the thought quickly. "Matthew's marks have significantly improved already." I sent the email from my drafts, then glanced at her. "Does this surprise you?"

"No! Quite the opposite! It was a brilliant idea to hire her. She is as well qualified in person as she is on paper," she gushed. I hummed my reticent agreement. "If I may . . ."

I let her speak, but made obvious my need to crack on with my work. I didn't expect her words to be worthy of my full attention.

"Getting to know her, she's a beautiful soul. Grounded, humble, more importantly, well-intentioned. I think you should give her a listen sometime. More than her advice, but also her experiences. Her *life* experiences," she rambled around her point. My eyes lifted to hers. "If I may be so bold to say . . . you have many similarities. Important ones, I believe."

My eyes narrowed. "Your meaning?"

Her hands wrung nervously. "I think she could help you. With more than just the children." She had the audacity to look me in the eyes when she said, "If you're ready to move on—*when* you're ready to move on—I think she would be good for you."

An icy rage spread through my veins, making me wish I could strangle the words from her fat neck. "*Move on?*" I repeated, the anger lowering my voice.

"Please don't be upset, I only meant—"

"How dare you?" The rage boiled up inside me. "Has all I've done for you and your family meant nothing?"

"Of course not!"

"You believe what, then? That I should simply forget Lara and begin my search for a new wife?" My body shook with my rage. Pain, perhaps. "Have you forgotten what I've been through? Have you forgotten what I've done?!"

Her face dropped. "No! That wasn't what I meant!"

Lies. The hag hadn't stopped making suggestions since before Ms. Nielson arrived. With a deep breath, I let my anger cool to something worse. "Do you know what she *is* good for?" I taunted her. "Doing your job better than you."

The tears filled her eyes. "Please. I didn't mean any harm."

"Didn't you?" I picked up my phone to make the arrangements for her departure.

"Please! I've been by you and the children through everything! I only want what's best for all of you."

"Yet this is how you choose to treat me."

"No!" she sniveled. "I love you and the children as I do my own family. You can't—"

"Except I can."

I was tired of the memories that haunted me during every quiet second or moment without distraction. I wanted to purge everything that stole my solace and to maintain some control over when the memories returned. Mildred's uninvited reminders brought the worst pain imaginable, and there was only one way I saw to control it.

"Colin will collect you shortly. I'll have your belongings packed up and mailed to you."

• • •

I barely slept that night. Very rarely did I regret the choices I made. However, I could admit my choice to fire Mildred may have been a bit rash. Her insensitivity was out of character in the worst possible way. Her behavior was an annoyance for which I had no time or desire to correct. I would be better off without her. The children, whether they knew it or not, would be as well.

The twins ran past me, skidding to a stop and returning to my side. I kneeled to pull them close, giving each of them a kiss.

"Go on," I told them. They did so without protest.

My guilt dissipated with the sight of their smiles. Their mother was always clear about what she thought was best for them—always urging me to give them every opportunity she never had. Aubrey provided the expertise they needed to succeed, but without the threat of Mildred's knowledge of my past. She was a perfect solution to an impossible problem. Or so I thought.

In the doorway, what I saw stopped me from taking another step.

Aubrey. Bent over.

I fixated on her ass instantly. She traced her perfect curves with her hands as she straightened up. My cock moved against my thigh.

What was there not to like? She was youthful, beautiful. *Flexible.* I brushed it off as I always did, attributing my reaction to basic biology.

She gasped. "Mr. Montgomery."

"Ms. Nielson."

"Good evening."

"Evening."

A flush warmed the bronze hue of her freckled cheeks. Her plump lips remained parted as she looked for words to cover her embarrassment. Lips I struggled not to imagine wrapped around me before I came onto her tongue. My cock throbbed once again.

"Was there something you needed?" she asked.

"I need you." I watched her eyes widen and realized my phrasing may have reflected my desires more than my intention.

As attractive as I found her, submissive women only satisfied half of my needs. Eventually, my self-hatred would lead me to seek more punishing forms of stimuli. This, too, would pass.

"Will you be joining us for breakfast tomorrow?"

• • •

Contrary to Aubrey's beliefs, I did not intend to harm my children. Keeping them safe and happy was my utmost priority; the reason for all I did. It was not her place to tell me whether my choices were to her standard. Not that it would stop her from telling me so.

The children had received the news as poorly as I expected. As planned, my trip would keep me out of their way for a week or so. It was best to let them sort through their feelings without them having to see my face.

"Are you leaving again?"

I looked up to find Aubrey in my doorway wearing the glare that only managed to make her more attractive. "Yes. To London."

"So soon? You just got back," she whined. I proffered no response. "You work so much your children hardly get to see you. Did you not plan to spend some time with them after taking their caretaker away?"

Spending time with the person responsible for their pain would never help them. She knew nothing. "They'll be fine. They have you, do they not?"

"I'm a teacher, not a nanny."

I kept myself from laughing. "You are whatever I pay you to be."

She came to my side and grabbed my bag from my hand. I looked at her in shock.

"You are fucking up your kids. You know that, right?"

I stared in disbelief. The gall of this woman. A mere stranger who believed she was entitled to an opinion on my personal matters.

"Your kids need regularity and structure. They need consistency. If they keep having people come in and out of their lives, they'll never be able to trust that someone will stay."

Her words sliced me, but I wouldn't let her see that. "You don't know what you're talking about."

"I know more than you think."

She frustrated me to no end. Always pushing, challenging, *talking*. My anger caused me to block out her next excuse. I was waiting for her to piece together that she meant less to me than the woman I just put out of my house. But instead, Aubrey kept on blathering until she gained my attention once more.

"They lost their mother, and their father is too busy working to acknowledge their presence. They need a real parent in their lives. Not a placeholder their father pays."

I stared at her in disbelief, then began laughing at her ignorance. "You have quite the pair of bollocks on you, don't you?"

"I don't need balls to know when you're being a prick."

My hand flexed as if I were trying to fight off my urge to bend her to my will. If only she knew all the ways in which I could correct her attitude, she'd lose that audaciousness the second I had her crawling at my feet.

"Stay until tomorrow. You owe them that much."

"I cannot change my plans each time my children cry."

"Then maybe you should stop being the reason they're crying at all."

I'd had enough of her and her mouth. I picked up my bag. When she pulled it from me again, I snapped.

I pushed her back, slamming her against the wall harder than I intended. But I didn't care. My hand moved to her neck, a fantasy of choking her flashing through my mind. "I am not someone to be fucked with, Ms. Nielson."

Her eyes widened a mere second before my vision went white. The pain in my balls nearly brought me to my knees. She caught me by the collar, glaring down at me like a woman I'd pay for a very different service. "Neither am I, Mr. Montgomery."

I stared up at her, impressed by her sudden confidence, and more so, the way in which she implemented it. A moan nearly escaped me when I fought to hide the way her anger made my blood rush south.

"I'm not fucking with you when I say your children need you. Stop worrying about work and start worrying about being a better father," she spat.

She let go, and I collapsed back against my desk, my hand darting to my balls. The pain faded into an intoxicating pleasure. My cock lamented her absence with a steady thudding.

"Enjoy your trip, Mr. Montgomery." Her hips swayed with confidence as she walked out. The click of her tall heels twisted my thoughts. My body ached to follow her and beg for more.

Mildred was wrong about everything.

Aubrey would be very, *very* bad for me.

Two

How did it get this far? How did I become so enamored by someone when it was the last thing I wanted?

It never happens all at once. Losing oneself is a process. Bit by bit, I was stripped of all that I knew of myself, my desires, my needs, until all that remained was . . . this horrid feeling.

It started that night. The moment I first gave in.

She enraged me, begged for my wrath with challenge after challenge. It consumed my mind. Every flicker of a moment between an email or a schedule reminder, my thoughts returned to her, and my blood returned to my cock.

Not in years had I had the desire to be with someone. Desire on its own, of course, but never directed at a specific person, especially someone in as close proximity as Aubrey. I knew I wouldn't be able to let go of those thoughts without proving to myself how insignificant she was, that the image I created in my mind was far greater than the reality.

So, I fucked her. Hard and well.

As I cleaned my cum from her stomach, she stared up at me in awe, her legs still splayed, her cunt dilated and wet from my presence.

I could not tell you what I was thinking—if I was thinking at all—before that moment. She got me to do something I hadn't thought I'd be able to do again: have sex with someone else. *Enjoyable* sex at that.

Drained and sated, I collapsed back onto my place in the bed. I had done what I meant to do and intended nothing else. And yet . . .

Her weight beside me gave a sense of familiar comfort; her scent, the calm reminder of how wonderful sex could be. I turned off the light, meaning to allow the oxytocin-spurred admiration to fade with sleep, hoping she would soon be gone with the last of my desires.

But, as the minutes passed, she stayed, lingering with the same boldness she always had.

Completely exhausted, she hadn't moved an inch. In the moonlight, the luster of her brown skin looked like velvet against my sheets. Carefully, I trailed my fingertips up the back of her leg, over the swell of her perfect ass, and along the curve of her lower back.

The masochistic part of me wished to curl up behind her, to hold her close and feel her breathing against my chest. Instead, I covered her with the blankets to put an end to my longing.

If only it had worked.

• • •

Months later, I was still attempting to do the same. Once all our sordid secrets were revealed, all our kinks aligned and well-practiced, I found myself tumbling to my knees before a malevolent goddess.

Cruel and benign all at once, I trusted her; trusted the

balance we found in each other's desires and limitations. Being inside her was my favorite place on Earth. She was my obsession, my crux, and I loved all the types of pain that came with it.

She had hit me, choked me, debased me, fulfilling all my unspoken wishes. But when she came out wearing *that thing*, I had questioned where my limits stood. She touched me where no one had before, fucked me relentlessly, and the pleasure, deep and consuming, overtook me. As if it had punched me in the face, I instantly felt drunk on the feeling. Just a simple touch was all it took for her to unravel me.

I couldn't explain why I trusted her so. Possibly because she was the only person who had brought me pleasure in years. I braced myself to accept it, trusting that, in her experience and her time with me, she knew better than to lead me astray.

Then I ruined everything.

The softness she always gave me after a scene fucked with my head, and she knew it.

"I've been thinking," she said, giving reason after reason for me to change my behavior yet again. Her attempt gave me a laugh.

"You think I can't tell what you're up to? Fuck me, then ask for favors?" I laughed at her feeble attempt. "You sound like Lar—"

My skin turned to ice the second I uttered her name. Regret turned my stomach until I felt I would be ill.

"Excuse me."

I left the bathroom, stumbled past the bed, and out of the room. Like a ghost, I fled to the only privacy I could find. My feet hadn't felt the stairs, my hands only felt the top of my desk when I leaned onto it for balance.

What was wrong with me? A stabbing pain in my heart came

whenever I thought of Lara. The painful longing and regret that consumed my life and left me a sordid shell of a man.

The nausea refused to subside. I pulled open my drawer and grabbed what I needed, taking it with me.

Outdoors, the wind breathed life back into my lungs, bringing me no comfort. I would rather feel nothing—rather die than feel even a resemblance of what I felt before.

That was why I ran to Aubrey, was it not? To give me a moment to be broken. A moment free of thought—a desire she fulfilled flawlessly each time. So, how did I find myself here?

"There you are."

It wasn't something I could do around Lara. I gave it up the moment I met her, then resumed the moment she . . .

I lit the end of my cigarette, letting the calming poison rush into my lungs. Aubrey lingered beside me but refused my offer. I returned it to my lips, inhaling my calm whilst hating the loudness of the silence.

"Lara is—*was* . . . my wife." Bloody hell. Would I ever stop living in the past? "I assume you've put that together."

"I have." Her voice was just a whisper. An apology without saying the words.

A twinge of pain returned. I inhaled deeply in an attempt to stave it off. "Thank you for tonight, but I'd like to be alone now," I said. Lying. "If that's all right."

"Of course, but . . . I need to make sure you're okay before I leave you." Her hand found my arm and I shied away from it. I didn't want her comfort or her sympathies. I wanted her the way she was a few moments before, and the pain that came with it. But it seemed I would always want what I could never have.

"I'm fine," I assured her. The look of worry on her lovely

face made me want to apologize. I did everything but that. "Goodnight, Ms. Nielson."

She disappeared, leaving me alone.

Only after two cigarettes' worth of toxins were in my lungs did I feel back to myself. Numb. Tired. I left the roof and went inside. Down the stairs, Aubrey's bedroom door sat ajar. I peered inside, finding her fast asleep.

I stood there for a moment, observing her from afar. She always slept heavily like that. Always on her stomach, haphazardly covered by her sheets. It didn't feel odd to know such a thing about her, just as it no longer felt odd to know I slept better with her beside me.

Unable to help myself, I crept into her room and sank to a knee in front of her, whispering to avoid startling her.

"Aubrey. Love. I've changed my mind." I brushed the stray tendrils of hair from her face. "Come back to my room with me?"

As always, she lay still, her quiet breaths slow and even. How she found such peace in a world so painful, I did not know. The only thing I fully understood was that being with her was the closest I ever came.

I ran my hand over her cheek, then traced my thumb over her plump lips, wishing I could kiss them again. "Sleep well, my love."

Regretfully, I left her. And when I flew out the next morning, I counted down the seconds until I could be near her again.

• • •

I was a bloody idiot. My lips betrayed me, exposed me whilst I was lost in victory and liquor. Now, Aubrey thought me a broken man in need of a shrink. I didn't need a doctor to tell me what was wrong.

I was a monster. Pure and simple.

Aubrey pried, she pushed, and I gave in every time. It was infuriating. And yet, it made me want her even more.

"Do you like fucking me?" she whispered into my ear, her fingers twisted in my hair. I found her foreboding gaze, the cold contempt she had for me that always brought me to my knees and left me begging to be between hers.

I thrust my hips, my cock still trapped in her tepid fist. "Yes."

"Do you like the way I make you come?"

My desire became audible. "Yes."

Her hand released me, and without a second's hesitation, I pushed my way inside her. Her wet heat drowned me in bliss as I buried myself deep. My senses lulled, feeling her fluttering grip around me.

My hand trailed down the butter-soft skin of her waist, the curve of her hip, and the plumpness of her thigh as I spread her wide.

"Do I satisfy you? Do I give you everything you desire?" she asked.

Her voice sent the blood rushing lower, making the softness of her wet center blind me to any other need or want. There were few things better than being inside her. "Always."

Her fingers fisted in my hair and pulled it hard. The pain was sharp. Lovely.

"Then why do you still not listen?" *Because it's oh so fun not to.* "Look at me." Her hand slapped against my cheek, leaving it ringing. My cock swelled in the hot grasp of her cunt. "Look at me!"

I did as she said. And why wouldn't I? Inside her, everything felt like pleasure. My pain, inflicted or preexisting, faded to euphoria.

It was only her perfect body, her tight cunt, and the power of it all.

As little as I wanted to admit it, she had me. Ensnared, awed, and in love with her splendor.

"You think you are in control, but you're not," she threatened me. "In this bed, you are mine. Out of this bed, you are mine. You do what I tell you. Do you understand me?"

A rush of pleasure left me in a moan. "Yes."

She slapped me once more. "Look at me." I bared my teeth at the impossible task before me. She expected me to listen and obey when my body was screaming to fuck hers into oblivion? Only she could force me to do so. "Yes, what?"

My cock strained. "Yes, mistress."

"Good." She pulled my face down to hers. I attempted to taste her lips, but she pulled away, choosing to stare into my soul. "Now fuck me. Hard. And don't you dare look away."

I lost my grip on reality as it faded to the heat roiling between us. With another slap, my attention returned at her demand. As I stroked inside her, as she forced me to obey her every whim, she *did* have me. All of me. And it threatened to shatter me. "Fuck, Aubrey. I—" I, what? *Love you?*

Frivolous words and twisted thoughts always came to me when I was with her. Part of my jaded shell crumbled away every time I allowed myself to trust her. The danger brought me pleasure, but the true fear . . . That would come if she ever learned about my past and left me.

A sound froze us in place. "Aubrey?" Matthew called for her.

"Shit," we muttered in unison.

Reluctantly, I pulled myself from her and collected her

garments from the array of locations in which they had been strewn. I covered myself and placed my laptop to hide my remaining erection. Matthew barged in not a moment later.

"Dad?" He spotted me and his eyes narrowed. I shared his contempt.

"Matthew. I'm glad you felt entitled to let yourself into my room."

"I can't find Aubrey, so I assumed you two were in here fucking each other."

The filthy way the phrase left his mouth made my mood even worse. "You're a tactless one, aren't you?"

"Learned it from the best."

True as it was, he had enough reasons to hate me without me stealing the object of his boyish desires for my own adulterated whims. "Well, she's not here, I'm afraid. You must have just missed her."

"Oh. Cool. Well, sorry to bother you with my presence." With the slam of the door, I looked to where Aubrey stood, obscured from my view. She waited until the other door signaled his true departure before opening it.

"This isn't happening," she said when I went to her.

"Why? I'll be quick."

"I should be with them. *You* should be with them, not hiding up here, using me to ignore the reason it hurts you to be around them."

And just like that, she was prodding again at what would take her from me. "Don't," I said.

"I didn't, Augustine. *You* did. But until you're willing to face that, we'll both be waiting patiently for the other to give us what we want."

She left. My anger returned with frustration, but soon after, my rationale.

I had become too reliant on her. Convincing myself it was simply the sex that kept me coming back to her was no longer working. I was incapable of relationships, undeserving of merely entertaining the thought of a partner in any sense. There was no realm in which my misdeeds and horrors did not taint my soul with indispensable guilt. To have any affection for Aubrey was reprehensible. I wished I had never found myself in this position.

Had Lara stayed. Had I known she would leave me before I loved her too much to let go.

The very thought sent an ache over my skin so deep I felt the acid rising up in my throat. Naked and alone, my thoughts laid bare in front of me.

Nothing in life was my choice. Nothing was in my control. Not really.

I suppose that was when I had it figured out. Aubrey would never stop filling my mind and fueling my obsession if I kept her close. I would continue to be in pain if she reminded me of what I lost and gave me the solace I did not deserve. As much as I did not want it to end, I needed to draw a line. I needed to keep this horrible feeling at bay.

Falling for her was the last thing I wanted to do, but unfortunately for me, I already had.

I loved Aubrey. And I hated myself for it.

Thank You

This work was a labor of love that tore open many of my wounds and forced me to sew some of them back together. To my readers who supported me and this story since its creation, thank you for everything. I wouldn't be in this place without you.

The Author

Embri Wilson is a millennial who loves warm blankets and boba tea. Her focus is sex-positive adult romance featuring Black and mixed-race female main characters. She is a Sagittarius, and for that, she is sorry. Embri hopes to reach an audience who feels seen and celebrated by her works.